SPIRITS OF CAVERN AND HEARTH

By the same author:

Masters of Glass
Iskiir
The Fisherman's Curse
Swimmers Beneath the Bright

SPIRITS OF CAVERN AND HEARTH

M. COLEMAN EASTON

ST. MARTIN'S PRESS
NEW YORK

Design by Glen M. Edelstein
Interior art by Clare Bell
Cover art by Tom Canty

Library of Congress Cataloging-in-Publication Data

Easton, M. Coleman.
     Spirits of cavern and hearth / M. Coleman Easton.
         p.   cm.
     ISBN 0-312-02287-5
     I. Title.
PS3555.A733S65   1988
813'.54—dc19   88-16891
                                            CIP

First Edition

10 9 8 7 6 5 4 3 2 1

ACKNOWLEDGMENTS

I am indebted to Russell Galen for his encouragement from the start, and to the following for their many valuable comments and suggestions: Kevin Anderson, Clare Bell, Michael Berch, Janet Gluckman, and Avis Minger.

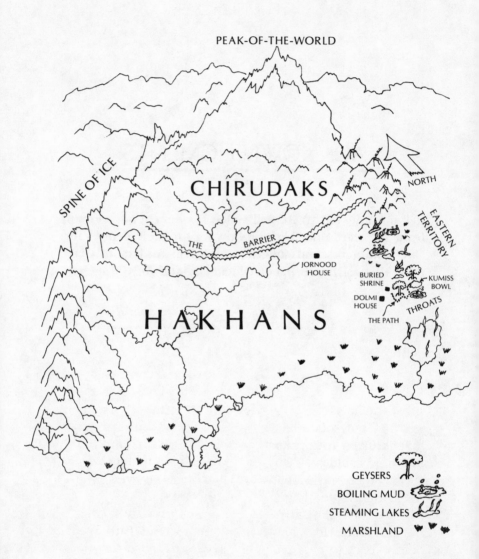

PEAK-OF-THE-WORLD

CHIRUDAKS

NORTH

SPINE OF ICE

EASTERN TERRITORY

THE   BARRIER

JORNOOD
HOUSE

BURIED
SHRINE

KUMISS
BOWL

HAKHANS

DOLMI
HOUSE

THROATS

THE PATH

GEYSERS

BOILING MUD

STEAMING LAKES

MARSHLAND

CB'88

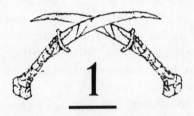

1

*Even the gods do not know all that is
to come.*

—*Shaman Dzaminid*

Ahead of the horseman
stretched a desolate landscape—a stark expanse of mineral-encrusted rock, punctured by steam vents and bubbling mud cauldrons. On his left a plume of boiling water
spurted, then settled back again into its yellowed basin.
On his right rose clouds of sulfurous fumes.

To Yarkol Dolmi, the scene was unpleasantly familiar.
Only someone like himself, who knew the Path well,
could expect to pass safely here. As a physician he often
tended laborers who were injured at work sites along the
Path. This morning he'd been summoned once again. But
now, halfway to his goal, he felt a vague uneasiness as if

he had forgotten something. He glanced down at his saddlebag, but recalled he had carefully packed it.

Some matter from home, perhaps? With three wives and a handful of children, an errand might easily slip his thoughts. Or was it the talk of war that concerned him, the threat of hostilities in the north? He shrugged, unable to find an explanation.

Then the vague sense of distress suddenly turned acute. He frowned as a spasm of pain coursed down his neck and gripped his shoulders. An active man, approaching middle years, he had known his share of aches and twinges. But this attack, coming with so little warning, made Yarkol rein in his mount. He reached up to probe the troubled muscles . . .

Then, unaccountably, the onslaught came—a torrent of invisible blows to his ribs, his back, his head. In anguish and surprise he tried to cry out, but the sound caught in his throat. The reins felt cold between his stiffening fingers. He was slipping from the saddle, his boots snagged in the stirrups.

For a moment the agony eased, and Yarkol found strength to untangle his feet and slump to the rocky ground. He lay with his face to the sun, closed his eyes, and felt his body begin to spin. Another spasm shook him, and he briefly forgot where he was. *In the Throat of Sorrows,* he recalled when he could open his eyes again. He knew no harsher place.

The wind shifted, bringing an acrid whiff of steam from a nearby fumarole. He tried to lift his head, but fell back, exhausted by the effort. *What cruel malady?* No commonplace ailment had felled him, he was certain. A fearsome word whispered in his thoughts.

Someone would find him soon, he expected, would carry him home to his bed, and then . . . The rest was too much to bear. Images of his wives and children hovered, unfocused. Already he heard weeping.

2

Yarkol knew of only one illness that progressed this quickly. Even now he felt the paralysis grip him, bringing also a slight numbing of pain. He struggled to move, to twitch the smallest of his fingers, if only to prove that he had not fully succumbed. No use. It was enough of an effort just to draw breath.

Around him all was silent but for the occasional nickering of his horse. He asked himself again if his conclusions could possibly be wrong. It was one thing to examine a stricken wretch, another to grasp one's own symptoms. For twenty years Yarkol had served both the wealthy and poor, and only twice had he come upon cases of soul-strike. He had seen two lives destroyed by this mysterious ailment. Now, he thought grimly, he would learn about it at firsthand.

Suddenly he heard voices shouting—rescue at last, whatever good that might do. He tried to speak, but could make only a wheezing sound as the dusty face of a work-gang captain leaned over him. *Take me home,* Yarkol wanted to say. The grimy man spoke to another, their discussion impossibly prolonged.

Then the physician left the ground, though he barely felt hands grasping him. The two men lifted him into his gelding's saddle, bent him forward, and somehow tied him in place with his arms about its neck. What a grim sight this would make for those awaiting his return!

Yarkol's face was pressed against the horse's mane. He could see with one eye if he cared to, but the view offered nothing but barren expanses and swirls of yellow steam. How he despised the Throats! Yet his family had lived on their border for twelve generations. And for the past hundred years, Clan Dolmi had labored to build a safe route—the long-sought Path—across this ruined landscape.

When that great labor was done, the Eastern Territory would be opened. The overcrowded Hakhans would at

3

last have the lands they needed for their sons and daughters. Yarkol would not witness this triumph of his clan. His children would see it, perhaps even join the eastward migration. But first they must mourn him—one who might have gone with them.

His eyes fell shut again, and his thoughts returned to his family—three wives, eight children. He wanted to weep, but even that was impossible now . . .

Yarkol woke in his own bed. Still unable to move his head, he stared up at the tasseled red canopy. Among the lingering scents he thought he discerned Merig's fragrance. Ah, Merig.

They don't recognize my illness yet, he thought at once. Otherwise he would have been banished from his family already and left to his fate on a heap of straw. Contagion was not the issue. His symptoms could not spread to another.

They will know my condition soon enough. Yarkol winced inwardly as a narrow visage entered his field of view. Of course, a healer had been summoned. But why Kushu? The stricken Dolmi watched his kinsman frown as he felt for the pulse at Yarkol's throat.

Why could it not be someone else? Yarkol and Kushu, so opposite in outlook and temperament, rarely spoke to one other. Now the news of Yarkol's fate was to come from Kushu's lips.

The fallen Dolmi could not see how many visitors stood in the room. Surely, he thought, his wives must be present. He heard muffled weeping and the cries of his youngest daughter. If only he could smile, offer a few words of comfort.

"He has not responded to the vapors," said Kushu gravely.

Vapors? Yarkol did not remember the treatment. Perhaps while he'd slept . . .

"The medicine I forced down his throat, costly as it was, proved useless." Kushu clucked his tongue and placed a hand over Yarkol's brow. Then he reached for a candle, bringing it closer until the brightness grew unbearable.

"All the symptoms are here," he continued, removing the flame. Of course, Yarkol's pupils were dilated; the test was unnecessary cruelty. "Yet we must wait two days more to be sure of his fate. Keep him clean. There is little else we can do for him."

At those words, the weeping broke into uncontrolled sobs. Yarkol struggled once again to move his lips. As he fought his unrelenting muscles, he heard the children being sent from the room. *Leave them here,* he wanted to cry. *Let me see them one last time.*

Only his third wife came closer. Merig's tear-stained face hung over him, and he thought for a moment he would rise up to embrace her. *Closer, Merig!* Perhaps she had aged over the past ten years, but to his eyes she was still the young beauty of Clan Zarad. In choosing his other two wives, he had followed the advice of his elders. The third match had been made on impulse, with Merig's eagerness as great as his own.

Yarkol's brother pulled her back, but the sounds of her grief were not stifled. Once more the stricken man sought to stir, to call out, but she was gone. The bed began to spin, and all his strength went into breathing. After a time, he noticed that the room had gone black.

He dreamed, and yet he was not quite asleep. A chain of mountains loomed ahead of him, and behind those snowy peaks rose others even taller. Yarkol knew, as he studied the panorama, that his body remained in the bed. Yet he felt himself pulled northward by the vision, along trails that lifted him ever higher, over treacherous passes and across ice-laden valleys. And always, as he looked north, he thought of the ultimate peak, the Mount-of-Mounts at the continent's center.

Already, I am called. He tried to fight the dream, for it hinted at notions that his people had long ago discarded, at beliefs that only the northern nomads kept alive. His illness, however sudden and inexplicable, had nothing to do with the Chirudaks' summit gods. Yet the visions continued, taking him over narrow ridges where the winds threatened to blow him from his saddle. Upward, always upward he went. Behind each range lay another, fiercer barrier. Beyond and above them all, shimmering in the impossible distance, lay the Peak-of-the-World where the gods held court. *Chirudak gods.*

His journey ended far short of those heights. He found himself on a broad plain sheltered between crags. Herds of sheep and horses and curly-haired goats roamed the brown, wintry grassland while hide-clad riders patrolled against wolves. At the valley's edge, beside a frothing stream, stood the yurts of the nomads in orderly rows. During his travels Yarkol had seen a few such round dwellings, their gray felt coverings tied to frames of bent canes. Now, for the first time, he glimpsed a large nomad encampment.

Misgivings rose as the dream propelled him toward the largest yurt, where warriors stood guard at the entrance. The felt sides here were pure white, the ends of the roof poles red. He saw the door flap pulled back, but resisted the force that drove him closer. Never had he entered such a place . . .

He woke trembling, soaked with sweat, his hands gripping the bedclothes. His heart was hammering, his breathing harsh. For a moment he could not push the dream image from his mind. But then he noticed that some

6

sensation had returned to him. He could *feel* the wetness on his body and the smooth quilt between his fingers.

He realized that the illness already was nearing its second stage. Yarkol tried to turn his head. The motion was stiff, painful, but he managed to survey the room. Yes, the paralysis had eased. And in time, as the illness ran its course, he expected to regain the strength of his body. But this physical recovery would bring no release from his woes. His life at Dolmi House was finished in any case. This room, and all it held, would soon be lost to him.

For possibly the last time he gazed at the great ancestor, the first Dolmi to cultivate the land. Mounted on a white charger, the patriarch surveyed with satisfaction the valley he'd wrested from Chirudaks. The soil bore crops now—grains, fruits, berries. No longer did nomads' cattle trample this ground.

On another rug three priests stood in a circle, their forked beards pointing at the child they blessed. The object of attention was no ordinary child, for later he would lay the first building stones of Dolmi House. In the background, shimmering as if seen through the infant's imagination, stood towers and high walls, crimson pennants streaming from battlements.

In the third and newest hanging yet another Dolmi visionary appeared. Standing on a precipice above the Throat of Sorrows, the figure watched a ghostly stream of riders cross the desolation. On all sides of the Path lay steaming geysers and bubbling pools. Yet the travelers to the new lands kept their heads high and did not falter. They advanced in a jagged line that vanished into the landscape. Yarkol sighed, for that hope was not yet realized.

He turned again to the first rug and studied the ripening fruit trees. By giving up nomadic life, the Hakhans had made themselves strong and secure. In those early days

7

there had been food for all, prosperity for Dolmi Clan after generations of wandering . . .

Reflecting so, Yarkol grew aware of his own hunger and thirst. He turned with great effort and found a drinking glass beside the bed. With halting movements he pulled himself up until his back rested against the headboard. He reached for the goblet with trembling fingers, grasped the stem, and lifted, slowly. At last he brought it to his mouth and drained the contents.

He licked his lips. *Wine? Cider?* No. The drink held a faintly bitter aftertaste. He sniffed a familiar odor in the cup and suddenly recognized the herbal compound that had flavored the drink—a restorative he should have known at once. What, he wondered, had the illness done to his memory?

Frowning, he turned his head as something scuttled across the shadowed end of the room. *A rat?* Impossible in Dolmi House, where ferrets were loosed nightly in the corridors. He squinted into the corner; a tiny man-like shape seemed to be crouching at the base of a chair. Yarkol pursed his lips in disbelief as the impish face made a grin. "Are my eyes ruined as well?" he cried out in anguish. He fell back, startled by the sound of his own voice.

When Yarkol had recovered further, the priest Murtok came, bringing with him a platter of cheese and bread along with a jug of cider. Yarkol reached hungrily for the food, though his hands were still shaky. He had little interest in what the priest would say to him.

"So," said the priest, toying with a round chunk of cheese. His face was fleshy and deeply lined. His dark blue robe was intricately embroidered in white, and Yarkol noticed brownish stains on the sleeve. "It's as

Kushu suspected, is it not?" said Murtok in a jovial tone. "I see tufts of your beard falling out already."

Yarkol's fingers rose to his face. He felt a few bare patches and could only scowl, for he knew the progression of his illness. *In the end, I'll be smooth as a child. And for that I must be banished.* The priest was calmly chewing, his own gray magnificence rising and falling with his jaw.

"So from your viewpoint I am no longer a person," Yarkol answered quietly. "That's what you came to tell me."

Murtok shrugged, licked his fingers, then reached for another tidbit from the platter. "The question I must answer for myself is *why* this has happened. Why does this affliction fall on an honored clan?"

Yarkol let his breath whistle through his teeth. "You wish to hear the telling of my sins?"

From the priest came the cloying odor of the incense used in his ceremonies. "You have offended the God-on-High. Why else would you be so stricken? But some good will come of it if I can use you as an example to the others. There are many who grow lax in their duties."

"I never missed my obligations," Yarkol growled. He tore into the crusty bread with a vigor that surprised him. "I followed your calendar, made the sacrifices you demanded, laid my offerings in your treasure house. Do not accuse me of impiety."

"The matter is more subtle than following observances." The priest poured himself a tankard of cider.

"I know where this is leading. I healed the sick, all who called me, including some you would have left to die."

Murtok pursed his lips. "Unbelievers have no right to aid from one who serves the God-on-High. I warned you often, and each time you dismissed me."

9

"The ones I served were Hakhans. I did not ask about their beliefs."

"And never, in all your days, did you aid a Chirudak?"

Yarkol laughed hollowly. "I break out in a sweat if I catch the stink of one. You know that well."

"I know more than that. For three days you lay in a Chirudak place of evil. Who can say what the demons did to you there—what slow-growing seed they planted?"

The physician gritted his teeth, trying to hold back the memory. "I was alone in that place," he said softly. "Alone and untouched." But after all the intervening years, Yarkol still could not be certain of what had happened.

He had gone exploring—a foolhardy venture of his youth. Near the edge of the Throats he had followed a speckled lizard through some brush and had come upon an opening in the hillside. An inexplicable urge had caused him to crawl through the hole and down into an underground chamber. There, in dim light that filtered through the entrance, he saw piles of human bones and above them masks carved into the rock. The eyes on the carvings glowed like tiny fires; he could not turn away from them. When night fell, he dropped into a stupor.

Later, he opened his eyes and saw Chirudaks dancing, their rank scent filling the chamber. Each man's hair hung in three plaits that lifted as he spun faster and faster until the braids stood out stiffly and the face became a blur. Then, suddenly, the dance stopped. All the men but one retreated. The last, a shaman in his robe-of-bones, advanced to the wall, plucked free one of the carvings, and held it to his face. The mask *became* his face, its fierce teeth glowing . . .

"I prayed over you afterward," the priest said with a shrug. "After the dogs found you. But why you didn't climb out of your own accord, I still don't know."

Yarkol smiled faintly. For years he had believed that Chirudak spirits had wrestled with him in the dark

10

cavern. He was convinced now, however, that fumes from the Throat had leaked into the chamber and intoxicated him. His young imagination, stimulated by frightening artifacts, had produced the visions.

Murtok tipped up his drink and swallowed the last of it. "Then you agree that there's truth to my words. The demons put the illness into your heart, left it there to grow so that it could strike you at the height of your days. A small revenge for what we did to Chirudaks."

Revenge? Yarkol recalled suddenly the troubling news from the north. After a long time of peace, the nomads had begun to stir again. Dolmi Clan had just made a substantial payment to support the northern defenses.

But old disputes over land had no bearing on Yarkol's problem. "I agree with nothing you say," the Dolmi retorted. "One man suffers fever, another the pox. To treat my case as different makes as much sense as the babble of your prayers."

The priest smiled coldly. "I am not the one who casts you out. Try to stay if you wish, and see how long you can remain within these walls. The madness will drive you away."

"You spend too much time listening to Kushu."

"I know from my own experience." Murtok waved his hand at the sick man. "This once happened to a fellow priest. You can imagine how the others were shocked. We tried to lock him up, and he broke through the door by butting it with his head."

Yarkol would not admit aloud that Murtok could be right about this. Yet the dreams lingered with him, the northward call growing stronger. The second stage of his illness was not finished, but already he felt himself a prisoner within Dolmi House.

He struggled against the feeling. *Merig. I must talk to her.* He closed his eyes and invoked the images of his children one by one. Something was amiss, for the intensity

11

of his feelings for them seemed diminished. He knew how their lives would change now. By Hakhan custom, they would become his brothers' children and would soon forget the man who had sired them.

The priest cleared his throat. "That Chirudak abomination—that so-called shrine—must be destroyed. What if someone else crawls in there?" Yarkol watched Murtok shake his gray head slowly. "I should have seen to it long ago. Tomorrow I'll send for workmen to fill the place with mud. We'll give them plenty to drink first and encourage them to piss into the hole." He grinned and gazed toward the ceiling, his heavy lips stretching across his face. Then he turned, snatched a last piece of cheese, and hurried from the room.

Yarkol cursed under his breath and wished that the foul scent of incense would disperse. *I am cast out, as Murtok says,* he thought bitterly. Yet his life was not over and he could only guess at what lay ahead.

He dozed, dreamed once more of a trek toward the snow-capped mountains. Every step took him to higher elevations and that much closer to the north. At last he stood again before the great yurt of his earlier vision, advancing to meet the man who waited within. *The Kag.* The one who calls himself Chief-Among-Chiefs. And this time Yarkol could not hold back.

Within the yurt, the glitter of gold pained the Hakhan's eyes. The Kag sat on an ordinary stool, wearing the simple felt trousers and hide coat of his people. But his face was covered by a gold mask, the cheeks studded with jade. From behind the eye-slits came the glow of moonlight on a dark pond.

What was the mask hiding?

This time, when he woke, Yarkol found himself in a room he did not recognize. He sat up. *Sat.* Yes, he moved freely; even the stiffness was gone. He felt that possibly ten days had passed since his first symptoms. He gazed around at the tiny room, which held only a pallet and a battered chair. Kushu had given a final diagnosis, and so Yarkol's family had sent him here. *A place where kitchen servants are left to die.*

But Yarkol, in body at least, was far from dead. His shoddy wrappings stank, and he peeled them off. Glancing down, he saw a trimmer figure, the fat on his belly and thighs gone. The other change he saw made him shudder, though he had known it must come. It had started with his beard. Now much of his body hair, even to the dark thatch at his groin, had dropped away. He would lose the rest soon, he knew, all but the hair of his eyebrows and head. His patches of new bare skin were as smooth as a child's.

A sound from without startled him. He covered himself with the filthy blanket. The door scraped against stone, opening slowly.

"Merig!"

"They said I must not come." She was pale, and her face bore lines of suffering, the once-bright eyes of gray cowled by sorrow. He thought she had taken on the years that his body had lost.

"Have you been ill?" He wanted to check her pulse, but he caught himself. He no longer had the right to practice his art. Perhaps his mind was not recovered, his training and experience shed along with so much else.

"You must eat again," she said, her hand smoothing her plum-colored gown. "I'll bring you food and drink. And something clean to wear."

"And water for washing."

"Yes."

He stared at her. "The children?"

"They have mourned you, as the priest demanded. It is finished now."

13

"Then I cannot see them again?" The realization should have brought a flood of misery. He felt only a single tear growing.

"They would not know you now. Why confuse them when they've accepted what they must?"

"And do you accept it?" He wished he could touch her, comfort her. But in his grimy condition how could he even step closer?

"I prayed secretly to the God-on-High," she said in a small voice, "that I might share your suffering. That I too might be cast out." She looked at her hands dolefully. "A sickness came, but it was not the same as yours. And now I am well."

"Be glad of that. Your place is with the children, not wandering the countryside." He tightened his fist. "The priest is right about some things," he admitted. "I cannot stay here, no matter how much I wish otherwise." For a moment he forgot his resolve and took a step toward her. One last embrace? The stench of the blanket rose about him, and his will faltered.

She reached out to squeeze his hand, once, quickly, then turned and fled the room. He heard her sobbing through the half-closed door; his knees weakened; he lay down and wept on his ragged bed.

Merig did not return, but she sent two servants with the promised supplies. Yarkol had expected no more. She had been courageous to come to him at all.

When the servants were gone, he leaned over the basin of water and tried to get a look at himself. The room was too dark for reflections. He opened the door and set the bowl where it caught the light. Now he could see his face, bits of dark beard still clinging, the rest as smooth and youthful in appearance as it felt to his touch. And the new purplish blotch that spread across his right cheek offered no surprise, though its cause was as mysterious as that of the disease itself. Twice before he had witnessed such a mark.

After he was fed and clothed, he found himself unable to remain still. The final phase of his illness was almost over, he realized. He paced the room, occasionally standing at the doorway to gaze into the muddy yard. From shadows he guessed the time to be late afternoon. A kitchen maid was carrying buckets from the well. Otherwise only a few broad-tailed chickens disturbed the quiet of the yard.

Merig had managed to send him his best riding boots, thick woven trousers, and a leather coat. She had also given him a sack of provisions and a waterskin. But she could do nothing to secure him a mount. He must steal one—*steal* his own gelding if he wished to ride off.

A rebellious thought came. He would spite the priests, expose their lies. Now that he was strong again, he would march into Dolmi House and demand to take up his former life. He would prove that he had not been cursed.

Striding into the yard, he advanced with sudden resolve toward the nearest stone building. *What a surprise for old Murtok!* But glancing up, he saw the high walls seem to sway and thought that they were about to topple onto him. He forced his feet to take a few more steps as he tried to imagine himself inside the closed rooms. The vision made him gag. Even before he entered, he knew that the air would be rank, suffocating. He dropped to his knees and held his face in his hands. *I am lost.* The old Yarkol was dead, already mourned; nothing could bring him back . . .

At last the new Yarkol rose and turned to the north that so urgently called him. The outer walls of the keep blocked his view, and he saw only sky in that direction, but he knew what lay beyond. A sense of purpose that he could not explain was already working against his despair.

15

He must leave now, quickly, before the past recaptured his spirit.

He returned to the room where his provisions lay, slung the sacks over his shoulder, then emerged into the shadowed edge of the yard. As he followed the row of shoddy outbuildings, he noticed something scuttle across his path, and he almost cried aloud. *Another!* He glanced down at the small grinning figure that paused at a dark doorway. The thing's arms were so long that its hands dragged on the ground. The toes of its hairy feet bore ugly talons.

"I don't believe in kobolds," he muttered under his breath. He studied the stables, thinking he must run across the open ground if he was to prove a proper thief. Glancing back, he saw the impish creature still watching him, its head nodding gaily. *The stuff of children's tales.* He kicked a stone in the creature's direction and was pleased to see it dodge. *Now I am drawn into this foolishness.* Angrily, he turned his attention to the problem of reaching his horse.

Suddenly he began to sprint. What new strength he had in his legs! The air rushed against his face as if he were already riding. Then he was across the yard and deep into shadows beneath the wooden roof.

He had not considered the dogs. Two mastiffs appeared—two he had trained himself. Would they recognize him now? he wondered. They did not greet him, nor did they attack or make a sound. They stood warily, seeming to ignore his soothing words. He took one step forward, then another, offering his hand to be sniffed.

As if by mutual agreement, the dogs turned away and padded off on other business. *My own pair, raised from weanlings.* They had ignored him, as if he were no longer a man. He wondered what he could expect from his horse.

But the gray stood for him and let him tighten the

16

saddle girth. He tied on the waterskin and provisions and led the gelding out toward the waning sunlight. Why must he feel guilty over this? In his years of service he had earned far more for Dolmi Clan than he was taking. Even so, he hesitated before rolling up a tattered blanket and adding it to his baggage. Then he swung into the saddle and trotted his mount out of the yard.

A cold wind sprang up, ruffling the horse's mane and the sleeves of Yarkol's coat. As he followed the winding road down from his clan's hilltop perch, he saw the Dolmi lands spread across the valley below. Here lay a scene that was not quite the one his carpet depicted. The grain was nearly ripe, but in sections a dark blight had withered the crop. From a distance the orchards looked well, but the apples, he'd been told, were small this year and unusually tart. Thank the God-on-High, he thought, that matters were not worse. The earth would carry his people through another winter, though the poorer families might face short rations.

In a few days the harvesting would begin. And afterward, when the work was done, how the great hall would ring with sounds of celebration! He could see his young daughter as she had been last year, her face gleaming as she spun in a dance. He could hear the music and the clapping, smell the smoke from sacrificial bonfires in the fields.

Yarkol blinked as his eyes began to grow damp. He shook his head, tried to will the memories away. *I must ride and think of nothing else.* The shadows of distant hills were growing longer, and he wished to be gone from Dolmi territory before dark.

Despite his mount's willingness, he came down the dirt track too slowly to suit his mood. He refused to turn back, to take a final glimpse at the great stone keep. Did his horse understand that they were leaving forever? The gray snorted once, shook its head, and trotted on.

17

Yarkol had an immediate destination in mind—one that lay northward but short of the mountains of his dreams. Before he abandoned himself to his wanderings, he must seek advice from Hirchil Zarad. Of all men he knew, Hirchil would be the last to turn him away.

Gazing across the fields, Yarkol saw only the rippling of grain as a breeze passed through. The laborers were all up in the orchards, gathering the fruit in hampers they wore on their backs. Looking across to the wooded hillside, he caught glimpses of movement.

Some workers would be at the road, but he saw no way to bypass them. He leaned forward, and the animal increased its pace. Ahead, in the distance, stood three wagons being loaded. The fragrance of apples grew stronger.

The laborers were all Chirudaks, from families that had settled on the fringes of Dolmi land. These people had given up the ways of their fierce northern cousins—the ones who troubled Yarkol's dreams. Now they wore the familiar garb of farmhands, trousers of gray for the men, long blue skirts for the women; no longer did they carry their deadly short bows. Why then did Yarkol find himself trembling as he approached them?

One farmhand after another looked up at the arriving Hakhan. Did any workers recognize him? he wondered. Some might recall his mount, but none would know his new face. He realized how strange he must appear, with tufts of beard still clinging in patches. Better to avoid most of these people, he thought, steering his horse off the road to bypass the largest crowd.

More Chirudaks appeared, their dark braids glistening where sunlight touched them. The men's chins were shaved, their cheeks bristly, their eyes bright. He saw mouths opening in surprise as shouts passed among the crew. An elderly woman dropped to her knees in a pose of reverence.

Wherever he turned he saw stares, and he knew what

was drawing such attention. For a moment he seemed to feel a burning sensation where the illness had left its mark—as if flames danced across his cheek. He had some notion what this sign meant to Chirudaks.

They had abandoned nomadic habits but still carried their ancestors' beliefs. And Chirudaks, Yarkol understood, viewed one with his affliction as *godstricken*, a person to be revered. He shook his head at that idea, finding it as absurd as his own priest's claim that he was being punished by the God-on-High. He wanted nothing to do with Chirudak superstition, yet nomads haunted his dreams.

At last, Yarkol maneuvered his horse past the laborers and back onto the road again. Finding the path open, he urged his mount into a brisk trot. The cool wind felt welcome against his face and he wished only to fly faster.

He crossed a low hill and then another. Then he realized, with relief, that he was no longer on Dolmi land. Below, the fields of the neighboring clan lay deep in shadow. Evening was coming on.

Yarkol headed for a stand of willows beside a shallow stream at the next hill's base. This was where he must spend the night. He thought of the warm bed he might otherwise be sharing with Merig and clamped his jaw. He could not recall when last he had slept beneath the stars.

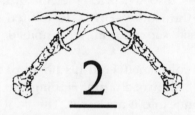

2

*A man who sleeps without dreaming
is a man who has no future.*

—*Chirudak saying*

Night had come to a town
that lay on the western border of Dolmi land. This was a
settlement of Hakhan shopkeepers, smiths and traders.
But Chirudaks, workers from the nearby fields, gathered
here after dark to share food and talk. Their meeting
place had neither walls nor a roof. A mere plot of ground
at the edge of town, it possessed tree stumps for seating
and a crude shelter at one end in case of storms.

The nomad woman, Etoudoori, and her two male companions had been visiting here often since their arrival
from the north in late spring. Now she stood by the fire
impatiently, watching another woman kneading dough.

Weedchewers! Etou's contempt for her southern cousins had not been softened by her days among them. How she longed for home, where people ate sensible food. Lately, of course, everything there had been in short supply. Even so, in nomad camps the smell of roasting meat filled the air every night. Here the Hakhans owned most of the few animals and sold meat to Chirudaks at unconscionable prices.

Over the fire grain-thickened soup bubbled in a misshapen cauldron. Etoudoori was hungry enough to look forward to her portion. But she recalled how she had refused even to taste such vile-smelling brews during her first days in the south.

Soup and bread. That was the best meal one could find in these parts. And Etou, who had always shirked women's chores, was expected to aid in the preparations.

The woman who was kneading looked up suddenly. "You need practice, Northerner," she said, standing away from the board that rested atop a stump. "Finish this for me."

The visitor frowned, but bent to the task. She had been told to make herself into a weedchewer—to learn their habits and ways of talking—so that she would attract no attention from Hakhans. Now she wore a long dress of crude cloth, though the garment was unsuited for riding. Her fine six-year-old roan had been turned into a carthorse, for southern women were not brash enough to mount a horse's back. Women not ride? Then they could never be true Chirudaks.

Etoudoori vented her frustrations on the dough, kneading it so furiously that her companion pulled at her shoulder. "You don't learn, my pretty one," she said. "What you are good for has nothing to do with our work."

The nomad woman hissed and stepped aside. It was true that she possessed other talents. Even as a child, she'd known how to escape the drudgery about the yurt.

21

While herdsmen stood watch, she had been the one to bring them skewers of roasted lamb and skins filled with yohourt. The men always cheered when they saw her bright smile and her eyes that glinted gold. As she grew older, she learned other ways to please men.

Now she was doing nothing but waiting. For weeks she had listened to the gossip here and in similar places, had questioned everyone who came for the knowledge that she so dearly wanted. Her companions, Oron and Baatibi, had also made rounds of the neighboring settlements.

But little could be learned, for the Dolmi soil-tillers were a secretive lot. They were happy to let Chirudaks work their fields, but kept them far from the Throat's mysteries.

After a time Etoudoori had begged to go home, but Oron stubbornly refused. He was the Kag's cousin, after all, sent here on a mission of great import. He could not return dishonored by defeat. And so he had persisted, even venturing to the edge of the Throat to watch riders brave the Path. Had the Hakhans caught him, he would have spent the last moments of this life in a boiling pool.

The Path wound farther than he could see. All he could tell was that many men came and went on it. So he stayed on here, trying to learn more—even a single useful fact— that he could bring to his powerful cousin.

The Kag! Etou shivered as she thought of the man whose influence had spread so quickly. The tribes fiercely valued their independence and rarely accepted a leader over all. Only in the past few years, as drought withered the herds and life grew harsh, had the chiefs rallied about one man.

It was the Kag's will that had sent her here, on a quest that she once thought hopeless. Now, unexpectedly, a new chance for success had arisen. Soon she might be going home.

Etou turned her back on the fire and looked toward the

empty road. Overhead hung the Wolfpack, a string of tiny moons across the eastern sky. Oron should be back by now, she thought. Perhaps this time he would bring the news they awaited.

"Etou, my sweet!" A rough hand grabbed her own. She spun back, eyeing the farmhand warily. She had long before established her skill at kicking a man hard enough to make him limp. The skinny weedchewer smiled cautiously and spread out his arms. "Just a hug, Etou. That's all I ask."

"Tell me what I want to know and you'll get more than that," she said harshly. "Otherwise . . . nothing."

"Aren't you tired of that refrain? Sometimes you need a little fun." His friends were drinking kumiss from gourds, and he tapped the nearest man on the arm. "How about some for the miss," he said in a loud whisper that brought peals of laughter.

"It won't change my mind." Etou smiled and reached for the gourd. The weedchewers' kumiss was inferior, made of fermented cow's milk because mare's milk was unavailable here. Nonetheless, she savored the tangy potion as a link with home.

"Have another," the farmhand said, a smile growing on his thin lips.

Etoudoori knew that she could quaff three full gourds without effect. If she drank more than that, the roisterer within would break free, taking over her body. Such a change she enjoyed at times, but not with these people. The man who had given her the drink took another step closer.

She shouted a warning as she tugged at her dress with one hand, lifting the hem so that her booted foot could swing freely. How she longed to exchange this rag for the practical trousers of the nomad. Now five weedchewers were closing in on her, and she could see from their faces

23

that they too had overindulged in drink. A quick glance behind showed several other men blocking her escape.

She wondered why had they grown so aggressive tonight. Generally the men traded banter with her and tolerated her rejections. Did they realize that she was leaving soon, that this might be their last opportunity? "More kumiss!" she cried. "More for everyone." She tossed her empty gourd aside and reached for another. The weedchewers seemed cheered by her concession and paused to watch her drink.

"Where I come from," she said haughtily, "a man drains three for each the woman takes. If he is still a man after that . . ." she paused, smiling. "Then he deserves what he gets."

By now it seemed that the entire assemblage of weedchewers had surrounded her. The other women stood at the edge of the crowd, some trying to drag their men away. The long leather sack containing the brew was thrust forward to the front of the throng; the challengers began to fill their gourds.

"Beauty of the mountains," said one, holding up his dipper in a toast. "When I see you, I think of . . . a sleek mare crossing a bright stream."

"Lovely Braids-of-night," said another. "You have the grace of the evening bird."

Five men stood shoulder-to-shoulder, each with his chest out, each offering an overblown compliment before he drank. Her eyes narrowed when she realized what they were doing. These five "suitors" were imitating the traditional competition for a maiden's first favors.

Forgetting her challenge to the men, Etou emptied another gourd. Was this her third or her fourth? She still felt steady on her feet, though she sensed her roisterer stirring. The weedchewer at the far end, she had decided, was the least objectionable of the lot. He had a surprising

24

gift with words; perhaps he fancied himself a poet. She smiled, readying herself for the next round of toasts.

"What are you doing, Etou?" Oron's deep voice! It fell like thunder over the crowd, and for a moment everyone was still. She turned to see a dark rider on the road, his silhouette blocking the stars. At once she heard grumbles of disappointment as the weedchewers began a disorderly retreat. Oron, with his rough northern ways, frightened these normally-timid folk. Even with their bellies full of drink they would not challenge him.

"Well, Etou?" the rider boomed. "Enjoying yourself?"

"I am waiting for you," she said evenly, stifling her urge to giggle. Oron was always so cold and serious. Never had she seen him laugh with joy.

"And what have you learned from your little friends this night?"

That my face is like a moon of heaven. She bit her lip to hold back those words. "I am no good for kneading bread. And too much kumiss makes me drowsy."

"Ah." His face lay in shadow, and she could not make out his expression. "Even so, one of these weedchewers would be glad to take you. For his *second* wife if his first would agree to it. She'd sooner put your eyes out and burn off your hair."

"And you? What would you do with me if you weren't so concerned with your honor?"

"Enough chatter. There's no time for delay. Our rabbit's out of his den."

Yarkol slept poorly that night. Often, he woke from dreams of mountain passes and high plateaus. In his nightmares he felt the cold wind biting through his thin clothing. Whenever his eyes opened, he wrapped himself more tightly in the tattered blanket.

25

One time he woke and thought he saw someone standing over him. He sat up suddenly, then remembered the knife at his belt. His fingers trembled as he grasped the weapon. His were the hands of a healer, not a warrior.

Perhaps he'd been mistaken. The heavens were bright with moons, yet he saw no intruder. Shadows lay beneath the trees. He squinted, but did not care to explore the darkest places. He checked that his horse still grazed nearby, then tried to sleep again.

At dawn Yarkol brushed himself off and stood up groggily. After a night such as this, sleeping on damp, hard ground, he expected to feel stiff in his joints and sore in his muscles. Yet his body moved easily and without pain. In a few moments he felt fully awake and ready to ride.

He whistled for his horse, and heard an answering snort. The animal, hobbled, had not gone far. "Do you grow used to your new rider?" he asked softly, rubbing his fingers deep within its mane. The gray worked its tongue and jaw to show its pleasure.

Yarkol made a hasty meal from his provisions. By the time he was finished, the sun cast enough light to permit him to study the ground. Had someone stood here while he slept? A fox had left paw prints by the stream. The only footprints were his own.

With a shrug Yarkol mounted, then took the road that led toward Zarad House. The valley was peaceful at this early hour, the farmhands not yet at work. With luck, he hoped to avoid encounters with Chirudaks this morning.

He passed several towns, and one larger settlement, its streets of wooden houses winding and crisscrossing in no clear pattern. This was a place he visited rarely, for the smoke of so many chimneys made his eyes water. How would these people manage, he asked himself, if the crops of the great landowners should fail? Yet the goods made here—the candles, cloth, and iron work—were in demand throughout the region.

26

Yarkol frowned as he considered what disasters might befall these people. But new lands would relieve the burden on the old. If the Path succeeded, he thought, then all would be well.

The roads grew busier as the sun rose, and he was glad to reach the border of Zarad land. His mount carried him from one rise to the next, passing grain fields almost ready for harvest. Suddenly Yarkol spotted Zarad's great keep, glinting, high walls awash in the morning's light. Around it spread more territory than the Dolmi clan controlled; indeed the Zarads once had dominated this region.

Only because of the Throat had Yarkol's kin come to the forefront. The Path was a Dolmi endeavor; no others were permitted to work on it. The cost had been great, but when the work was completed, the Dolmi place in history would forever be assured.

Yarkol's pride faded as he recalled his own situation. Would Hirchil consent to see him? He did not know how best to approach the Zarad physician.

He made his way up the long track, meeting puzzled stares from the few riders—all Hakhans—he passed. He touched his face, and a few final wisps of beard fell away. Perhaps his appearance was not so startling now, so obvious a sign of recent illness. But he knew that the mark still lay across his cheek.

He would not, he decided, seek admission at the front door. Though he had married a daughter of this clan, he no longer could claim kinship. So he turned past the stables and found an entrance where kitchen servants came and went. One woman, he realized with dismay, was a Chirudak, her braids tucked up under her cap. She studied him with widening eyes as an empty bucket slipped from her hand.

"I must see Hirchil Zarad," he whispered to her

27

urgently. "I am . . . was an old friend." He spoke his name slowly and asked if she could remember it.

The woman seemed unable to reply. He watched her lips move silently before she turned and hurried into the house. *Do you also think me godstricken?* he wanted to shout after her.

Yarkol dismounted and tied his animal to a post. The stone walls here, he saw, were coated with a thin layer of moss. He let his hand rest against the soft, fine tendrils. Surely, he thought, the walls at home were similarly covered. Why had he never noticed this? Now he found that such small things fascinated him. His eyes followed tiny cracks in the mortar.

"Yarkol!"

He turned, startled. Hirchil had come! Merig's father stood staring, as if he could not decide whether to embrace his visitor. "It is you, Yarkol?"

"Do you not know my voice?"

The old physician's white beard fluttered in the breeze. His eyes squinted, and he shook his head sadly. "I cannot bring you inside. Come." He took Yarkol by the arm and strode toward an outbuilding at the far end of the yard. "I saw you while you lay in your sickbed. A sorry sight. But now you are different again, healthier certainly."

"You were in Dolmi House?"

"To attend my daughter. Kushu knows his medicines but has little sense with people. I gave her the reassurance she needed."

"I saw her once before I left." Yarkol felt his eyes stinging.

"I can guess why you came. From Kushu you'd have gotten small comfort. As for the priests—" He gave a sharp laugh. Hirchil halted before the stone shed, gave a signal to the mastiffs who stood guard, and waited while they moved aside. He opened the narrow door, letting out a dusty smell of grain.

28

The Zarad stepped into the chill, gloomy interior and beckoned for Yarkol to follow. "Here we can speak freely," Hirchil explained. "I want no questions from my wives."

"So long as Merig is cared for, they should be happy."

"Yes. But they worry. About your so-called sins and what effect they might have on the grandchildren."

"At least you don't believe the priest's rantings. You're the only man I trust to tell me what to expect."

"Ah, Yarkol." The Zarad's short, bulky figure was barely visible in the shadows. "Men are felled for no reason. Illness does not choose its victims. But to be stricken in this way may be a different matter. Have you seen your reflection? You are a young man again."

"And for what? That I may spend my days wandering?"

The elder sighed. "I have listened to what the nomads say about such cases."

"Chirudaks!" Yarkol spat out the word. "With their gaggle of gods at the world's peak. Must I believe that *they've* touched me?"

"I won't take sides, Yarkol. But remember that Chirudaks and Hakhans were once the same people. Their gods were our gods. The priests tell us to forget the old notions, but the past remains with us."

"Will you tell me next that you believe in sprites and kobolds?"

Hirchil laughed. "I know that grain vanishes from this storeroom even when we leave dogs standing guard."

Yarkol paused, hesitant to make his confession. "What if I told you that I have *seen* such things?" he whispered. "Imps with arms so long that their hands drag on the ground." The Zarad stirred, shuffling his boots on the stone floor, but did not reply. "It is true," Yarkol continued. "My eyesight is keener than ever, yet twice I've seen apparitions. Twice, since the illness touched me. Is this another symptom?"

"It is said," Hirchil began cautiously, "that sprites flock to the stricken."

"Chirudak talk!"

"You asked me what I know. We are beyond facts now. Perhaps you did see an imp, though the rest of us deny them." Abruptly his tone changed. "There are some large rats around!" he added jovially. "In shadow one might fool you."

"Then you cannot help me."

"I cannot say what your affliction means or where it will lead. Yet I always look for hope in the grimmest situations. Your family has suffered cruelly, but on the other side of the balance may lie a chance for good. Think not of the next life . . ."

"But of the one after that." Yarkol repeated the refrain automatically. What could such sentiments mean now? The Zarad had a mystical streak about him, and Yarkol could not prove the man wrong. "Hirchil, I thank you for your words."

"I wish I could do more." The old man embraced him in the darkness and let out a mournful sigh. "Stay here a moment. I'll bring your horse. And I ask you to visit me again if you can. If nothing else, send word of how you've fared.

Yarkol nodded, but could not speak. He remained beneath the roof, though he found the air stifling. The wanderlust tugged at him; already he longed to be in the saddle. Why was Hirchil not back yet? At last he heard the familiar voice. "Go quickly and with blessings." Hirchil's words followed him as he sped back toward the valley.

The Dolmi felt as if he were emerging from stupor. He had gone to find advice and had come away with only a few words of comfort. What was he to do now? All he could say was that the road beckoned as it wound its way through Zarad's grain fields.

A town lay ahead, and he wished to bypass it. To one

30

side, however, lay rocky terrain; swampland bordered the other. And so he set his face forward, determined to ignore the stares of all who must see him.

Entering on the main track, he saw that he was approaching a crossroads. Perhaps he might yet find a way around the busiest thoroughfares. Unfamiliar with this area, he slowed to get his bearings.

At the junction a Chirudak rider was staring at him. The man, exceptionally tall, was mounted on a northern pony of chestnut color. He was dressed like a southern laborer in full trousers of gray weave and a short blue tunic. Yet something about this stranger—perhaps the unruliness of his sidewhiskers or the stubble on his chin—made Yarkol think of wild northerners he knew only from hearsay. He had seen such people in his dreams . . .

This man had a deeply tanned and weathered face. The hair above his forehead was thin, as if growing back after tonsure. Yarkol frowned, for he had heard that nomad men shaved the hair above their brows. Unlike the farmhands, this Chirudak gazed at Yarkol calmly, and for that reason the Hakhan was encouraged to speak to him. "I'm looking to bypass the town," he ventured.

The other rider stretched out his arm and pointed a long finger. Something about the northerner's face seemed familiar. Could he possibly have been working the Dolmi orchards? If so, what was he doing here? Yarkol did not ask these further questions aloud, however. He nodded at the Chirudak's response and turned his horse.

Despite his route, Yarkol was obliged to ride past a row of wooden shops. He found the street busy with horses and carts, all belonging to Hakhans. A few men glanced his way. Only one stiffened, as if the Dolmi's marked face meant something to him.

Perhaps Yarkol had misjudged these townspeople. For a moment he toyed with the notion of trying to settle in such a place. If he could pass as a youth, then perhaps some craftsman would accept him as apprentice. Even better, he might find a healer who would take him on, and then he could try to start his life over.

Intrigued by his daydream, he paused to study the scene. Two men were lifting heavy grain sacks into a wagon. From behind them came steady hammering at a forge. Then a priest emerged from a shop carrying a small parcel under his arm, his forked beard quivering as he walked. He turned at once toward Yarkol as a ferret turns to its prey. The priest's small eyes seemed to probe, and then his mouth fell open. He raised a fist, nearly dropping his bundle, and shouted an incoherent warning.

Somewhere else, thought Yarkol as he jerked the reins with annoyance. He could find a new life only by winning free of priests. His horse also seemed to sense the lack of welcome, hastening away between the ranks of carts and wagons.

Yarkol crossed another valley, pausing for refreshment at the far side. His eyebrows raised when he reached for his provisions, for an unfamiliar sack hung beside the one that Merig had sent him. *The old man.* Yarkol undid the fastenings, found cheese and dried meat within. And hidden beneath the staples lay a silver money chain of a dozen links. "Hirchil!" He shouted the name aloud in dismay. Glancing over his shoulder, he considered riding back to return this unneeded largesse. Now he understood why the Zarad had taken so long to bring his horse.

The Dolmi thought of the long ride and shook his head. He knew Hirchil. Returning the gift now would prove impossible. Perhaps later, if he established himself in a trade, he could send the money back to its source. Today Yarkol could not retreat, for the road drew him onward.

He passed one town and then another. Sighting across to the next valley, he realized that he was traveling northward without any conscious intent. Why must I give in to these urges? he asked himself. The north did not appeal to him, especially with winter coming on. Perhaps to turn west would be sufficient to satisfy his wanderlust. He recalled the names of places he had never seen.

As he pondered whether to continue or turn, he noticed three Chirudaks halted on the road below. They had been waiting, it appeared, but now they approached him at a leisurely pace. He stiffened, wondering what they might want of him.

The first—the tall one with a dark face and narrowed eyes—he had seen before. This was the man who had pointed the way at the crossroads. And perhaps Yarkol had met him earlier, but not in the Dolmi orchards. Yarkol's pulse quickened as he thought of the possible night visitor to his camp.

The second man, chunkier then the first, also rode a northern pony—a mottled creature that was stout of neck and stocky of leg like its rider. And the third Chirudak was a woman who drove a rickety cart laden with bundles. She too was garbed in southern fashion, her dress the color of the sky and surprisingly clean. Her face made him think of a woodfox he'd once come upon in a meadow.

The three halted, effectively blocking the road. Yarkol felt confused and strangely lightheaded as he confronted them. The afternoon sun was strong, reflecting from their crimson saddle cloths. The woman held something bright in her hand—perhaps a shiny bead or a bracelet. Yarkol wanted to address the tall rider, who was probably their leader, but his gaze remained fixed on the flashing bauble. "Why . . . why do you stand there?" he asked in a tone that failed to carry his indignation. "Have you never seen a face like mine?"

"You are godstricken," said the woman, whose voice bore an accent of the north. "I know what that means to you. Your people turn you out."

The Hakhan wished to shield his eyes from the light,

but his hands felt heavy. He could not summon the will to turn his head. "I ask no help from you. I wish to pass, and you are in my way."

"Your people ignore the truth, and now you suffer for it," she continued. "I know what happens to you. You wander and wander and never know rest." Her voice droned on. Yarkol, feeling dazed, barely listened to her words. Other Chirudaks had passed him by. Why did these three take a special interest in him?

"Move your horse," he said weakly. But he'd grown so drowsy that his eyelids fell shut. He tried to rouse himself, to break away from these nomad meddlers before they could steal Hirchil's silver. Despite his intentions, his eyelids would not open. And the woman was still speaking, her voice both seductive and cold.

"You are chosen," she was saying. "Chosen by the gods, but for what goal we do not know yet. You need help to find your way. I am your guide."

I want no guide. The last words of protest never sounded.

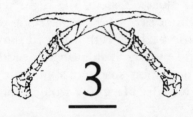

3

*The taawik—that magnificent white
bird—is, as all agree, the highest
incarnation that a human can aspire
to. But what is the lowest? Some say
the gnat, others the snake, others the
flesh-gnawing worm. I say that only
the gnat, the snake, the flesh-gnawing
worm can know for certain.*
    —Shaman Dzarum (Whitemane tribe)

When Yarkol woke, he sat
up hastily, glancing one way and then another without
recognizing his surroundings. On two sides steep walls of
a ravine rose toward a twilight sky. In the center a brook
flowed quietly past tumbled gray boulders. Near the
stream bank the Chirudak woman knelt, poking at a fire.

35

"Where is my—" His voice trailed off when he saw his horse cropping at weeds that bordered the brook. His mount was safe and apparently unharmed, but what about himself? When he stood he felt queasy. Perhaps a touch of his illness had returned.

"You rest," the woman said. A small, blackened pot sat unevenly on a stone in the fire's center. She stirred the contents once. "Tomorrow you feel better."

Tomorrow? Must he spend the night with these straners? He could not say if they were trying to aid him or to steal what little he had. Yarkol forced himself to walk to his mount and put his hands on the saddlebags. He did not wish to betray his suspicions, but with his fingers he could probe for Hirchil's gift. Through thin leather he felt hard links of silver.

"Sit by the fire," the woman said. "I'm making soup."

Yarkol was not sure that his stomach wanted food, but he began to feel ashamed of his mistrust. After all, these people could have left him by the road and taken the horse along with all it carried. They had troubled to bring him here.

He returned to the fire and sat on the ground. "It was good of you to help me," he said cautiously. Dusk had fallen. Firelight danced on the woman's face, highlighting her cheekbones, her flared nostrils, the curve of her chin. She possessed a wild beauty, he admitted to himself. *Ah, but so does a she-wolf.*

"What of your . . . companions?" he ventured. One Chirudak seemed tolerable for the moment. He did not know how three would affect him.

"They come." The soup was boiling furiously now, threatening to bubble over onto the flames. The woman stared idly at the frothing pot but made no move to rescue it. Finally Yarkol grabbed a poker and knocked several burning sticks aside.

The woman smiled with evident chagrin. "I am

36

Etoudoori," she said, "She-who-shatters-the-winter's-heart. I'm careless tonight. Distracted by your presence."

"You are a northerner," Yarkol replied. "You take the local guise, but I see the nomad in you."

Her expression hardened. "I visit my cousins. Now I go home again."

"And the men?"

"They visit cousins too!"

He lowered his gaze. So far as Yarkol knew, most local Chirudaks shunned their northern relations. Moreover, with their leaders threatening war, nomads were not welcome in the south. As he pondered what true purpose his captors might have, he heard someone approaching.

"Etou!" A deep voice. The shorter of her companions emerged from darkness, dropped a load of firewood, then began chattering in a patois that left the Hakhan bewildered. This man was stocky, solidly built beneath his laborer's shirt. If it came to a struggle, Yarkol did not think he could overpower the nomad.

The conversation continued, and the Dolmi began to catch occasional words and phrases, gathering after a time that the man was called Baatibi. Yarkol tried to guess what such a name might mean in the nomads' tongue. *He-who-rolls-over-asleep-and-squashes-wife?*

Baatibi pulled the stirring stick from the soup, blew on it, then sucked noisily. "We make you into real cook soon," he told the woman. "But not there yet."

She answered angrily, and the Hakhan did not need to grasp each word. His stomach felt settled now. If he was staying, then he might as well eat. But when Baatibi brought a wooden bowl from his saddlebags and tried to dip it into the pot, Etoudoori slapped it aside. "Wait for Oron," she insisted.

Baatibi sat down sulkily and stared across the fire at the Hakhan. He lifted his hands as if holding a small box,

37

made a shaking motion, then raised his eyebrows. Yarkol, puzzled, did not reply.

Soon the tall nomad, Oron, rode into camp. When he dipped his own bowl into the pot, nobody challenged him. He sat crosslegged, sipping at the broth with a refined manner that surprised Yarkol. Oron barked an order; Etoudoori provided another bowl for the guest. Baatibi hastily scooped out his share, and the woman, with less enthusiasm, did the same.

Yarkol held the warm bowl in his hands. The watery contents had a gamy aroma that troubled him. He had heard that nomads ate lizards and beetles when no other food was available, and this recollection did not help his appetite.

He asked himself how he could sit here calmly, beside three northerners who might strangle him at any moment. Yet they showed no obvious hostility. At last he tasted the steaming liquid, found the flavor as strong as the smell. Oron's gaze seemed to pierce him, and he wondered if he dared not finish his serving.

"You receive great honor," said the tall nomad, attempting the southern mode of speech. "And you wish to return it to gods." He waved a long-fingered hand. "No need to tell me that. I know Hakhans."

Yarkol looked down at his soup. Was this meal the honor he refused? His face flushed as he realized his stupidity. The man was referring to Yarkol's affliction.

"Others like you waste this new life they get. Stubborn." Oron nodded deeply, twice. "Waste chance to do what a man cannot. And in next life, what do they expect? Not good. Be a lizard, maybe." He took a last appreciative swallow from his bowl. "Hakhan does not heed Chirudak. Hakhan thinks Chirudak stupid. Is man stupid because he does not let walls hold him? Ha. Tell me how you like your houses of stone."

Yarkol could not answer. The illness had changed him,

made his old life repugnant. Surely the nomad knew this and was baiting him.

"Your eyes answer," Oron said. "You see Chirudak has sense under his hair." He held out his hand. "Give me bowl. We leave something for water-sprite."

Yarkol gave up his unfinished portion with relief. He watched Oron stride to the edge of the stream and pour a libation into the running water. At once, a luminous face appeared just below the surface, its mouth gaping to catch the offering. Yarkol looked away hastily.

If the others had seen the thing, they gave no sign. The Hakhan could not rid himself of the image—a toothless mouth, a hairless head, a chin sprouting long strands of water-weed. An angry imp, it was said, could make a horse slip on a rock and break its leg. Surely he didn't believe that!

By the time that Oron returned to the fire, Baatibi had something new beside him—a cracked wooden box covered with carved images, so old that the relief was almost worn away. Yarkol made out a few demonic faces, nothing more. Baatibi loosened a strap and pulled off the lid.

Oron shouted something at the shorter man, and Yarkol caught the tone of disapproval. Baatibi shrugged, began to lay out the contents—thin slabs of bone cut into various shapes. Here were disks of several sizes, each marked in black with curious figures. Two oblongs were incised with bird-wing designs. Smaller irregular pieces bore animals—a horned ox, a pony, a shaggy goat. The largest disk showed a stylized soaring mountain, and Yarkol wondered if this was the Peak-of-the-World. When the tokens were neatly arranged, Baatibi pointed a thick finger at the Hakhan. "You play before?" he asked.

Yarkol frowned and shook his head.

"I teach. Here. This is God-of-Good-Pastures." The face of the piece was etched with several crisscrossed lines.

"And this is Bringer-of-Ice." As he named each chip, he replaced it in the box.

The Dolmi continued to stare, though he grasped little of what he was shown. Perhaps these nomads had a strange sense of fairness, he thought. Rather than taking his money outright, they would force him to lose it in a gambling game. He expected Baatibi to start by laying valuables on the ground, but instead the man closed the box and began to shake it. After a few sharp rattles, he opened a slot on the side and allowed the pieces to slide out one by one.

Oron, seemingly annoyed at this pastime, turned his back on the game and began to puff on a cheroot. Etoudoori, drawing closer, grinned when she saw how the tokens had fallen. "You always think your luck will change," she said, slapping the shorter man affectionately on the knee. "But you are Baatibi, always Baatibi."

The man pushed her arm away and began to separate the pieces that had fallen face-up from those that showed only a blank surface. She leaned across his legs to see and rattled off a quick summation that Yarkol couldn't grasp. Baatibi grabbed several of Etou's braids to pull her out of his way. She swung an ineffective blow at his head, then stood up laughing. "Now let the Hakhan shame you," she said.

Baatibi spent a few more moments surveying what he had drawn. Then he sighed, replaced the pieces, and handed the box to Yarkol. "Game-of-Fate-and-Honor," he said. "Shake first. Four times. North, south, east, west."

Yarkol had seen no stakes proposed for this match. He noticed the woman watching him intently. "Four times," he repeated. The container was surprisingly light. He remembered how to open one slat and let the tokens fall.

Etoudoori shouted with excitement as she began to arrange the results. Here was the horse, there the wolf. The Lady-in-Green showed, but the Bringer-of-Ice lay beside

40

her. At last all the tokens had been paired, with none left over. "A perfect balance," declared Etou with surprise. "Strength against weakness, prosperity against doom."

"A trick of sprites," snorted Baatibi. "They want to keep us stupid."

"The bones don't lie," she countered. "If every sprite could change them, what use would they be?"

"What use now? Who can say if Hakhan withers or thrives?"

"Even so, there is a forfeit to be paid." She stared expectantly at Yarkol.

"Have I lost then?" That the nomad had beaten him was no surprise. Yet in the play he had seemed to come out ahead.

"Your future is uncertain, but Baatibi's is clearly bleak." She spoke as if explaining to a child. "That makes you the most fortunate, so you pay. To console him in his misery."

Yarkol sighed and got to his feet.

"You have henga?" The stocky nomad looked at him eagerly.

"Henga root," Etou explained. She held up her thumb as if showing what was meant.

The Dolmi pondered a moment before he recognized what they wanted. The herb, valued as a restorative, was only available from traders who ventured north. He had heard that Chirudaks used it regularly, either chewing the root or brewing a stimulating tea. "I have none," he admitted. "But I can give you a cake of salt."

Baatibi's rapt expression faded. He held out his fleshy hand and waited for Yarkol to return with the prize. As soon as he received the pale lump, the nomad whistled for his pony.

Oron still sat with his back to the dying fire. Only Etou watched the Hakhan now. Yarkol felt strong enough to ride. Perhaps if he drifted toward his own animal, he might quietly mount and be gone . . .

The woman approached him as he stood between stream and embers. She put her hand lightly on his arm. "Your dreams hold the answers," she said softly. He noticed a different smell about her—not the odor of horse that surrounded the men. The scent was pungent, mildly unpleasant, perhaps emanating from oil she used on her braids. "The bones are no help," she said. "Tell me your dreams, and I can see the way you must follow."

"I'll take my own way, find a distant town and a trade." He had been on the verge of leaving camp. Now, for some reason, he felt his boots rooted to the pebbly ground.

"Trade? How can that be? You can never stay more than one night in a place."

"There are roving trades." Yarkol sighed, for he knew that his plans had no substance. The words she had spoken on the road were true. He would wander, perhaps not only toward the north, but he would find no peace.

But what was the force that compelled him? Only Chirudaks claimed to understand it, and Hirchil Zarad did not dismiss their answers. Despite his suspicions, he wanted to hear what the woman might tell him. "Listen," he said grudgingly, his anguish darkening his tone. "When I dream, I see northern peaks. Yurts beside a brook. Herdsmen protecting the flocks. What do I, a Hakhan, have to do with such places?"

"Only the gods can know. But remember that the fates are balanced for you, and soon the scales swing one way or the other. You must learn why you are chosen." She paused, staring into his eyes. "Have you no more dreams?"

Yarkol hesitated to tell her the rest. In nightmares he had found himself within the largest yurt. How could he guess what this vision signified? "I saw a man masked in gold," he whispered.

"The Kag!" She shouted and clapped her hands. Oron stirred, suddenly turning to see what the commotion was about. Etoudoori rushed to her companion and spoke excitedly but in hushed tones. Oron sucked on his cheroot, then blew out a great cloud of smoke.

"At dawn," he said, the words exploding from his lips. "At dawn the newborn learns his way."

Etou returned to the Hakhan, her face still aglow with excitement. "When the sun rises, we go to the top of the ridge," she said, pointing up the ravine. "There we find your answer."

Yarkol nodded agreement, but realized at once that he would not stay until morning. The urge to ride had gripped him again, and soon he must take leave. Yet, despite his misgivings about Chirudak beliefs, he was curious to pursue what Etou had told him. Later, he thought, he would seek further advice from nomads.

He made a pretense of preparing for sleep when the others unrolled hides and stretched out on the ground. Only a few sparks still glowed from the fire; the heavens, alas, were maddeningly bright. He wished for clouds. Where were the storms of autumn?

The drowsing Chirudak men appeared restless. They started at every sound—the hoot of an owl, the distant barking of dogs. The Hakhan knew he must wait until the nomads fell into heavy slumber, but his own weariness began to overtake him . . .

Again, in dream, Yarkol stood within the nomad leader's yurt. The two men were alone amid the rich trappings of office—cups of beaten gold, rugs of the finest colors. But the Kag's residence also held reminders of his humble origins—a battered fur hat, a wooden table whose top was scored and weathered.

The Kag's mask hid his expression. Yarkol had once seen the bright eyes behind it, but now those eyes were growing dim. Inexplicably, the chieftain's body swayed,

43

began to fall. His head described a slow arc; he drifted down like a dead leaf. Only when the nomad lay still, his mask facing the roof, did Yarkol notice the blade protruding from his chest. Blood oozed from the wound, spreading over the outside of the Kag's hide coat.

The Dolmi cried out in surprise, for he recognized the knife as his own. He woke with his heart racing and stared at the sky. The stars had moved! He'd slept far too long.

Yarkol tried to rouse himself to action, but the nightmare held him where he lay. This was his most vivid dream since the illness had started. He could not shake off the image of the body tumbling. Though he had not seen his hand strike the blow, his knife had surely slain the man. It was a mere dream, he kept telling himself, until at last he felt calm enough to stand.

All sleepers were quiet now; he heard their steady breathing. His chance to flee was not lost.

Yarkol rolled up his blanket and walked cautiously toward where he'd last seen his mount. A handful of small moons provided more than enough light. And yes, the animal, its flanks gleaming faintly, stood grazing on the far side of the brook. Yarkol advanced to the bank, searched for a stepping-stone but found none nearby. The memory of Oron's libation troubled him.

Why not roll up his trouser legs and wade across? In the moonlight he could not judge the depth of the water, so he picked up a long stick and poked it into the flow. At once, a bald head appeared. Below it Yarkol discerned a slender body matted with water-weeds. From impossibly thin arms extended hands that possessed only two fingers each—not human fingers but ridged, bony claws.

The imp's thick-lipped mouth curved into a malicious grin. Yarkol gritted his teeth and jabbed his implement at the creature. The sprite's image wavered, but the stick touched nothing solid.

44

Smiling in triumph, for had proved the sprite a mere illusion, the Hakhan withdrew his wooden prod. But when he glanced down at the twig, he noticed that only half remained in his hand. Jumping back from the flow, he nearly shouted from surprise. His horse, on the far side, still grazed quietly. Yarkol retreated, fearful that the animal might see him and try to cross.

The Hakhan's legs were shaking. He sat on the ground and tried to convince himself that his eyes had fooled him again. He touched the stick's end, felt a cleanly cut edge. Bitten by a muskrat? he asked himself. Surely no sprite had done this.

Yarkol pounded his fist against the ground. He was a victim of delusion, he thought. The nomads, with their talk of water-sprites, had made him see what was not there.

As a physician, he had taught women to bear children without feeling pain. Now Yarkol was determined to free himself from his own troubled senses. He must clear his thoughts if he wished to recover his horse.

He closed his eyes and focused on his breathing. Deeply and slowly he took in air, counting the breaths. The body must vanish, along with its cares and delusions. The spirit within was all that mattered.

Deeply and slowly . . . Yet, despite all, he heard a faint voice calling, too shrill to come from any human throat. Yarkol forced wind to whistle through his nostrils, but he could not drown out that other sound. "Come, Ulaansh," it wailed. "Come wrestle with me. Show me your strength."

Suddenly he felt torn asunder as if he had become two people at once. His body still sat on the ground, its lungs heaving in a slow rhythm. But another part of himself broke away, crept forward a short distance, and halted. Seeing with eyes that were not eyes, he turned to look back at a man in trance. Yes, that was Yarkol, hunched

45

over, marred face visible in the moonlight. But this other who watched was also Yarkol. Spirit and flesh had somehow parted.

Had he gone too far with his exercise? Never had Yarkol heard of such a result. He turned his spirit eyes toward the glimmering water and saw the sprite's glowing face at the surface. Even in deep trance he could not shake off the illusion.

"Wrestle with me, Ulaansh," the imp asked again. Its eyes were round as full moons, but totally dark within. Its small ears were membranes that resembled fins of fish. "A quick match, Ulaansh. If you win, I'll let you cross over to your horse." The claws came out of the water.

Wrestle? Using what? Yarkol looked down to discover that he could *see* the spirit form in which he had separated from his body. The shape was a man's, but only white bones showed. The sight of his fingers stripped of flesh so shocked him that he scrambled backwards, rushing to regain his earthly form. In a moment his awareness merged again with his senses.

"Hakhan, you disappoint me," came the high-pitched voice again. "We must reach an understanding, your kind and mine." Yarkol's real eyes sprang open, but his attention was diverted from the persistent sprite. He turned to see a dark figure—human, at least—looming over him.

"You are awake already. Good." Oron's deep voice. "On your feet then. Hurry. Dawn is here soon."

Dawn? Then he had missed his chance for escape after all. The Hakhan felt too disoriented to argue with the northerner. Etou had gone ahead, walking along the ravine toward higher ground, and he felt compelled to follow her. He recalled the promise of guidance and realized that now he must hear her out.

The way became steeper. Overhead the stars were fading. But he had not rid himself of the water-sprite; whenever he glanced at the stream, the imp's head rippled just beneath the surface. Could nothing hold it back? A tree had fallen across the flow, creating a miniature waterfall. Yarkol's eyes widened as he watched the creature flatten itself and slide up the thin cascade.

Soon the party reached the canyon's rim, a point higher than the surrounding landscape. Surveying the shadowy plains below, Yarkol saw no familiar landmark.

"Sit with your face to the rising sun," Etoudoori urged in a throaty whisper. Yarkol noticed that the two men were departing, walking briskly along the ridge as if eager to be far from him. From the woman's neck hung a large oval hoop with a skin stretched over it, a shaman's drum, he surmised.

"Close your eyes," she demanded. He found himself doing as she bid. Etoudoori stood behind him, resting her hands on his shoulders, her touch raising goosebumps.

"Tell me what you dreamed this night," she whispered.

The Hakhan tightened his lips. He could not answer.

"Tell me." She began to massage his stiff muscles, producing a warmth that spread downward.

"I . . . I saw the Kag. As before."

"The same as before?"

He felt light, almost capable of floating. She pressed close to him, her musky smell filling his senses. If he confessed the truth . . .

"I . . . stood in his yurt. He wore his mask of gold, but his eyes were changed."

Her smooth cheek touched his own. A warmth sprung from her flesh, melting Yarkol until he could hold nothing back. "And the rest?" she insisted. "No harm will come to you."

"I . . . killed him," the Hakhan wailed. "He fell, pierced by my knife!"

At once he felt Etou spring away from him. He opened his eyes, turned to see her pained expression. She swung her head wildly, looking first toward the distant men,

47

then back at the quickening dawn. "Sit down," she managed, her voice quavering. "Sit down and do as I tell you. The first light must fall on closed eyelids."

The Dolmi sat. Once again he felt her hands on his shoulders, but this time he sensed a faint trembling. She began to sing softly, a melody that spoke first of grief and despair. An image came to him of a snow-covered plateau, where a group of weary nomads and their sheep struggled against a storm. New snow came down heavily, deepening the drifts. The animals were faltering, and the men could find no shelter.

Suddenly a towering figure appeared in the midst of the tumult. He shouted orders, rode back and forth tirelessly, until the herders and their animals were moving in another direction. Then a high cliff appeared, with a cave beneath it where all might take cover. Again and again, the newcomer brought stragglers to safety, sometimes carrying a child beneath each arm, other times picking up fallen sheep and brushing the snow from their coats.

Who was this hero she sang of? the Hakhan wondered. Perhaps he had heard tales of such a man—godstricken—chosen to serve in a moment of crisis. But this legendary rider had nothing to do with Yarkol's plight.

At last the song ended, giving way to a faint drumming—a rhythm of eerie, hollow sounds. He recalled the shaman's drum he'd seen strung about her neck? It was said among Hakhans that human skin covered such instruments and that the skin came from a babe strangled by its mother. He shuddered, dismissing such cruel talk, but did not turn to study what the woman held. The drumming grew louder, accompanied now by a rising chant.

"The north draws you," she whispered, her breath warm and moist against his ear. "The north beckons, and you have no choice but to follow." He felt her finger pressing against his lips, knew he must stay silent.

Again she tapped at the drum. "The Kag awaits you,"

she said in a singsong voice. "The Kag prepares to welcome you as a friend."

Yarkol stiffened, recalling the most recent dream. Had he mistaken the obvious meaning? Perhaps it was a warning of what might happen if he should fail in his task—whatever that task turned out to be.

"Your goal is to bring peace," sang Etoudoori. "Hakhans and Chirudaks must not fight."

His lips parted, but he forced them shut again. The Hakhans wanted only peace, but surely she knew that. Her own people were the ones who threatened an invasion.

At that moment he noticed a pink glow through closed eyelids. Sunrise! The woman continued to drum as brightness grew.

"Go north and be a bringer of goodwill," she chanted. "Tell the Kag that the Hakhans wish his tribes rich pasture and fat herds. Offer him a gift."

Yarkol felt the sun's first light on his face. Etoudoori drummed on. Bring a gift? he asked himself. What had he to offer? But these doubts fled as the drumming continued, accompanied by words that flowed ever more quickly. Often he could not understand what she sang, but one refrain came again and again until he grasped it as a single sound.

"Embrace the Kag as a brother!"

4

Pupil: Why must we ask spirits to carry our pleas? Why do we not pray to the gods directly?

Teacher: Why does a fish not breathe air?

—*Chirudak tradition*

The sun's rays had not yet dipped into the canyon, but Etoudoori was almost ready to depart. She paused in her work to watch the Hakhan as he dazedly mounted his horse. A pang of guilt gnawed at her, and she wished it away. Must she pity this wretch—this spawn of a soil-tiller?

Etou had been told to speed the Hakhan northward. To do so, she had twisted the meaning of his dreams. Now she could not foresee the consequences.

"Tell me this if you will," the newborn asked her as his ten-year-old plains gelding shook its head impatiently. His smooth face was a boy's, open-eyed with curiosity, but his wiry figure was a man's. "Do you know the meaning of this word—*ulaansh*?"

Etou smiled. "That is you. *Reborn.* Gifted with new life."

The Hakhan's lips twitched, as if he hadn't expected such an answer. He continued to stare at her while holding his mount in check. Another question came from him, but so quietly that she had to draw closer to hear it. "Last night, when we poured the libation, did you see the water-sprite?"

This time she could not hold back her laughter. He was indeed the child he appeared to be! Once, when she was young, Etou had imagined she saw tiny eyes glowing among the coals. She had called her sisters and brothers to see the "imp," and they had taunted her cruelly. Finally her mother had explained that spirits do not show themselves, except in dreams. "Go on your way, Hakhan," Etou shouted with a wave of her hand. "I've nothing more to tell you."

He hesitated, and she feared he might question her makeshift ceremony or her use of the shaman drum. The southerner gazed into the brook a moment longer, as if waiting to see a water-imp thrust out its talons. Was it possible, she wondered, that an *ulaansh* could see what ordinary eyes missed? She had heard that in a tale once, but the prospect made her shiver. She was relieved when finally he shrugged, turned his mount, and rode off.

"Hurry with your packing," commanded Oron, already astride his horse. His saddlebags bulged, and she realized that he had lightened her cart.

"I'm not ready," she murmured. "I must make an offering first. Ask forgiveness of the ones I've wronged."

"You've no time for that. Listen. Here's my plan." On

51

his eight-year-old gelding, Oron made an overbearing figure. He sat in shadow, a fresh breeze rippling his trousers. "Baatibi must take care of a small errand. After that, I'm sending him directly home to tell what we've snared. I'll be following the Hakhan's heels, making sure he holds to his journey. But you'll be too slow to keep up with me."

"You leave me to travel alone?"

"I'll drop signs for you. Rise early and ride late if you want to reach my camp."

She tossed her head. "Maybe I'd rather follow Baatibi."

"So he can waste time rutting with you under a blanket?" A cruel smile showed on Oron's face, and his hand patted the place where his sword, now packed away, normally hung. "Maybe I should cut off his worm to be sure he'll have no distractions."

"She won't follow me," Baatibi cried at once. "See. I'm gone. I'll take the steepest trail north." He was already riding up the canyon, his horse laboring under his bulk.

"You forgot your sleep roll!" Etou called after him. The squat rider doubled back hastily, grabbed the hide from her hands. As he passed, she noticed the borrowed spirit drum hanging from his saddle. She could still feel the tingle of its vibrations as her fingers struck the skin. Now, perhaps robbed of power by Etou's misuse of it, the instrument would go back to its owner.

Oron followed Baatibi, the two riding quickly in the direction that Yarkol had taken. Etou shook her head in disgust. "What do you care?" she shouted after them, recalling the men's retreat during her drum-beating. "*My* soul's at risk. You ran away to stay clean." Some might say that her soul had long ago lost all hope for a decent next life. But Etou knew that the total of her past transgressions could not compare with what she had done today. For, despite his soil-tilling ways, the Hakhan was godstricken. She did not know what purpose the high ones meant for him, but her meddling had altered his destiny.

Now he would become the Kag's tool . . . provided only that he reached the north in safety.

She must make what amends she could. The gods would not hear her pleas; even shamans could not directly soothe their wrath. But spirits might intercede for her. Here, in this ravine, she planned to begin her penance.

With a pointed stick she scratched out a circle in the gritty soil. From the food stocks that the men had left she took a leather pouch of crumbled salt. She knelt in the circle's center and leaned over so that every grain would fall into the freshly scored earth. "Underground spirits, take this gift," she chanted. "Kobolds, rally to my offering." Four times she turned about the center, remaining on her knees despite sharp stones that bit through her skirt. Then with her thumb she carefully sealed up the rent she had made in the soil. "Be kind to me, kobolds," she pleaded. "I am easily led astray by men. From this salt, make tears of pity for my foolishness."

When that was done, she sprinkled a handful of grain into the brook, begging the sprites there also to come to her aid. Froth danced on the water, and she remembered the Hakhan's question. Of course she couldn't see the sprites, but she knew they must be there. She listened to the current's hiss and imagined answering voices.

Finally she tossed pinches of herbs to the morning breeze as she called on the spirits-of-air. "Hear me, swift ones. You who are free can carry my message." She spun four times, naming the winds.

A series of melodious bird calls interrupted the last of her offerings. Etoudoori glanced up to see a pair of long-necked taawiks roosting on a sunny ledge. The largest bird had just landed and was folding its white pointed wings; it stared at her as if in rebuke.

You too know my shame! She could not face the bird's

gaze. Whispering a last plea to the wind, she turned to finish her packing.

Yarkol found himself riding again, first across rocky, untillable land, then down into marshy regions. His direction was northward, and now he did not question his drive. In a few days he would reach nomad territory, yet even that prospect failed to daunt him. He wondered if Etou had soothed some of the fears that lingered from his childhood misadventure.

He felt gooseflesh prickling when he recalled the sound of her spirit drum. The ceremony had affected him, he realized, though he could not say how. In any case, his worst suspicions had proved false. The northerners had done him no obvious harm. With his marked face for protection, he believed he could travel safely into the high country.

The incident with the water-sprite troubled him, but he chose not to dwell on it. His thoughts turned instead to practical matters—to the task he had adopted. He intended to serve as an emissary of peace, yet lacked any official standing. To offer the Kag friendship he needed agreement from the Barrier Alliance.

The man who could help him was Hyar Jornood, leader of the northernmost Hakhans. Responsibility for defending the south from nomads rested with Jornood and the Barrier clans. Yarkol had seen Hyar from a distance once, but knew nothing of the man's temperament. Furthermore, he had only a vague notion of how to find Jornood House.

Somewhere in the north a great bulwark, a construction that took five generations to finish, stretched from west to east. Yarkol had tried to imagine this earthen barricade, this monument to Hakhan tenacity. Soon, perhaps in a few days, he would see what the Barrier clans had achieved—the wall that held the nomads back.

Yarkol squinted from the top of a knoll, but discerned no peaks against the overcast sky. He sensed a storm coming. In the west the clouds looked dark.

He urged his horse into a steady trot and hoped he'd find shelter in a town ahead. On both sides of the road grain stalks swayed in the quickening breeze. But the storm did not come, and for a time the sky brightened.

The Dolmi passed several settlements, stopping to ask directions now and again. Jornood land, he discovered, lay two days ahead. The woman he asked gave Yarkol a puzzled stare, but did not retreat from him as other Hakhans had done. Perhaps, he thought, his affliction was little known in this region. If his appearance drew no attention, then he might comfortably stop in a town and enjoy a soft bed with thanks to Zarad's generosity. He was not sure, however, that he could tolerate a night beneath a roof.

Afternoon arrived before the sky darkened again. When he was halfway across a valley, Yarkol saw his horse's ears prick up. A faint flash of lightning showed in the western sky.

Suddenly his mount began to fight the reins, speeding up as thunder rumbled from behind. The gelding plunged from the road and into a field. Yarkol saw a crude shelter, four poles supporting a roof of branches, at the base of a brambly hillock. The animal evidently sensed a chance for safety, for it turned with a whinny and charged toward the place.

The first heavy drops were falling as he neared the shed. Yarkol saw movement within; a few Chirudak farmhands had taken refuge here. They moved aside warily as he fought the gray to a stop and dismounted. The horse rushed inside ahead of him. The four Chirudaks, a youth and three young men, gaped at Yarkol's appearance.

The Hakhan's attention turned at once to his mount. The animal was shivering, not from the few raindrops on its coat but from its fear of the storm. He stroked the side of its muzzle and spoke in a soothing tone.

The horse remained skittish, tearing free to watch the progress of the storm. It stood looking outward with its head lowered, its feet firmly planted. The gelding had been caught in thunderstorms before, Yarkol recalled, without suffering a serious fright. He wondered if his own strangeness was to blame for this odd display.

A loud clap of thunder evoked a new whinny of fear. Yarkol glanced about helplessly, afraid that the animal might plunge wildly out into the weather. The Chirudaks had edged closer, he noticed, the youth coming within a stride of him.

"Sing to your horse," said the boy, whose narrow face made his ears look oddly enlarged. "Sing like this." He began a low, nasal drone, the sound rising and falling in a repeated rhythm that appeared to have a soothing effect. As the boy continued, Yarkol noticed his mount's quivering begin to ease. The gray did not even seem to mind the water that dribbled through the roof onto its neck.

The squall passed quickly, giving way to a steady, light shower. Soon the horse poked its head outside and began to crop at nearby stalks of grass. By then the youth had stopped humming and stood directly in front of Yarkol. He reached up hesitantly, then suddenly touched the Hakhan's blemished cheek with his rough fingers. The Dolmi started in surprise.

The older Chirudaks rebuked him, but the boy stood his ground and smiled. "Changed one," he said. "Man who is no man."

One companion whistled, beckoned the boy away with

a large sweep of his arm. "I want to see," the youth protested.

"You see enough," said the older man. "You want your soul cursed for troubling him?"

"But he's a *Hakhan.*" The two spoke as if Yarkol could not understand them, though they used the southern dialect.

"He's protected by the gods." The taller one strode forward, grabbed the youth's thin arm and pulled him aside.

Yarkol shook his head in angry bewilderment. "Am I no longer a person?" he demanded. "Am I a creature to be discussed but not spoken to?"

The Chirudaks retreated from his outburst.

"The boy was kind enough to help with my horse. For that I thank him. But you others—"

"We wish you no harm," one replied hastily. Despite the continuing rain, the four backed out of the shelter. They glanced at the sky, then began to run.

"So you call me no man!" Yarkol shouted bitterly, though he knew they could not hear him. "Do you run from a *woman* then? Or is it a beast that I've become?"

Wrapped in a thin cowhide, holding the reins in chilled fingers, Etoudoori shivered as the downpour continued. Her six-year-old roan mare, pulling the creaky cart, plodded without complaint along a muddy track. The smell of wet horsehair smothered all other scents.

Oron was far ahead by now; she had seen his sign at every crossroads—a row of stones whose number told when he had placed them and whose direction pointed out his route. The sun did not show behind the clouds, but she thought it must be eight parts across the sky—late afternoon.

Undaunted by puddles, the pony continued along the

57

rutted road. "You are no ancient cart-horse," she said softly to her animal. "But you do this out of love for me." She longed to saddle the mare and ride it the way she had always done. Why maintain her pretense of being a weedchewer? To catch Oron she must travel well past sunset. If the sky remained cloudy, she would not find her way.

Etou tasted rain on her lips and thought the drops salty. Had her offering been accepted? she wondered. Perhaps the spirits were shedding tears of sympathy for her plight.

No. She did not believe she could win favor so quickly. More offerings were needed. To balance the wrong she had done might take years or even prove impossible. In that case she must suffer the punishment of the gods, returning in her next life as a rabbit or a lowly grasshopper.

She passed through a village, where the wooden boards of the houses were dark from rainwater. Wistfully, she gazed through the open doorway of a stable at men talking amid a scattering of straw. What if she got rid of the cart? she asked herself. She could trade it for supplies, saddle the roan. Then she could rest awhile and catch Oron when the storm ended.

Etou felt a cold trickle down the back of her neck. How much more discomfort must she endure? Her idea of riding seemed sensible, despite Oron's warnings, for she was leaving the southern country now. The need for pretense would soon be over.

But she could not expect to trade her cart to a Hakhan; he would laugh, offer a hard loaf of bread or a rancid cheese, and threaten her if she refused him. A weedchewer, one of her docile cousins, would surely treat her more fairly. And Etou knew where to find weedchewers—in the shabbiest quarter of every settlement.

This town, however, showed no sign of Chirudaks. Pressing her lips together angrily, she tried to adjust her cap and hide wrapping to better keep out the rain. Passing into farmland again, she glanced toward a cluster of birches at the edge of a field. To her surprise, she saw a familiar horse—Oron's chestnut mount standing beneath the branches. A moment later she made out the warrior's commanding form. "Our Hakhan's gone to ground," she told herself softly, grateful now that she'd not been hasty to change her mode of travel.

She pulled in on the far side of the copse so that her rig would be less visible from the road. "His horse spooked," Oron said casually, as if she'd been there all along. "Lightning-shy. Poorly taught. The man seems to be in no hurry."

"He should know that winter is creeping down," she answered, nodding in the direction of peaks now hidden by clouds. "If he hopes to see the Kag—"

"I'll make certain that the Hakhan finds my cousin."

Etoudoori scowled. The newborn would reach his goal, she believed, but she would gain little from it. The Kag did not know her, nor would he care about her fate. She had served him, and now she mattered less than the droppings of his goats.

"The soil-tiller's been asking his way to Jornood's keep," Oron added, his voice now carrying an edge of concern. "You know what that means? He'll be talking to his cousins. Might still change his plans."

"His dreams won't stop troubling him." Etou knew those nightmares were more dangerous than Oron could imagine.

"Even so, he may need more help," the warrior said. He cleared his throat. "Another ceremony."

"I won't do it again," she answered firmly. "I'd be useless anyway without a drum."

"After one lesson, are you an expert on sorcery?"

Etou hissed. She had learned what little she knew of mysticism from an old woman living in a cave farther

59

south. The woman claimed to be a shaman, but would such a person lend out her drum? The payment had been generous, of course, but a true shaman wouldn't be swayed by wealth.

"Look there," said Etoudoori suddenly. She had been watching the shelter at the field's far end. "He's coming out. Maybe he's in a hurry after all."

That night Etou woke from frightening dreams. Her heart was thudding so loudly that she thought Oron would be roused by the sound. Only a few memories of the nightmares lingered. She'd seen a great confusion of people and animals—herds out of control, riders thrown from their mounts. The air had been murky, the ground treacherous.

Unable to sleep now, she lay staring at the dark sky. The rain had ceased, but heaven's lights failed to penetrate the clouds. Why had she been tormented this night? she asked herself. Surely because the gods remained angry with her.

She must make another offering, she decided, and plead with the nearby kobolds to intercede for her. Etou sat up, reached for the sachet of rare pollens she wore about her neck, and loosened the thong that held the pouch shut. Taking a pinch of the contents, she lowered her fingers to the damp ground. "Accept this gift, underground hobs," she whispered. "Ask the gods to hear my penitence." She tried to doze again, but found herself still awake when dawn came.

Oron trotted off after the Hakhan, leaving her alone to jounce along the rutted track. The sky was clear, the morning air cool and filled with the scents of earth. Occasionally a taawik flew overhead. She cringed whenever she heard one calling, for these ancestor birds knew the

60

mood of the gods. The winged ones were chiding her, warning of punishments to come.

To be reborn as a taawik was the greatest hope a Chirudak could have. In the past she had always viewed these white fliers with awe, thinking that someday, after many lives, she might join them. Now she could not dare such a thought. But how she envied their freedom.

Over and again she railed at her slow means of travel. Why continue in the sluggish cart, when on horseback she could readily keep up with Oron? The Kag's cousin offered little companionship, but she felt some comfort in his presence. Crossing the hills and fields with no one to talk to left her imagination open to wild fears.

That night she fell to arguing with Oron while their small fire burned down. They had stopped in a mossy hollow, a short way past Yarkol's camp. "I'll get rid of this cart tomorrow," she declared. "Saddle the roan and ride with you."

"When the time comes for that, I'll tell you."

"Tomorrow."

"So that soil-tillers can recognize what you are? Do you want soldiers dragging you into a field? They'll have fun with you there."

She tossed her head. "I might also have fun. More than I'm having with you."

"What you need, woman, is a herd of billygoats to keep you happy. Mere men can't do it."

"You're the one who sports with animals." She squealed with laughter as she dodged Oron's blow. When he came after her, she darted into shadows. But she was breathing heavily and knew he could hear her.

He faced her but did not follow. "Maybe this stick can fill you up." He lifted a stout branch from beside the fire. "Should I smooth it for you with my knife?"

The taunts flew awhile longer. Then he left her and

stretched out for sleep behind bushes near the road. He slept lightly, she knew. Yarkol would not slip past him.

Etou lay down near the fire and found herself quickly drifting off. Nightmares came again. She saw horses rearing, cattle charging out of control. Solid ground broke open, swallowing men and animals while yellow steam fogged the air. In the midst of confusion she saw the Kag, unmistakable astride his huge stallion. The mount lost its footing, stumbled, fell with frenzied cries into a boiling pool.

She woke and found that she had almost rolled into the embers, her hide and blanket left behind as she fought the dream. Trembling, she felt about for kindling to build up the fire. She had not slept long, she realized, but she dared not close her eyes again this night.

What the dream foretold for herself, she thought, was an early and violent end. This fear so gripped her that at last she went to Oron's saddlebags and found his wooden shoy box. He had forbidden her to touch this, but what did such petty rules mean now?

The box was smaller than Baatibi's, its carvings newer and finer. Seated by the fire, she rattled the contents gently, afraid even this noise might wake Oron. Glancing toward the road, she made out his sleeping form and tried to calm herself.

First she performed the preparatory shaking, facing in turn each quarter of the world. If she kept the bones clean, she thought, Oron would never suspect that she'd used them. She opened the slat, let the pieces fall softly onto the blanket. Why were so many landing with their faces down?

Etou stared in disbelief at the result she'd drawn. Hastily, without daring to tally the score, she stacked the tokens back into their container. Even as she replaced the set in Oron's bag, she still saw engraved faces grinning cruelly. Not a single hopeful sign had appeared.

How could she doubt her grim position? First night-mares, then an an ominous foretelling. Her thoughts fled to a summer of her youth when a plague had struck the herds. Her entire tribe had worked to dig the sacrificial pit, line it with layers of leaves and flowers, and place within it a wealth of gifts. Every family had poured kumiss over the offering and pleaded for the sprites to summon aid.

Etou shook her head. By herself and in darkness she could prepare no such sacrifice. But suddenly she knew how she might soothe spirits of both air and earth. She would give them a thing of undisputed value—*the cart.*

Hastening from the fire, she found where her mare was grazing. "Now you'll be a proper mount again," Etou whispered. She took her saddle from the cart, along with the bags and bundles, and began to ready the horse. When the roan wore its customary trappings once again, it held its head high and stamped with evident pleasure. Etou led the animal aside, and tethered it to a tree far back from the fire.

She found her riding trousers and pulled them on be-neath the hated weedchewer dress. Then she dragged the empty cart toward the flames so that its wheels straddled the coals. Here was the sacrifice she meant to offer.

The wood was old and dry. Small tongues of flame spread over the bottom and crept up the warped sides. A fragrant smoke rose. She stood back, watching with a smile. "Take this gift," she said softly to the sky. Then she picked up a pointed stick and began to dig a small trench. She would bury the ashes as a gift for underground spirits.

The blaze grew, brightening the dirt where she was scratching. She had almost forgotten Oron, asleep be-neath his bush. But suddenly she felt a blow that knocked her to the ground. A tall figure stood over her; she saw a face contorted by rage. "Woman, you have less sense than a headless sheep." He tried beating at the flames with a

63

blanket, but he had come too late. One wheel collapsed; the cart's remains tipped over and continued to burn.

Etou, still trembling from Oron's attack, stood up warily. Her mare was ready, the saddlebags loaded. If she left now she was done with Oron, safe from repeating the deception he had forced on her. She hurried to the roan, pulled her skirt high and swung up into the saddle. He was still beating futilely at the fire and did not turn to look at her as she rode off.

Low in the sky, the Wolfpack hung in a tight cluster. Mother Moon was up, a fat yellow crescent in the east. Etou could see the road clearly, though she had to blink away a few tears. She did not care where she was going.

5

*When the rains are scarce, we burn
offerings to the spirits of air and ask
their assistance. But one summer, the
pleas of Mossbend tribe went
unanswered. "The spirits do not hear
us," said the people. "They must be
elsewhere, attending better sacrifices."
To lure back the sprites, the people set
fire to the forest. The blaze raced
across the mountainsides and sent
smoke to fill the sky.*

*By the next day the entire forest had
been destroyed. Soon the sky grew
cloudy and rain began. "The spirits
answer us," the people cried with
delight. The rain continued until
creeks overflowed and began to flood
the valleys. "Enough!" cried the
people, but now the spirits seemed*

deaf again. The tribesmen drove the
herds to high ground, but the water
kept rising. Finally, when everyone
was crowded onto tiny islands, the
rains stopped. After that, the
Mossbends understood that too much
can be worse than not enough.

—*Chirudak tale*

Etou rode on, paying little heed to the paths she was taking. She held the reins slack, letting the roan enjoy its freedom from the traces. It had suffered the cart long enough.

In the moonlight the woman saw shadowy settlements and a few larger towns. She did not care to know their names. All that mattered was her direction—north. In a few days, if she kept going, she would reach Chirudak territory.

Her thoughts flitted from one trouble to another. Oron's brooding face would not leave her, though she denied any fondness for the man. They might have had good sport together, but nothing had happened between them. She sighed, for the warrior's goat-headedness had cost her more than brief pleasure. She had meant to bury the ashes from her offering; now, how would she placate the kobolds?

When dawn came, she paused to rest her mount at a wooded stream. Taawiks roosting in the branches gave her no peace. "What do you want from me?" she shouted at them, throwing a handful of pebbles into the copse. Then she began weeping, pressing her face to her roan's

66

neck for comfort. In her anguish she had attacked ancestor birds!

At last she composed herself and began to ride again. Sage advice, she knew, was what she most needed now. Perhaps, even in weedchewer country, she might find someone who understood the nature of spirits.

Etou began paying close attention to the fields and soon found a party of farmhands starting work in a vineyard. The weedchewers gave her puzzled stares; she suspected that they had never seen a woman astride a horse.

She rode up to a stoop-shouldered man whose sidewhiskers were streaked with gray. The elderly laborer frowned, his gaze shifting from her trouser-clad legs to her face and then back again. "Will you help me, grandfather?" she asked in a plaintive tone. "I need to find a shaman. Do you know of one in these parts?"

The old man did not speak. Behind him, purple grapes hung in glistening clusters.

"Grandfather, please. I'm without friends here, and my soul is in danger. Surely there must be someone."

The roan's shadow fell over the man as he pursed his lips. "Look at you," he said at last. "More than y'r soul's in danger."

She tugged at her dress, which was hiked up by the saddle, but could not pull the hem down to her boot tops. She slapped at the conspicuous trousers—proof that she was a stranger here—sighed and lowered her head. A rich grape smell drifted on the air and made her think of soil-tillers' wine. Ah, if she could lose herself in drink and let the roisterer free!

"Get yourself home, girl. Keep riding and don't stop."

"That's just what I intend to do. But I must see a boneman first." She found courage to glare at the old farmhand again, and this time he seemed to soften. "If I

67

don't find one," she insisted, "there's no point in going home."

The grandfather shook his head slowly. "One of your drum-beaters passes through here now and then," he admitted. "You keep asking folks. Maybe up north a way you'll have some luck. But take my advice and get moving. This is still Hakhan country—no place for your kind." He pulled a curved knife from his belt, then turned to his vines and began to cut.

Etou rode on, bypassing settlements where Hakhans might notice her. Occasionally she approached field crews or dusty hovels, receiving rebukes and little information. By the time noon passed she began to feel weary from lack of sleep. It would be wiser, she knew, to doze during daylight and travel at night. But, stubbornly, she continued.

The day was seven parts gone when she reached a small village she had heard about. At once she dismounted and smoothed her dress down into place. Now she thought she could pass as an ordinary weedchewer leading her man's pony.

She noticed the mare's ears swivel toward a row of huts. Etou cupped a hand to her own ear and thought she heard a faint, high-pitched voice. Someone had told her that a woman was sick here, that a shaman had been called to provide a cure.

Etou advanced and heard the chanting grow louder. The huts were poor affairs of mud-and-wattle, each roofed by a thin layer of thatch. Between the huts she glimpsed places where the ground had been dug up—sites of offerings to kobolds, she guessed. Peering into an open doorway, she saw a figure swaying and bending. Sunlight streamed through the entrance, cutting a swath across the dark earthen floor.

As the dancer moved between light and shadow, she caught glimpses of his peculiar garb. Leather fringes

68

swirled as he turned; his high-peaked cap was a blur. When he paused, raising his hands to shake a pair of gourd rattles, she saw patterns of bones affixed to the front of his tunic.

And for a moment she glimpsed his eyes—full of madness in the midst of a face that might otherwise belong to a herdsman. He had a narrow countenance, a jutting chin, a thin, beaky nose. His fingers were long and slender, his wrists bony, his lips edged by foam.

Etou's mouth fell open, for she had not seen such a person since the previous winter—at the time of her mother's death. Her tribe's shaman had filled the yurt with the choking scent of his incense, had danced until he fell into a twitching heap. Later he proclaimed that the dead woman's soul had risen and would live again in a newborn child. Etou's mother had not earned her white feathers.

That news had brought tears to the family, but now Etou was glad that her mother was not yet reborn a taa-wik. She would be spared, for now, the knowledge of her daughter's shame. And perhaps, by the time her new body grew old enough to know the world, Etou would find a way to redeem herself. Perhaps . . .

A nudge from Etou's mount brought her back to practical concerns. She found a watering trough, then tied the animal to a post. Returning to the open doorway, she noticed the object of the shaman's ministrations—a still form on a pallet. As her eyes adjusted to the dim light, she saw more clearly the woman lying with her face to the roof, her long gray braids spread out beside her. A girl squatting at the foot of the bed paid no attention to the visitor.

The room held a few stools, a low table, some cooking pots and vessels. Tattered hides covered part of the floor. Sensing no objection, Etou entered the hut, sat with her back against the rough wall, and listened to the chant.

69

The words were in a language only shamans knew, with sounds like the cries of a hurt animal or the droning of wind outside a yurt. The hairs of her nape stood up as she listened.

Then the dancer lifted his oval spirit drum, its hoop even larger than the one that Etou had borrowed. And the sounds from this instrument, she realized, were far subtler than those she had produced. His drumming made her forget hunger and thirst, lifted her to a place where she was free of earthly concerns, made clear visions spring from darkness. She saw a snow-covered crag jutting impossibly high.

The Peak-of-the-World! She wondered if she might witness the very gods. The mountaintop was wreathed in mist, but she saw luminous figures in the distance, hints of grace and beauty that lasted only moments. If she could draw closer, she might bask in the High Ones' glory. If only the visions would hold still. But the tantalizing images faded into formless gray, and suddenly a new and massive shape emerged from the fog. The thing was solid black, its bulk huge enough to blot out the sky.

Two moon-sized eyes of heated iron glowed in an enormous skull. The head turned slowly until the eyes fixed directly on Etoudoori. She felt torn apart, exposed, as if the skin had been peeled from her frame. Etou screamed, and the sound she heard was a chorus of anguished voices.

She opened her eyes, saw the sick woman writhing, her mouth wide as she gagged in fright. The girl was huddled beneath a blanket, wailing. And the shaman had collapsed in the center of the floor, his arms and legs jerking like limbs of a crushed spider.

Etou was still quaking from what she'd seen but she managed to crawl to the old woman. "It is over," she said soothingly, half-surprised at her concern for this stranger. "The evil's been frightened out of you. You can rest now." More than the evil had come out. Etou smelled that the woman had wet herself.

Etoudoori understood the vision she had seen. The image of the god Demonsbane was usually sufficient to drive away common ailments. In this case she was certain that she had sensed the departure of the malevolence—in a rush of pain that struck everyone in the room. Now she felt humbled by the shaman's power.

She comforted the girl, and between them they put a dry robe on the grandmother. The others in the family were still in the fields, Etou learned. They would not return before dusk. And meanwhile, the shaman remained in trance.

Etou did what she could for the household, despite her distaste for the work. The floor coverings were badly in need of cleaning. She took the hides outside and beat them against the walls of the hut, raising dust clouds that dispersed slowly in the still air. Using a leather bucket, she lugged water from the well—some for her mount and some for the cookpot. Meanwhile, the sick woman showed signs of improvement and asked for a bowl of yohourt.

As dusk approached, the shaman stirred from his slumber in the middle of the floor. He rubbed his hands to his face, slowly sat up, and stared groggily at Etou. "So," he began in a hoarse voice. "You've been looking for me."

Her pulse leaped in surprise. "Do you know *everything?*" she asked, half in dismay, half in relief. "Then I need not explain."

He smiled. In the dim light she could barely make out his features, but he seemed a different man than the frenzied dancer. "Do you take me for a sorcerer?" he chided. "Of course you must explain. But later." He turned, gave his patient a passing glance, then called to

71

the granddaughter. "Come, Nuuni. Where's the game we were playing?"

The shaman reached into one of the many pouches hanging from his waist. Etou heard a click of iron against stone, then watched a spark grow into a tiny flame. In a few moments, the boneman had a stubby candle burning.

Clutching a handful of long straws, Nuuni shyly crept forward. "It's my turn," she said quietly.

The shaman laughed and nodded. She dropped the bristles in a heap, then began to pick them up one by one.

In the candlelight Etou studied the boneman's expression. He seemed to have shed his years, for his delight in the game seemed no less than the girl's. Each time she succeeded in pulling away one more straw, he clapped gleefully. But at last her small fingers slipped, and she disturbed the pile.

"Ah," he said, as if anticipating a rare delight. His long, thin fingers were well-suited to this game. He took away one, five, seven more bristles as the girl's face fell. Then his hand hovered in midair while Nuuni began to grin.

Etou could not help leaning forward to study the pile. She saw no obvious way he could continue the game without forfeiting his turn. "Five straws remain," he said laughingly. He cast a glance toward Etoudoori. "To me, that means there are five of you. Five seekers of wisdom. Touch one, you jostle another." He reached into the heap's middle, pulled out one bristle only to scatter the rest. "See!"

"I win," said Nuuni. She picked up the remaining straws quickly, then jumped up and did a small dance around the shaman, twirling in imitation of his own movements.

Etoudoori puzzled over his words, for she did not know which five he had meant. She and the Hakhan were surely seekers, but who were the others? Oron? Baatibi? The Kag? She wished the shaman would give her more than a passing nod, but he seemed to prefer the child's company.

From outside came voices. Etou turned to see a man and two women—all three farmworkers covered with dust—hurrying in through the doorway. The man, large-jawed and long-necked, dropped his load of firewood while the women knelt at the pallet. The grandmother managed a weak smile. "Better," she whispered. Pointing to Etoudoori and then the shaman, she seemed to be saying that the two were together.

The women built a fire on a stone hearth in the middle of the room. Smoke rose, drifting out under the eaves, while a pot of soup began to boil. Nobody addressed Etou directly, yet they filled her belly with a welcome meal.

Later, neighbors came in to see the condition of the invalid. One brought a large bowl of kumiss, and Taki-jaly—the shaman—was the first to indulge. Everyone had a sip, but the boneman took far more than that. It was only as he moved about the crowded room that Etou noticed his slight limp. In the dance he had shown no awkwardness, yet now he favored his left leg.

Takijaly seemed to enjoy the company, striking up conversations with everyone he saw—everyone except Etoudoori. His narrow, grinning face appeared wherever she looked. Here he stood telling loud stories. There he lifted delighted children to his shoulders, letting them tower over their elders.

When the merrymaking ended and the family members wearily unrolled their sleep mats, the shaman stepped out into the cool evening air. Etou, suffering from lost sleep, followed him nonetheless.

"Ah. I'm pursued by the northern beauty." He turned at the end of the row of huts, his face showing palely in Mother Moon's light.

"What do you know about me?" she demanded.

"Only what I see and hear."

"And of the Kag and his gelding cousin?"

"Only what you tell me."

For a moment she felt like beating her fists against his chest. What sort of man could conjure an image of Demonsbane, then play at jackstraws with a child? She raised one hand in angry frustration, but the bone images on his robe glowed in the yellow light and she could not bring herself to touch them.

"Let us walk." Despite the limp, his long strides outmatched her own. She scurried to keep up with him as he entered a narrow lane.

"I . . . I seek advice," she said hurriedly.

"The world is full of advice-givers."

"About the gods . . . my soul . . . the misdeed that was forced on me."

"Forced?" They continued briskly, reaching a field of tall grass that stood beyond the settlement.

"The men. You know how they are. They promise, they bluster, they wheedle. I agreed to come south with them—to gather news, nothing more. Then we learned about a godstricken Hakhan."

"Ah." The shaman halted and turned to stare at her, his expression suddenly solemn. "Godstricken, you say? Tell me about him."

Etou could not bear his scrutiny. She looked at the dark ground and spoke almost in a whisper. "The kitchen servants knew first," she began, "servants from the big stone house. They told their friends. After we heard about it, Oron and Baatibi began to watch the Dolmi road . . ."

Only when she told of the spurious ceremony and of her efforts to mislead the Hakhan about his visions did Takijaly react strongly. He whooped with mirth at her description of the two men retreating while she was left to tap the drum and speak the words. "So they thought themselves safe from the High Ones' wrath? Wait until

74

their next lives. Crawling on their bellies will teach them otherwise." He took her arm gently. "Come. Dance with me in the field, and I'll ask forgiveness for your folly."

Dance? Was that all the gods wanted? Etou watched the shaman throw aside his peaked cap, letting his long braids swing freely. She had not been able to judge his age before. Now he did not appear old—certainly not of a grandfather's years. He pulled off his high boots and bid her do the same. She turned away from him and removed the riding trousers as well, for the brisk walk had made her warm.

Now she seemed to hear a drum beating, though he'd left his instrument behind. The grass was cool and moist underfoot. The air had the fragrance of damp leaves. Etou, weary earlier, felt charged with surprising energy. Her body was suddenly light; each leap she made seemed higher than the last.

The shaman sang a little song, not at all like the chanting he'd used in the hut. Above, the moons also appeared to be dancing. Takijaly's hand clasped her own and they whirled without missing a step, his limp no impediment. The drumbeat grew louder, quicker. The field became a blur.

At last they fell down, laughing, gasping for breath. He hugged her to him, and she felt his chest heaving from the exercise. Her face felt hot; her whole body tingled with new life.

"Is this what the gods demand?" she asked merrily as she felt his supple fingers reaching under her dress, sliding up her bare legs.

"Not at all," he answered. "We do this for ourselves. To gain the peace we need for contemplation." His lips touched her ear, his moist breath bathed her cheek. His hands were cool and soft where they caressed her.

75

*　　*　　*

Etoudoori was ready to travel long before dawn. "Go!" the shaman told her. "Go where your ulaansh is headed. I'll finish my business here and catch up with you at Jornood's keep." He handed her a stubby henga root. She bit off one tiny piece for strength, packed the rest in her bag.

She planned to confine her travels to darkness, for she had already taken too many risks. As she followed a forest track, she watched the sky brightening. It was time to stop, she knew, recalling the shaman's advice. But now she did not feel sleepy. And how fast, she wondered, was the Hakhan moving? Might he not reach his destination— the keep that Oron had mentioned—well ahead of her?

Though she had slept only briefly, the henga kept her from feeling exhaustion. The light grew; still, she did not stop. When she passed a ride or a wagon, she rarely evoked more than a puzzled stare. Perhaps her caution was not needed.

The country grew wilder, less often farmed. Between the settlements lay rolling pine forests and calm lakes. Goats wandered through rocky fields. *More like home,* she thought, and pressed her roan onward.

Late in the day she halted, thinking she would dismount and rest for a short while. The ground was soft under the pines; the insects chirped quietly, lulling her into sleep. When she woke and saw that the night was half gone, she slapped the side of her head in annoyance. The Hakhan was surely beyond her now.

Etou drove her mount hard, passing several villages before morning. She ate biscuit, chewed henga, and rode on. A sizable town lay ahead; she did not bother seeking a way around it.

The sun was one part high, the shadows long as she rode down the broad main street. At the edge of town

76

stood a mill, a round stone building beside a creek. Wagons were being loaded with bulging sacks while Hakhan soldiers stood about, some joking with each other, others watching the road.

"What's this?" one called, staring at her approach. She tried to dodge his advance, but another man leapt out into the road and grabbed her bridle. The soldiers wore brown, high-collared tunics; short swords hung from their belts.

"She rides like a man," said one with a streaked beard. "Wonder what else can she do?"

Another flipped her dress higher and fingered her woolen trousers. "Look at this. She's got to be a *crude.*"

"A nomad this far south?" The first shook his head. "Pretty one, though, if you like that kind."

Etou berated herself silently for her carelessness, but forced herself to sit straight in the saddle. "Let me pass," she said, in a calm voice.

"There's no hurry." One man was tugging at her trouser leg and seemed intent on pulling the garment off.

"I wouldn't mind a little fun," she said, maintaining an even voice. The soldiers crowded around, each vying for a better look at her. "The six of you together wouldn't keep me busy for long."

The men grinned and exchanged glances. Behind them the miller's assistants were still lugging their sacks.

"Even so," Etou continued, "Hyar Jornood will ask why I'm late. So if you'll be kind enough to tell me your names—"

"Jornood?" A few soldiers moved out of her way.

"Why would Jornood be waiting for her kind?" Streakbeard remained skeptical, but his companion poked him with his elbow.

"Why would anyone be waiting for that one?" He grinned and waggled his hips.

"Jornood? Never. He's got five wives—two of 'em

young. A man his age? How could he have anything left?" The soldiers began to close in again.

Etou had lost the advantage of surprise; now she must take a bold chance. "His young wife's the one who summoned me," she declared. "Called for a midwife. With luck, she doesn't need me quite yet."

The men stared at each other and frowned. Etou knew that many Hakhans called Chirudak midwives to attend them. Whether a lady of a great house would do the same she could not say. And if these men were well-acquainted with the family, then they might catch her lie.

Sweat stood out on the soldiers' foreheads. Clearly she had them worried. "Let her pass," said streak-beard angrily, releasing his grip on her trappings. The others backed away slowly, with much grumbling and kicking of dirt.

"Another time," said Etou, showing a faint smile. She advanced at a brisk trot and did not turn her head.

Soon after, she made her way deep into a forest, threw herself down in a hollow, and wept angrily. She tried to blame others for her plight—first Oron, then Takijaly. Why had the warrior pushed her into deception? Why had the boneman sent her to travel alone? At last she found sleep.

By sunset she was moving again, watching for landmarks that the shaman had described. That night the sky was bright with moons, and she found her way readily. As dawn came, she stood gazing up at a craggy fortress— Jornood House, by all she had heard. The solid gray towers loomed like giant sentinels; the walls between them were capped by thick crenelations. Morning's first light shimmered on pennants of red and gold. She recalled her tale to the soldiers, and an old nomad saying sprang to her lips. "May your wives have many sons," she mouthed quietly.

Jornood House. Yarkol looked about him at the high ceilings, at walls hung with finely-crafted rugs, at glittering candelabra. He could not bring himself to sit in the elegant stuffed chair that the servant had offered. Yarkol the wanderer felt out of place in such a room.

He had not expected to be allowed inside this Hakhan stronghold. But when he'd gone to the kitchen door and spoken to a servant, a Jornood wife had come out to speak with him. She had looked him square in the face, seemingly unperturbed by his appearance, as he told her his name and asked to see Hyar Jornood.

Yarkol had thought to explain himself further, but something about the woman's delicate features had reminded him of Merig and he could not find his tongue. Now he stood in the huge room waiting nervously for his host.

A bowl holding fruit, ripe pears and apples, sat on a table beside him, but he dared not eat. He imagined seeds dropping onto the immaculate carpet, juices dribbling from his hand and mouth.

Hyar was evidently occupied elsewhere, for Yarkol had time to study every hanging and work of pottery. The air began to feel thick and musty, the walls to creep closer. Would his affliction leave him no peace?

Suddenly he recalled a new and troubling dream from the previous night. He had stood in the Kag's camp, with mounted tribesmen all about him, as the first snows of winter began falling. The nomads were waiting for something, their faces turned in a common direction.

Out of the swirling downfall a rider emerged, and Yarkol stepped back as he recognized the gold mask. The Kag's stallion halted, blowing out steamy breath, while the burly nomad leaped to the ground.

The Chirudak said nothing, but made his intentions clear. Using the toe of his heavy boot, he drew a line in the thin snow covering. Then he spread his legs and crouched menacingly, his arms bent, his fingers spread.

The object of the match, Yarkol understood, was for one opponent to drag the other across the mark. This was how the two men must settle their differences. Yarkol also crouched; at once they began to grapple.

In the first moments the Hakhan's front foot was pulled over the line. Yarkol strained, managed to ease back his heel to safety. The men stood locked for a time, neither gaining on the other. Then, with a sudden wrench, Yarkol unbalanced the chieftain.

The nomad went down on one knee, but was far from beaten, for Yarkol could not budge him from that pose. Meanwhile, the snowfall ceased suddenly, and the clouds dispersed. Sunlight cast long shadows across the white ground. It was early morning, Yarkol realized, as he caught the sun's glare directly in his eyes. Squinting, he took in the landscape that the storm had hidden. A precipice at the edge of a vast canyon lay at the nomad's back. If the Kag pulled Yarkol over the line, then both would tumble into the depths . . .

The dream had gone no further, for Yarkol woke with true daylight shining in his eyes. And now, after half a morning's ride, the nightmare still troubled him. He had accepted the role of a peacemaker. Why, he wondered, must his dreams show otherwise? Hearing footsteps he put these thoughts aside and turned toward a wide corridor. At last Hyar Jornood had arrived!

The elder was not unusually tall, but he walked with an air of authority that made him appear as solid as his watchtowers. His beard had almost gone entirely gray; his white hair was thick and neatly groomed. One could sense, beneath his silver-buttoned tunic, a man who had kept his body firm and well-exercised.

Hyar halted when he was several paces from his visitor. His eyebrows lowered, his look of anticipation giving way to a frown as he studied Yarkol's face. "I did not know," he said in a voice of regret.

"Perhaps I should have stayed outside—"

"Not at all." Jornood interrupted. "You are welcome here, Dolmi. Don't mistake me for one of your southerly cousins."

Yarkol nodded. He brushed off the back of his trousers, lowered himself cautiously into the chair. But he could not relax. He sat stiffly, while his host took an opposite seat.

"Forgive my surprise," the elder said, "but I hadn't heard of your plight. And I've been preoccupied, as you may know."

"With the nomads . . . yes."

"Their new leader is the problem. It's rare that the tribes can unite behind a Kag. This one, we hear, has most of the tribal chiefs behind him. By spring, he may be storming the Barrier. We haven't much time."

"This is what I came to see you about." The words sounded odd to Yarkol, as if spoken by another, yet he persisted.

Hyar's shaggy eyebrows rose. "You're a physician by training, I understand. Have your interests broadened?"

Yarkol laughed bitterly. "Yes, but not by choice. I'm doomed by my condition to wander. And I can travel where I will, even to the high country. Chirudaks won't harm me so long as I go without malice."

Hyar's head fell back against the headrest, and he seemed deep in thought. "You might do us good service, then. Our sources of information are few. You could travel the north country, learn the size and placement of their forces, the mood of their leaders—"

Yarkol shook his head. "That's not precisely my intent.

81

I would prove a poor spy, I assure you, though I do intend to seek out the Kag." *But not to wrestle with him!*

"The man's elusive, from what I hear. Tell me your purpose."

In his memory, Yarkol heard Etou's words again as she tapped the spirit drum. "To bring him a goodwill offering. To ask for friendship instead of war."

"Friendship?" Hyar leaned forward, his expression puzzled. "How can we forget so many generations of hatred?"

Yarkol sighed. "Perhaps it is possible. The Chirudaks . . ." He hesitated to finish, yet Hyar had shown himself tolerant of his guest's affliction. He touched the blemish on his cheek. "They think me godstricken," he said in a hushed voice. "The mark will make me welcome among them. And I feel drawn—drawn to the north."

"You may find the Kag, and he may give you an audience. But I can tell you that his people are belligerent. They need better lands, and they think only of taking ours."

"I must bring him something," Yarkol persisted. "You are our highest authority in the north. Let me carry some token of your good intentions."

"And what will result from such an offering? He'll merely think us weak, afraid to fight."

"He may see the wisdom of avoiding bloodshed. The Barrier has held for a long time."

"And it must continue to hold." Hyar closed his eyes for a few moments. "I view your plan as futile, but it's not in my power to stop you from traveling. Whether I'll help your cause is another matter."

"A gesture is all I ask. If he responds, then a meeting might be arranged."

"Meeting?" Hyar smiled and looked around, as if imagining the Kag's presence in this genteel setting. "Here is your answer, Yarkol. I'll give you a letter with my seal— an offer to join him at the Barrier for discussions of mu-

82

tual interest. That is not quite what you want, but the best I can do—a gesture with no concessions. If there is any chance of a settlement, he'll accept my offer."

The Dolmi nodded. "A fair reply."

"But I ask something in return. You're no spy, I grant, but whatever you observe may be of value. When your path comes back this way, stop here and see me, if only for a moment."

Yarkol smiled and plucked a ripe pear from the fruit bowl. He would save it to eat on the trail. "If my travels bring me to these lands, noble Jornood, I'll certainly accept your hospitality."

The shaman sat crosslegged on a westward-facing slope as the sun's last rays reddened the landscape. He stared at a handful of twigs he had snapped from the trunk of lightning-struck pine. Methodically he studied the sticks, comparing the tiny bends and knobs of one against another, then shook his head. If these offered a message, he could not find it. Even rubbing his fingers over the rough surfaces provided no enlightenment. Daylight faded slowly and at last, in disgust, he threw the twigs aside.

Sometimes inspiration came quickly. An odd bit of bark or an irregular leaf might present a discernible pattern, and patterns were the basis for all divination. In this case Takijaly had failed. Though he'd known for some time that a Hakhan had been called—that a new ulaansh had arisen—the gods' purpose eluded him.

The ulaansh himself was nearby. Takijaly leaned back against a rock and considered how best to approach the man. Etoudoori could be of help, he admitted, though she had started out by muddling the issues. Had she not interfered, he might already understand the gods' intent.

Ah, Etou, it is hardly your fault. The shaman had used his own means to locate Yarkol Dolmi. Now that the

83

Hakhan had reached—and passed through—his cousin's domain, Etou also should have caught up with him. She had planned to watch for Yarkol by the road to Jornood House. But when Takijaly opened his senses, seeking the troubled thing that was her soul, he found it far behind him. He sighed, knowing he would have to ride back for her.

The shaman rose, climbed down the hill to the copse where he had concealed his mount. The twelve-year-old spotted mare greeted him with a toss of her narrow head. "How are your shoes?" he asked her softly as he checked the hide coverings on each foot, feeling for cracks. He was counting on these shoes to disguise the animal's prints, for at least one traveler in the vicinity might recognize them. He must not let Oron discover his presence here.

He waited awhile longer, until twilight faded. Then, garbed as a farmhand, he rode south to meet Etoudoori. He sensed no others on the trail ahead. After some time, under moonlight, he glimpsed the towers on the hill above the road. "Etou!" he whispered, as he peered at a tangle of thorn bushes and vines. He called again and heard an answering crackle of brush. "You have missed him. The newborn is past you."

"I watched!" came the mournful reply. "I watched all day. He went in—"

"And came out again." Takijaly sensed her weariness and believed she had fallen asleep. "Never mind what happened. I know where his camp is."

"Then we have him." She emerged from her hiding place, plucking at a few tendrils that still clung to her. "But Oron may be watching."

"I will take care of Oron. But I may need your help with the ulaansh." They began to ride, and the shaman considered the course he had planned. The Kag's cousin had done better than Etou; he had trailed Yarkol to his camp this night. Now Oron must be left behind.

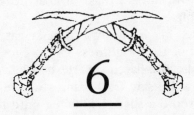

6

Be wary of an ulaansh who does not know his way. He is a two-headed wolf.

—*Shaman Torla (Pinebole tribe)*

Watching the last embers of his fire, Yarkol found his eyelids growing heavy. Now that he carried Hyar's letter for the Kag, the Dolmi felt a quiet satisfaction. With a sigh, he unrolled his blanket onto a bed of dry leaves and stretched out. Through bare branches he looked up at a handful of stars. The night air was clear and chill, but not cold enough to keep him awake . . .

Suddenly he saw again the snow-covered plain, the horde of mounted warriors watching him. The Kag, a burly figure in his padded coat, marked off the line of battle. Once more Yarkol was forced to grapple with the chief. The Hakhan's foot slid over the snow-covered ground; this time he could not pull it back. "I bear a letter of peace," he shouted, but the Kag did not let up. And behind him, Yarkol knew, lay the abyss that would swallow them both.

Then the clouds parted, and sunlight dazzled him. How far to the cliff's edge? The Hakhan could not see for the glare. He felt the nomad make a final heave. Both men began to tumble . . .

Yarkol woke, his body awash in sweat. The sky remained dark, but the brightness in his eyes was real, for fire had inexplicably flared up. He had left only coals in his hearth; now he saw fresh flames where none should be. He wondered if a spark had fallen onto his pile of dry wood.

His first concern was to put out the blaze before it spread to the surrounding forest. But when he tried to leap up, his body refused to obey him. Some new affliction? He lay rigid, gripped by a paralysis that he could not explain.

Then he saw, at the edge of the fire, a small, grinning figure watching him, its tiny hands at its hips. The Hakhan wanted to believe that he was still dreaming, but the sensations were far too real. The heat was already beginning to sear his skin. His eyes watered from the smoke.

The hearth-sprite—for what else could it be?—itself seemed to be alight. Its body was oddly misproportioned, the chest broad, the arms and legs spindly. And flames danced along every limb.

Yarkol raged silently as he watched the imp beckon. "Now I have you, Ulaansh," it taunted. "You got past my friend Laalu Wetbeard, but you won't escape me."

The Hakhan gave no answer. He continued to draw breath, but beyond that he could not move. Then he recalled the startling result of his breathing exercise at the ravine. His body was useless now, he admitted to himself. He did not know what he might accomplish by slipping out of his flesh.

The memory of that first experience troubled him. But if he remained as he was, he could only watch the flames draw closer . . .

In. Out. In. Out. He focused on a tiny glowing spot in the fire's heart. *In. Out.* Could he manage the trick again? He confined his thoughts to one bright place, lost himself in the hissing of breath. At last he felt the bonds melting, flowing. In spirit-form he crept from his rigid husk.

He tried not to glance at the shape he now wore. The sight of finger and wrist bones unnerved him; the rest he could easily imagine. "What say you now, imp?" His voice carried a deep rasp. In his skeletal form Yarkol no longer felt the campfire's heat. He advanced toward the burning sprite and swung a blow at its head. The creature continued to grin, for the bony hand passed cleanly through it.

"You are nothing but a wisp!" Yarkol said angrily. "I'll waste no time on you." He turned to the blaze, thinking that he could knock down the pile, spread out the burning logs, and thereby undo the sprite's mischief. But when he struck at the heaped-up wood the blow merely jolted his spirit-bones. The pile did not budge.

Yarkol's hand felt made of putty, spreading around the log instead of toppling it. He struck again, watching how his spirit-bones flattened when they hit, then sprang back into shape. Could he move nothing while in this form? He grasped the end of a rough branch and pulled with all his strength. The wood gave just slightly before he lost his grip and fell back in exhaustion.

"You'll do yourself no good that way, Ulaansh." The sprite was now dancing atop the pile. Yarkol made another futile swipe at him.

"I'll give you a chance," said the sprite. "Answer my riddle, and I'll set you free."

"And if I lose?"

"Then you're mine!" The imp's grin showed glowing teeth that wavered like candle flames.

"I've no patience for riddles." As a child, Yarkol had heard too many tales of hobs and their tricks. The spirits promised one thing, but always gave another. Only rarely did a human come out ahead.

What else did the stories say about hearth-sprites? Yarkol turned from the creature and tried to compose his thoughts. A question nagged at him. How did the sprite appear here, in the forest, at a place where no fire normally burned? It had to come up from underground, and so there must be a hole.

The Hakhan was not sure what he was looking for, but he bent down and put his skeleton's fingers into the coals of his original campfire. The remaining bits of char were far smaller than the logs he had tried to handle. To his trance-body even these things felt like heavy stones. Yet the coals responded to his touch, moving aside as he pressed against them. So he was not totally helpless! "What are you after, Ulaansh?" the imp asked in a voice that sounded uneasy. Yarkol kept silent as he continued his search. "You'll find nothing in there," said the sprite.

Suddenly Yarkol shouted in triumph. In the ground, at the center of his original hearth, lay a tiny opening. "Why do you interest yourself in a snake's den?" the imp screamed. "Hear my riddle and be done with this!"

"I have enough riddles of my own," the Hakhan murmured. Continuing his explorations, Yarkol found a pebble just the size he needed. It felt to him as heavy as a sizable rock, but by cupping it in his bony palm he discovered he could move it.

"You will burn, Ulaansh, if you ignore me. Nothing will be left but a heap of ash."

Yarkol shook his head. He recalled now that every hearth was supposed to conceal a passageway to the sub-

88

terranean realms. Closing the tunnel would trap the sprite. "And what will be left of *you,*" the Hakhan asked, "if you can't get back underground? Once the flames are out, you'll be helpless up here."

The imp planted its glowing foot in the way of Yarkol's pebble, but the stone shoved the creature aside. "Ulaansh, this is a dangerous mistake!" it shouted. "I can go to your home, set fire to your loved ones."

Yarkol gave one last tug so that the pebble settled into the tunnel's mouth, closing off escape. He leaned back, satisfied. "Can you dance across open country?" he asked. "How do you leap over barren stretches where nothing can burn?"

The imp raged. It hopped back and forth, setting alight a nearby pile of dry leaves. Seeing the flames spreading, the Hakhan turned protectively toward his fleshly form; the sight made him gasp. He had viewed in reflections his new beardless face with its marred cheek, but in the orange light all seemed changed. The expression was rigid, a death mask. The eyelids were open, but within the sockets lay only the darkness of the grave.

"Take out the stone, Ulaansh," the hearth-sprite pleaded.

"I'll do it when your fires are all cold."

"But I'll die!"

"To be reborn as a crueller imp."

The sprite answered in a somber tone. "I have no soul, Ulaansh. My kind cannot be reborn."

Yarkol hesitated. "Then leave a single ember. Douse the rest." He forced himself to turn from his body. The imp was rushing about frantically, waving its tiny hands. Wherever it touched now, flames sputtered out. And the creature itself grew smaller at every step. It was knee-high, then boot-high. Finally only one coal glowed beside Yarkol's stone. The imp had shrunk to a thumb-sized figure that cowered pitifully beside its route to safety. The

Hakhan thought he might scatter the last ember and end this imp's pranks forever.

"Hurry, Ulaansh."

Did Yarkol dare break his own promise? Destroying one sprite, he thought, would merely enrage all the others; he needed no impish enemies. "Don't call on me again," he warned at last. "And tell your cousins the same." Reaching down, he shoved the pebble aside, then closed the tunnel as soon as the creature was gone. The last coal faded out, and he hastened back to his body.

An intense smell of smoke was the first sensation to strike him. His skin still tingled from heat, and his eyes streamed with tears. But his body was his own again, he realized, as he scrambled away from the dark hearth. He began to doubt the whole incident, yet he could not dismiss the lingering odors.

Moonlight filtered through the bare branches. He turned cautiously to the place where his spare wood had been stacked. *Charred and still warm!* He picked up handfuls of leaves and breathed their burnt smell.

He had not dreamed the incident. And he was wide awake now, with no hope of sleeping more this night. He gathered his blanket and supplies, whistled for his mount.

"Newborn. Wait."

Another sprite calling? Yarkol turned and stared angrily toward the sound. He saw a faint glow, but the face this time was human.

The nomad woman! What was she doing here? She held a candle as she approached on foot. Behind her came a man whose appearance was hidden by shadow.

"A bad thing has happened," she said as she stepped closer."

Yarkol eyed her with suspicion. "I don't know how you found me. As for troubles, I nearly burned up in my campfire."

Etoudoori frowned and sniffed the smoky air. "I should

have come to you sooner," she said. "I was watching at Jornood House, but you slipped past me." She turned as her companion, dressed in a farmhand's tunic, came closer and took the candle from her. Yarkol had not seen this northerner before. He was a tall man of middle years, his face thin and lightly bearded. The Hakhan saw a wildness about his eyes that did not fit with his garb.

"What do you want from me?" Yarkol asked uneasily.

To his surprise, Etou knelt before him and took his hand. "You must forgive me, Newborn," she said. "I beat the drum for you, but I could not see your true destiny."

"What you told me was sensible. I followed your advice. Now I bear a message for the Kag."

"Even so, my guidance was not enough. You have more to learn before you continue your travels. The shaman will help you."

Shaman? Yarkol turned suddenly to stare at the man who stood behind her. His face, smiling gently in the yellow light, seemed more comical than threatening. Yet the Hakhan recalled his vision in the old shrine, the shaman who danced.

"I am Takijaly," said the stranger softly. "Would you prefer to see me in my robe-of-bones?"

Yarkol shook his head. He could easily imagine how the man would look in his ceremonial garb. "I was satisfied with my plans," the Hakhan said nervously. "Now you bring doubts."

"Then come to our camp," Etou pleaded. "Takijaly can give you proper advice."

She rose and tugged gently on his hand. Yarkol fought his old memories. The visit to the buried shrine, he reminded himself, had been colored by his imagination. It would do no harm to hear a shaman's views. "Bury your fire first," he insisted. "Tonight I'm wary of flames." He squinted into the candle's glow, fearing that even there he might find a tiny sprite.

"We've no fire. Only cold ground."

"Then I'll come with you, but not for long." He whistled for his mount again, and this time heard an answering whinny. With the animal saddled and ready, he could feel more at ease.

Emerging from beneath the branches, he looked up to see stars in bright clusters. He had learned their names as a child. The Firewheel was a dazzling array of reds and golds and blues. The Great Horse hung near the top of the sky, its seven foals prancing close behind. Why did the sky fascinate him this night? He forced his attention to his real horse as he led the animal up a rise.

Finally he perched on a smooth stone with the candle glimmering before him. "How did you learn where to look for me?" he asked Etou again while shadows played across her face.

"You did not know your way to Jornood House. You stopped often to ask the route."

Yarkol nodded. "Even so, you went to some effort to find me."

She made what he took to be an uneasy smile. Beside her the shaman was staring skyward with childish rapture. He too seemed captivated by the heavens tonight. "Tell us what new dreams you've had," she asked softly. "Then we'll know if our efforts were wasted."

As Yarkol described the contest on the snowy plain, he saw Etou frown. Takijaly showed no reaction until the Hakhan was done. Suddenly the shaman sat up and clapped his hands. "The time was morning and the sun was in your eyes," he exclaimed, as if reciting a deep truth. "You were trying to drag him toward the west!"

"And he was pulling me the opposite way."

Takijaly raised one long finger. "You were the sensible one in that struggle. In the east lies death for Hakhan and Chirudak like. But in the west, the tribes may find life."

"Life?"

"There is a passage," said the shaman, "a way across the Spine-of-Ice, an opening into the western lands. The Kag's people are withering now, but on those rich plains they can prosper and grow."

"I've never heard of such a passage. Why don't the nomads use it?"

"Ah." The boneman began to grin. "Simple reason. The way is narrow and steep. A strong man can crawl through, yes. But what of the sick, the old ones? What of the herds? They cannot go."

"Then that is no answer," said Etou. "There is nothing for the Kag in the west."

Takijaly again gazed at the heavens as he reached a hand toward the woman. "We'll find out," he said dreamily, touching her shoulder. "Maybe something unexpected. The gods are subtle, my wild beauty."

Yarkol had intended to move on, but now he felt more curious than threatened. The shaman possessed knowledge of the north that might prove useful. For a time, however, the boneman's attention stayed with the stars as he named constellations that no Hakhan recognized. The Goat and the Shepherd's Crook. The Broken Bow. The Bowl of Kumiss. Yarkol laughed at some of the figures, though he wished he could turn the conversation to serious matters. At last Takijaly, still propped with his face to the sky, began to sing quietly, his voice so soft that the Hakhan caught only an occasional syllable. Yarkol could not help straining to listen, and the melody grew slowly louder.

The tune made him drowsy. Leaning back against hard stone, he allowed his eyes to close briefly. He would only doze, he promised himself. After a short nap, he'd feel refreshed . . .

Suddenly he started, slapped his hand to his neck. For a moment he'd felt a tiny sting, like that from an insect. He opened his eyes to see the boneman watching him, his lips still showing a smile as he sang. The stone at Yarkol's back softened; then he felt himself floating just above the ground.

He heard voices, two men speaking. One voice belonged to the shaman, but who owned the other? His bed of air was comfortable, and for a time the Hakhan did not concern himself with questions. Sometimes he listened to the conversation, but the words seemed unimportant. After a time, he noticed a brightness all about him and felt he was waking from a long dream.

In the still dawn air Yarkol smelled pungent smoke. The boneman was puffing on a thin cheroot, his expression of good humor scarcely changed. "So, Newborn. You look rested."

"What did you do to me?" the Hakhan asked angrily. Probing his neck, Yarkol found no trace of irritation. Yet he was certain that the shaman had pricked him—with a thorn dipped in some arcane extract. Here was a compound that Hakhan physicians knew nothing about.

"I made it easier for you to talk." Takijaly blew out a cloud of pale smoke.

"But I don't know what I told you!"

"Ah. A few surprises to go with what Etou said. You don't understand the Kag's interest in your Path."

"*My* path? It belongs to Dolmi Clan. Nothing about it concerns Chirudaks."

"That is not the Kag's view. He has hopes."

The Hakhan struggled to his feet. He felt a bit lightheaded, but otherwise strong enough to defend himself. The whole pattern was suddenly clear, including this final bit of treachery. Why did Chirudaks take such an interest in him? Only because he was a fallen Dolmi—a wretch who might betray his people. Perhaps he'd already said too much.

"Calm yourself, Newborn." Takijaly glanced up without

changing expression. "The gods chose you for a reason, and anyone who interferes risks heaven's wrath."

Yarkol, in his fury, was starting to tremble. "Tell me why your chief concerns himself with our Path."

"He seeks new territory for his tribes. Hakhan and Chirudak have been hemmed in since the birth of time."

"Then let him take the west."

"As you try to force him to do in your dream. Wise advice. But the herds cannot go that way, he believes, and so he turns to the Throat. The eastern lands beyond will sustain his people."

"You speak as if the decision means nothing." The Hakhan thought of the knife he carried and wondered whether he might dispatch this mild shaman. To kill a man, except to defend himself, was forbidden by his Healer's Oath. But to protect his clan's secrets . . .

"The matter is of great concern to me," the shaman protested. "I look to you to do something about it. I fear the Kag will march by spring. You must convince him that the Path is incomplete."

I revealed that much. Yarkol grimaced, wondering what more he had said. "I don't understand your Kag. To accomplish his aims, he'll have to break through the Barrier, then fight his way south. Those two feats are possible, I suppose. But leading his people onto the Path is madness. They won't get across."

"You'll tell him that."

"Will he listen to a Hakhan?"

"To one marked, like yourself, perhaps. If not, then your dreams will show you what to do."

Yarkol answered in a throaty voice. "I have already seen such dreams." He glanced toward the north where a few peaks gleamed now in the sun's first light. "Your loyalties baffle me, shaman. You send me to challenge your highest chief."

95

Takijaly laughed. "I have no such privilege. That right belongs to the gods, and even they cannot force the issue. The High Ones call you to the north, and I offer you my advice. But you alone must make the decision."

Yarkol shook his head gloomily. His resolve to go north was unchanged. But the shaman's warning made his task more urgent and far more difficult than merely delivering a letter. "I must continue my journey," he said, "though I cannot say how it will end." He turned to look for his mount and saw Etoudoori standing just behind him.

"The north has many trails," she said quietly. "You would do well to travel with a guide."

Her comment—seemingly an offer—surprised him. "After you beat the drum for me, you sent me off on my own. Am I suddenly incapable of finding my way?"

"There is something I must confess, Newborn." She bowed her head and stared at the ground. "You were never on your own. Oron has trailed you all this time. As soon as you crossed the Barrier, he planned to make you his captive."

Yarkol stiffened. "And now?"

"Come see for yourself." At her insistence, he followed her on horseback a short distance across to another low hill. Gazing down over a scattering of rocks and bushes, Yarkol saw the nomad warrior, apparently in deep slumber, lying beneath an overhanging tree. "Come closer," she urged, seemingly unconcerned about waking her former companion. The horses picked their way carefully down the shadowed slope. To the Dolmi's surprise Oron remained asleep.

At last she stood directly over the dozing man. Yarkol watched from a distance, but he could see Oron's chest rising and falling slowly while his hand rested on the hilt of his sword. Etou laughed, broke off a dangling twig, and touched the end to Oron's cheek. "He will sleep for two days," she explained, "thanks to the shaman. Now we can leave this ox far behind."

"What am I to think of you?" Yarkol asked bitterly. "You confess that your friend plotted against me. Surely you were part of his plan."

Her expression darkened. "The gods will punish me for my failings. But I ask your forgiveness, Ulaansh."

"You told me to seek peace. Should I now ignore what you whispered? I have a letter—"

"It may prove useful."

"And what if your chief persists in his plans? Do you understand that I must stop him?"

Her answer came slowly. "If that is the gods' will . . . yes. My duty is to bring you to the Kag. The rest is your concern."

Yarkol narrowed his eyes, but remained silent as they rode back the way they had come. Last night, beside his fire, he had known a few moments of contentment. Now his expectations had been overturned once again. Yet, above all, he felt the urge to be traveling. He had already wasted too much time here.

He reached the shaman's camp and halted briefly when he saw Takijaly staring at him. "Do we ride together then?" the mystic asked Yarkol. "I am also heading north." The shaman's spotted mare, bearing several bulky saddlebags, tossed her head impatiently.

"I have offered to be his guide," Etoudoori repeated.

"Then it is settled." Takijaly finished adjusting his baggage, then quickly mounted.

But I have not agreed. Even so, Yarkol followed the nomads as they turned onto the trail.

The Hakhan rode last, his thoughts in turmoil. At times he felt he would accept Etou's apology; at others he wondered what else she might be hiding. He would decide

97

tomorrow, he told himself at last. But he kept to the rear and did not converse with the nomads.

The road passed isolated farms that were separated by ridges and pine forests. By afternoon, the sky had changed from sunny to dark. Soon a steady rain began, but the travelers plodded on.

Late in the day Yarkol heard sounds of a party approaching—loud talk, laughter, whistling. *Soldiers?* "Don't be alarmed," he told the Chirudaks, though his own pulse quickened. "Stay back and let me deal with them." He hastened ahead just as the first riders appeared, their faces half concealed by hats with down-turned brims. This was one of Jornood's patrols, he realized. The first man, who seemed their leader, halted and scrutinized the travelers. "We meet strange people on the roads," he muttered. Then, in a louder voice, he barked a challenge.

Yarkol offered his document with its green wax seal. The soldier turned it one way and another, making no attempt to keep the parchment dry. "Hyar Jornood chooses odd messengers," was all he said as he returned the folded packet.

"We need to cross the Barrier," said Yarkol. "Can you direct us?"

The soldier's mouth twisted. Rainwater was dripping steadily from his hat onto his soaked tunic. "Turn that way when you can't go on." He pointed over his shoulder. The Dolmi nodded and the soldiers rode quietly past.

Daylight was failing by the time the dark earthwork loomed ahead of them. They drew closer until Yarkol could discern the weeds and shrubs that rooted in its heaped-up soil. The rounded wall was as high as he had expected—a fearsome sight—but with forests on each side of the road he could not get a sense of the structure's expanse. From a hilltop, he imagined, one might better appreciate the Barrier.

The path along the mound's base was overgrown with

vines, all dead now from frost. Occasional footpaths led to ramparts atop the wall. As night came on, the gloom thickened, and soon he could make out no details. Suddenly he smelled wood smoke, saw a flickering light ahead. The murmur of voices grew.

He neared a hide stretched between tall poles, with a campfire sputtering beneath it. Soldiers milled about a large cauldron. "Who goes?" shouted someone.

"I carry Hyar Jornood's letter north," the Hakhan said coolly. "If your officer wishes to see it—"

"Great Horse," shouted the soldier to his friends. "He's got crudes with him!" Pointing his sword at Etou, he slapped her exposed trouser leg with his free hand. Then he glanced at the shaman. "What about these two?" the guard demanded of Yarkol.

"My guides." The Dolmi offered his document again.

"Go on," the soldier shouted. "Get them back where they belong. Now!" He waved all three riders by.

Yarkol found himself bristling at the soldier's attitude and wondered briefly what had happened to his own loyalties. His attention turned at once, however, to the crossing. A narrow brook flowed under the high wall, and the tunnel through which it ran offered barely enough headroom for a rider. This breach, he believed, was used by patrols who kept the wall's northern side in repair.

Yarkol let the two nomads go ahead. His horse appeared nervous, its ears pricking forward as it peered at the opening. A torch flared beside the entrance, and the Dolmi noted how the tunnel was shored up with heavy logs. In case of attack, he imagined, the supports could be felled to seal the narrow passage.

He glanced cautiously at the stream. Seeing no unwelcome swimmers, he urged his horse into the flow. It took a few steps forward but halted short of the tunnel's mouth. Never before, to his knowledge, had the animal faced such a crossing.

Yarkol tried coaxing, but the gray would not budge. He saw soldiers at the guard post watching him, snickering with delight. Had they never seen a balky mount?

The Dolmi sighed and stepped down into the shallow water. He strode forward boldly until he stood beneath the low ceiling, then turned to his animal. "See!" he said loudly, so that all could hear. "It's safe. Look. Look at me." The gelding's ears swiveled back toward the growing sound of laughter. Perhaps driven by that raucous clamor, it advanced a few steps more.

"What a brave horse you are!" Yarkol called, pulling from his pouch a piece a biscuit for reward. The soldiers, shouting and jeering, had gathered behind the animal. Evidently it could stand their noise no longer, for it suddenly plunged forward, squeezing past its rider and splattering him with water and mud.

Yarkol turned, fuming but pleased with his ruse, and splashed after the vanishing creature. The air was musty, scented with damp earth. Within the tunnel the torchlight dimmed; he could barely see his way. Yet something glowed along the path ahead. He advanced warily.

He caught a whiff of fresh air and realized that he had almost reached the tunnel's end. But at each side of the opening a kobold crouched, long fingers trailing in the water. He must pass between the imps to get out.

"Ulaansh, you are far from home," said one.

He stared at its pendulous ears and elongated feet, recalling the imp he'd seen outside Dolmi House. He'd kicked a stone at that one. Could this be the same creature, come to exact revenge?

"The way is slippery," said the other. "You may stumble."

"And I may have kobolds for dinner." He spread his legs wide to straddle the flow. The ground felt muddy at the edges, but reasonably firm. He advanced in a swagger.

The imps, directly in his path, grinned coldly. They have no strength, he told himself.

He felt barely a whisper as he booted the hobs aside. But somehow he lost his balance and fell headlong into the chilly flow. "May the High God roast you on his long spit," he shouted as he pulled himself upright, the cold already seeping through his trousers. "Imps! Sprites!" He slogged out onto dry ground and whistled for his mount.

7

Pupil: Why do the gods allow imps to torment us?

Teacher: To make us strong.

Pupil: And how are imps made strong?

Teacher (angrily): The yurt grows cold. Go collect dung for the fire.

—Chirudak tradition

Yarkol, dripping, stood in the gloom on the northern side of the wall and listened for his horse. He whistled once more.

"Over here, Newborn." Turning toward Etou's voice, he caught a glimmer of light. Climbing to higher ground, he saw the northerners crouched beneath an overhanging rock ledge. A flame from their stubby candle cast wavering shadows.

"My mount ran off," Yarkol complained as he ducked into the shelter. He smelled burning tallow and wet clothing.

"We caught him," Etou answered. "But your plains horse won't do for mountain country."

"He's all I have."

"Tomorrow you'll trade him."

"Trade?" The Dolmi frowned at her casual dismissal of his mount, an animal he'd grown fond of over several years. The gray gelding was his only link with the past. If he took to riding a mountain pony, then perhaps he should plait his hair as well. Nothing would be left from his life as a Hakhan.

He did not care to pursue the argument. For now, keeping warm was his main concern. He glanced down and saw that the nomads had brought in his saddlebags. Grateful that he would not have to go out in the rain again, he knelt, took out his blanket, and wrapped himself from ankle to chin. Etou offered a biscuit, and he worked a hand free to accept it, thinking all the while of the soldiers' cookpot. He imagined that he smelled its aromas wafting over the mound.

At last Etou covered the damp ground with hides. Stretched out, the three travelers barely fit beneath the overhang. Everyone tried to sleep, but Yarkol kept waking to find rainwater dripping onto his arm or boot.

By morning the clouds were gone. The Hakhan stood gaping as the sun's first rays struck the Barrier. Now he better understood why the wall had proved so effective. Along the base on this side ran a broad trench from which much of the rock and soil for construction had been dug. An attacker would have to cross the ditch first, then ascend a sheer wall that bristled with spikes.

Despite its imposing bulk, the wall had weaknesses.

Though the mound was patrolled regularly, Yarkol understood that Chirudaks had tunneled through it on several occasions. And constant vigilance was needed where streams and rivers breached the wall.

"Newborn!" Etou was already astride her roan. She had discarded entirely her southern garb, he noted, and now wore a short padded coat and tapered leggings; her braids were tucked up under a fur hat that had flaps to cover her ears. Takijaly had donned similar clothing—what Yarkol took to be nomads' everyday garb. To the Hakhan only Takijaly's eyes hinted at his mystical vocation.

Yarkol saw no choice but to continue traveling with the northerners, for he did not know his way in this country. Ahead he saw a rough trail, narrow and rocky, far poorer than what his horse was used to. The Hakhan shook his head sadly, convinced now that this must be their last ride together. His gray could never reach the Kag.

The path ascended steeply, then began a gentle decline. Yarkol's gaze turned often now to the view of the mountaintops before him. The nearest peaks were white-tipped, glistening, and behind them rose another jagged range. This vista he had surely seen before—in his nightmares. Even the wind that rippled his jacket was familiar.

Here and there a modest homestead lay along the path. Settled Chirudaks occupied these, Etou told him. They raised cattle or tilled the rocky soil, following a way of life that nomads sneered at. The Hakhan noted occasional plumes of smoke and learned that some men here smelted metals for trade with passing tribesmen.

Later, from the top of a sharp ridge, Yarkol saw the land ahead sloping down into a broad river valley. Small farms clung to the nearest side, but the rest was open country. And at the far end he saw something that chilled his heart: a nomad settlement like those of his dreams.

Etou pointed and began chattering too rapidly for him

to follow. The shaman, riding behind her, seemed lost in his own thoughts and did not react. But Yarkol could see even from this distance the rows of gray yurts, the scattered herds, the riders guarding the horses.

"Winter camp!" shouted Etou for Yarkol's benefit. When she turned to him, he glimpsed her bright face and moist eyes. The first time he'd seen her he'd thought of a fox. Now, he saw more beauty and less savagery in her features. Wondering briefly if he could ever be drawn to a Chirudak woman, he at once heard Merig chiding him. No, such an attraction wasn't possible.

To Yarkol's relief his companions did not hasten to the nomad encampment. Instead, Etou led him to what seemed the most prosperous farmhouse, enticed the family's elder outside and began praising the virtues of Yarkol's mount. The Hakhan stood gloomily beside her and wished for a quick resolution.

The old man appeared to pay no attention as she pulled back the animal's lips or ran her fingers up and down its sturdy legs. The elder's eyes remained fixed on Yarkol's face.

"Grandfather," she said finally. "Think of this. You can have a mount that belonged to an ulaansh. It may bring your family great fortune."

At those words, the farmer's craggy face broke into a grin that showed his few remaining teeth. He approached Yarkol, leaning close to scrutinize the blotched cheek. "You?" asked the old one, his breath reeking of cheroot smoke as he pointed first to the animal and then to Yarkol. "Your horse? You ride far?"

When the Hakhan nodded, the elder's smile grew even broader. He waved the visitors to follow him to his pens where a dozen mountain ponies milled. A few stood with their heads drooping; one was gnawing at a rail. But a young mare, of dappled tawny coat with a white muzzle, looked particularly spirited. Etou pointed to the animal at once; the graybeard frowned.

Moments later, other members of the family arrived. They clustered about the Hakhan, children and elders equally curious. A few reached tentatively toward his horse's coat or even tried to touch Yarkol's boots.

The Hakhan wished that Etou had gone alone to carry out this chore. What had she made of him? He recalled bizarre, misshapen creatures that were sometimes caught on the borders of the Throat. Now he felt on display like such a beast, surrounded by people seeking a brief amusement.

Etou and the grandfather began to negotiate in earnest. She seemed possessed of an energy he hadn't seen before, waving her arms and tossing her head as she spoke. The elder frowned sometimes, smiled sometimes, but said little.

Finally, without moving, the old farmer raised a long forefinger. That was enough signal to send a youth over the rail fence into the pen. The chosen pony dodged him several times, but soon the boy clambered onto its back. Yarkol wondered, as the dappled mare tossed her head, whether she might not be *too* high-strung for his needs.

Another boy brought a Chirudak saddle, permitting Etou to inspect it. She fingered the worn leather, frowned, then watched carefully as it was fitted in place. The rounded skirts were longer than those of Hakhan saddles, Yarkol noted, and the faded crimson blanket reached well down over the pony's sides. Only when Etou had tugged at the girths and poked her fingers under every rim, did she nod acceptance. Yarkol unstrapped his saddlebags.

He did not want to watch his own horse being led away. Cautiously he approached the new animal, which the tallest youth now held firmly by its bridle. Yarkol blew his breath softly at the nostrils in the white muzzle. The pony stamped a forefoot.

106

All about him Chirudaks were jabbering, and he understood barely a word. Somehow he must gain the trust of this animal. He dug from his pouch one of the morsels he carried for his own—his former—horse. The new pony took the morsel eagerly, leaving his fingers sticky. Smiles spread across several faces.

Yarkol saw how the mount's tawny coat glistened in the sunlight. Cautiously he put one hand on the thinly-padded pommel. Why did he think the animal would not accept him? With sudden resolve, he stepped into one stirrup and swung his other leg over. At once, the pony began to run.

"Ho!" the Hakhan shouted as he was carried across the muddy yard. The mare leapt nimbly over a ditch, skirted a puddle, raced out onto a broad, open field. Of her own accord, or possibly responding to his reins, the creature halted and began cropping at the stubble on the ground. Yarkol heard laughter from the direction of the paddock.

"We're going to get along," he told the mare firmly. This time, when he twitched the reins, she accepted his will and trotted back toward Etou. The grandfather was grinning and winking as he spoke into the woman's ear. Yarkol assumed that he was offering a more docile creature in exchange.

Etou shook her head, took one more glance at the Hakhan, and returned to her roan. Most of the family had lost interest in Yarkol by then; they clustered around their new southern horse where it stood in its pen staring back at them. The Dolmi sighed and turned his mare toward the road that led northward.

The trail took them into rocky country again, and Yarkol quickly saw the value of his new mount. His gray had picked its way awkwardly along such stony paths. This creature stepped with confidence, avoiding obstacles with seeming disdain. It did not balk at steep climbs or descents or at crossing swift currents. He imagined that it

107

would have plunged willingly into the Barrier tunnel and spared him the cold bath he'd suffered.

Etou's roan performed similar service, but Yarkol grew puzzled as he watched the shaman ride. Takijaly seemed to stiffen whenever a steep drop edged the trail. He constantly tried to force his mount inward, inducing an awkward gait. Fear of heights was not an uncommon trait, but Yarkol suspected that the shaman's case was extreme. A journey such as this was more of a hardship for him than the Hakhan had realized.

Soon Yarkol noticed the scenery changing, the landscape growing wilder. On exposed ridges the trees bent almost parallel to the ground, with their branches swept back from the wind. Here he felt the onset of winter's chill, but in the occasional sheltered valley he found the sun still warm and the breeze pleasant.

As evening approached, the travelers came down toward a broad winding stream that reflected the glow of sunset. Along the banks yurts clustered in a dense encampment. Flocks of sheep and goats, herded by children, were being watered downstream. And in the far distance, ponies moved languidly across a brown meadow.

Etou and the shaman conferred briefly. Yarkol gritted his teeth when they turned to approach the busy camp. He was under no obligation to follow them, he reminded himself. But his mount trotted forward eagerly, and he found himself drawn also—by a mixture of curiosity and dread.

As he neared the yurts, the Dolmi smelled woodsmoke and aromas of cooked meat. The prospect of a hot meal was not enough to ease his misgivings. In every direction he saw the Chirudaks of his visions. Young men, their foreheads tonsured, their long braids dangling behind, were brushing the dusty coats of ponies. Women wearing quilted jackets were carrying chunks of freshly butchered meat. Many nomads paused to gaze at him; he could not face their stares.

By that time mountain shadows completely covered the valley floor. The last bands of yellow sunlight lay draped across the high ridges. The sky was dusky blue, almost cloudless. Yarkol wished he could float up to those serene heights, and for a moment he lost himself in contemplation.

Shouts of youngsters brought his attention back to the ground. He saw several children running after him, pointing and calling to their friends. Now the news of this "godstricken" stranger would quickly spread throughout the camp.

Etou rode boldly on; he wondered where she was leading him. She passed through the main ranks of dwellings to a yurt that was larger than all the others, standing alone on a raised piece of ground. Yarkol's forehead broke out in sweat as he stared at the covering of white felt. But this was not his destination; the Kag's camp lay much farther north. Even so, Yarkol heard blood pounding in his ears as Etou halted. A single guard stood outside the dwelling, his sheathed sword dangling from his belt.

As Etou dismounted, a youngster rushed forward to take her reins. Yarkol was reluctant to follow, but she turned, hissed loudly and motioned for him to come down. This yurt, he knew, held a mere tribal chief. But his legs felt unsteady as he presented himself to the guard.

Etou engaged the warrior in a quick exchange. He shrugged, planted his feet wide apart, and rested his hand on his sword's hilt. "Chochiid is not to be disturbed," said the guard as his face reverted to a frozen expression. She argued further, but the expression did not change. Behind him, the door flap was suddenly thrown back.

The flickering illumination from within backlit a tall, thin figure. Etoudoori touched a finger to her lips, then to her forehead, then bowed from the waist. She spoke humbly now, pointing first to Yarkol and then to the shaman. Chochiid stepped back from the doorway, beckoning all three visitors to enter.

This chief wore no mask, Yarkol noted with relief, but showed his weathered face plainly. His beard was close-cropped; his gray braids fell to the small of his back. About his forehead he wore a decorated band of yellow cloth inscribed with dark figures.

Layers of rugs that felt springy underfoot covered Chochiid's floor. Low tables and narrow chests stood beside the walls, and a bewildering array of artifacts—sacks, pots, tools—hung from the roof. In the center, beneath the smoke hole, lay a ring of stones about the fire. Two women, one younger than Etou and one looking as aged as the chief, peered with undisguised curiosity at the newcomers.

The tribe's elder motioned Yarkol closer. Supplementing the firelight, a triple candelabrum of carved bone brightened the room. Chochiid, without hesitation, touched a finger to the Hakhan's cheek. Yarkol willed himself to suffer the indignity as the chief traced the outline of his disfigurement. The old man marveled for a few moments, then barked a few orders to the women. The young wife scurried from the yurt.

"My guests . . . this night," Chochiid said. He ushered the visitors to thin cushions that lay about the hearth. Takijaly's face showed a dreamy look as he gazed into the fire. Etou, meanwhile, gave a shortened account of her journey.

The young woman reappeared, accompanied by two others who might have been her sisters. The first carried chunks of raw meat on skewers, the second a bowl of brown-skinned tubers. The third brought a tall leather sack, open at the top with a stick protruding from its neck.

110

The skewers were laid across the hearth stones. Fat hissing into the flames produced an aroma that made Yarkol wet his lips. For days he had survived on biscuits and water and shreds of dried meat, though he had minded little at the time. Since his illness, he'd paid scant attention to what he ate; small amounts of food and drink sustained him easily. This night, when the meat was taken from the fire, he found that despite the good flavor he could not finish his portion. Takijaly, licking his fingers, was glad to have Yarkol's leavings.

Chochiid's youngest wife stood before the leather container. She held the sack upright with one hand, and with the other began to pump the stick up and down. Yarkol heard liquid sloshing within. This churning went on for some time, until the meal was finished and the guests had wiped their hands on a square of damp cloth. Finally the woman poured the foaming kumiss into a polished wooden bowl.

Yarkol had heard of this drink—fermented mare's milk—but had never tasted the potion. This was the social drink of Chirudaks, he understood, and to refuse it would be an insult to his host. When the bowl reached him, he found the odor far stronger than he'd expected. The drink was sour on his tongue. He forced himself to swallow.

The bowl passed around the circle several times, and Yarkol did not find its taste improving. The growing loudness of talk and the smiling expressions of his companions suggested that the drink was having an effect. Yarkol thought its potency similar to that of wine; he felt no lightheadedness.

When the bowl was half-empty, the wife rose to fill it again. Yarkol found himself taking more at every pass. Etou, seated beside him, was speaking rapidly to the chief, and yet the Hakhan seemed to grasp what she was saying. Had he learned her variant of the language so quickly?

111

"He is like a child," she said, her cheeks glowing in fire-light. She put her arm about Yarkol and drew him to her. He leaned over awkwardly, his head resting on her shoulder while she stroked the back of his neck.

Chochiid laughed and said something that Yarkol failed to grasp. The Hakhan felt a sudden rush of affection for Etoudoori. Despite her questionable motives she had done him a good service, he thought, helping him come to terms with his affliction. For a short while longer he enjoyed her touch, but he felt foolish in this position and quickly sat up.

When the kumiss was gone, the host stood drunkenly and led his guests outside into the cold evening air. He pointed to the Fish Moons, two golden orbs that shimmered in the east, and shouted praises to various spirits. Each visitor, in turn, was encouraged to mouth ever wordier compliments. Yarkol's thoughts had grown fuzzy; he could not summon a single phrase. He leaned close to Etou, let her whisper in his ear, then repeated her sentiments in a loud voice.

At last, Chochiid made a formal bow of farewell just as the youngest wife arrived carrying a conical candle lamp. She smiled and led the travelers to a nearby yurt. This smaller structure was more modestly furnished than the chief's dwelling. Even so, with thick rugs on the floor, it offered far more comfort than Yarkol had known of late. He realized that some family had moved out—presumably to share cramped quarters—so that the visitors could occupy this lodging.

Feeling slightly dizzy from too much drink, the Hakhan pulled a sheepskin over his head and immediately fell into sleep. He woke sometime later to hear squealing and laughter that gave way to rhythmic sighs. The candle was out; he needed no light to tell what Etou and the shaman were doing.

How could he keep his thoughts from the past? He

112

covered his ears, but failed to ward off memories of Merig's warmth beside him. He lay with wet cheeks, unable to sleep until the last groans of pleasure died away.

Even after his companions fell quiet, he remained awake. At last, he threw aside the sheepskin and went out into the chilly night. The pair of Fish Moons had moved higher. All about him the camp lay still.

For a whole day he had seen no imps, and he wondered if he had finally shaken them off. Uneasily he gazed toward the broad, quiet stream. From this distance he saw nothing unusual, but he was loathe to walk closer. Then something caught his eye just behind the row of yurts. A cairn of stones, wide at the base and narrow on top, gleamed faintly in the moonlight. He thought he saw small creatures frolicking about the pile.

Resolutely, he turned away. Was that a kobold lurking by the doorway of his yurt? In anger he picked up a stone, but he quickly dropped it. If these creatures were real—and by now he could scarcely think otherwise—then ignoring them seemed his wisest course.

He recalled several tales he'd heard as a child. Kobolds were said to live underground and in houses and barns. They kept vermin away if they were kindly disposed. A forest hob could lure game to a hunter, but expected a gift of tooled leather in return. A hearth-sprite kept the fire from blowing out . . . Yarkol shook his head, wondering how much truth lay in these beliefs.

With imps abroad, the Hakhan could find no peace outside. He returned to the yurt, crawled across the floor, and felt his way to his bedding. When he woke again, dawn had come; he saw gray light filtering through the smoke hole. Takijaly was snoring softly. In the gloom Yarkol could not be certain if Etou still lay beside the boneman.

The Dolmi stepped outside to clear his head. Even the thin walls of a yurt became oppressive after a night. He was eager to get moving but reluctant to wake Takijaly. Perhaps, for Jornood's sake if no other reason, he would have a look around the camp.

Behind him he heard sheep bleating as children led them to pasture. Curious, he approached the edge of the flock where a tall youth stood watching. Even in the dim pre-dawn light Yarkol could see that the animals were thin and bedraggled. With such scanty coats, the sheep might not survive winter. And the goats would be good for little; at best they would make tough eating.

Grazing in the north had been poor this year, he understood. For several years running, the herds had declined. Now he saw firsthand the nomads' plight. But he recalled also how the Kag planned to provide for his people—at Hakhan expense.

Turning from the dust and smell of the animals, he strolled back to the cairn he'd seen under moonlight. This was a shrine, he realized, a place where offerings were left for sprites. Tucked between the stones he saw glittering bits of jewelry and scraps of weaving. He could not help squatting to search for tiny footprints; he found only pawprints of animals and laughed at himself.

Moments later, Etou was calling him, and he wondered how she had readied herself so quickly. Yet she and the shaman already sat astride their ponies, while a boy led Yarkol's dappled mount. The Hakhan nodded and took the reins.

As soon as he began to ride, Yarkol felt charged with new energy. He sped across the plain, cold wind chilling his face and whistling past his ears. The run exhilarated him; he wished never to stop.

Soon, however, the horses reached the winding mountain trail and were forced to resume their customary pace. Near noon the riders met a tribe that was coming down to its winter camp. On the narrow path northbound travel became slow and tedious. Yarkol was grate-

114

ful for his nimble mount as it sidestepped a train of woolly oxen.

The shaggy mountain beasts carried rolls of felt and bundles of rods—disassembled parts of a yurt. Other oxen bore looms, carved stools, spare saddles. As they went, the creatures bobbed their huge heads, their horns waving menacingly, their neck bells clanging. But these beasts also had suffered hunger, he realized; their ribs showed plainly through matted hides.

Some elders and infants traveled in litters borne by the larger beasts. The other nomads, including small children, all rode ponies. Both men and women carried bow-cases, slung over their backs or hanging beside their saddles. Yarkol knew of the northerners' reputation for archery skills, but this was the first time he'd seen their weapons at close quarters. If Jornood had to fight these people, the Hakhan thought, he might find himself seriously disadvantaged.

At last the trail split, allowing the three riders to get away onto a quiet path. They rode until evening, settling in finally with a small encampment. A group moving south had separated from its tribe and stopped for the night on a narrow plateau.

Yurts were not erected at this temporary camp. Everyone cooked in the open, while crowded animals lowed restlessly nearby. A line of children, aided by black, long-haired dogs, stood at the edge of a precipice to chase sheep back into camp.

The travelers found no chief to greet them, no welcoming meal. They were happy to share their own food with a humble family and sit about a smoky fire. Etou began chatting with a young husband. His one wife kept eyeing her with disapproval while the man's attitude progressed from shyness to open fascination. And Etou encouraged him, touching his arm or knee as she spoke.

Yarkol could not understand Etou's behavior. Was not

115

one lover enough for her? Takijaly seemed oblivious to the flirtation; he sat between two young children and amused them with finger tricks, manipulating small stones to their evident delight.

When the meal was done, several men lit cheroots in the flames of the campfire. Etou's new friend, however, stood up and went to his saddlebags. He brought back a gaming box, a modest version of the one Yarkol had seen before. Turning to his scowling wife, the nomad indicated that he wanted her to compete with Etoudoori.

As Etou stepped forward, she knew that the woman would prefer a simple brawl to this contest. But here was a more civilized way to settle a grievance, and the wife would be forced by custom to accept it. The tribeswoman took the shoy box angrily, and for a moment Etou feared she might refuse. Then, with a look of determination, she shook the contents in each of the four directions.

From the sidelines came murmurs of encouragement. Kneeling beside the fire, the wife let the bones slide out quickly, not seeming to care that they fell onto dirt and ashes. She made no immediate move to arrange them as her family gathered about her to view the results.

Etou, now seated cross-legged beside the wife, reached impatiently toward the game pieces and received a blow for her efforts. The woman spoke sharply, then proceeded to collect the tokens and lay them in neat ranks. Etou's eyebrows rose as she saw sun and rain and good pastures standing clear of dark influences. Impoverished as she appeared to be, this woman had decent prospects.

At last came the moment that Etou had worked for all evening. She knew that the shaman did not approve of shoy, but she hoped to disguise her interest in the game through this appearance of bitter rivalry. She shook the box, mixing the pieces as well as she could.

The tokens slid out and lay in the dust—Taawik and Windstorm and Bringer-of-Ice. She shivered as she recalled her last attempt at divination. Was she any better off now, after the shaman's assistance, after confessing her misdeeds to the Hakhan? Taawik was neutral, a bearer of good tidings or bad. Windstorm meant destruction, and the other face-up pieces appeared equally foreboding. Etou felt her eyes begin to sting.

The young wife smiled coldly, her chin held high. It was clear that she'd won handily. The tribeswoman must pay Etou a forfeit, of course, but what could that matter?

"You may have him for the night," the wife said indifferently, gesturing at her husband. "He'll not see you again."

Etou started. She truly cared nothing for the man. All she had wanted was an excuse to consult the bones. "You are too generous," she answered. "A bit of salt will do. Or a pinch of herbs."

"Those things aren't easily replaced. There's no dearth of man-juice."

Etou had thought herself bold, but her face reddened at this woman's outspokenness. The husband was gazing at Etou eagerly and all the camp's eyes seemed on her. *The price of a game of shoy.* What could she do but smile acceptance?

8

The women of Warmbed tribe give birth only to daughters, and the tribe has no men but those being entertained for the night. One year, the women neglected their shrines and stopped making offerings to the kobolds. Deciding that a lesson must be taught, the imps agreed on a plan of revenge. From then on, whenever a man entered a Warmbed yurt, the imps chased away his mount. No matter how carefully the animal was secured, the kobolds found a way to set it free.

When news of these pranks spread, the Warmbeds found themselves without visitors. Soon, they told each other, they would have no more daughters, and the tribe would die. So

118

the women prepared a great sacrifice,
burying much treasured jewelry and
cloth. The kobolds relented, and at
last men returned.

Since that day, the Warmbed
women have always been generous
with their offerings. And no visitor to
the tribe has ever had to search for his
horse.

—Men's Tale (Leatherhat tribe)

Next morning, Yarkol found the trail crowded again by tribes heading for their winter camps. He made his way past shaggy oxen, fierce black dogs, and countless plodding sheep. He tried not to notice the curious gazes of oncoming riders.

Occasionally he glanced up to see Etoudoori well ahead of him, her roan's head swaying as the animal breasted the flow. Annoyed by Etou's behavior at the evening fire, he hadn't spoken to her this morning. He still did not understand his feelings toward her. Was he merely embarrassed by her flirtation, or was he also suffering a pang of jealousy?

Etou rode alone, for the shaman had lagged far behind. Yarkol sensed her remorse from the way she slumped in the saddle. He had a vague wish to comfort her, but held back. This woman remained an enigma to him. He wanted to trust her, yet his doubts lingered.

Angry with himself now for wasting so many thoughts on her, he concentrated on the obstacles of the trail. He struggled through a flock of goats, then bypassed a long line of oxen. For a time he paused, making way for a tribal chief with his wives and children and burdened beasts. But finally the downhill traffic began to thin until only occasional stragglers appeared. Grateful for solitude, Yarkol made better time now, speeding his mount up a gentle rise.

He heard shouts and barking dogs ahead. Suddenly he saw why the path had grown empty. A broad, pebbled stream that crossed his trail was holding back travelers on the far bank. Such a shallow flow should be easy to ford, he thought, yet the animals had stopped short of its edge. Sheep bleated; cattle lowed. Even the well-trained mountain ponies danced nervously and would not approach the water.

The Hakhan became puzzled. Many animals and riders had crossed earlier; he had seen them on the trail below. Why should this trouble start now, just as he arrived? Glancing up, he saw more travelers trying to come down the narrow defile. If the impasse continued much longer, he realized, the animals would begin to trample each other.

Dismounting to look closer at this unlikely obstacle, he tethered his pony to an overhanging tree. The water level was low, exposing glittering round pebbles. Stepping down onto the stones, he saw that one earthen bank was deeply undercut. He crouched, peered into the dark cavern, but could not tell how far under it went. From within came a musty odor of damp moss and decaying wood.

Something about this place drew his suspicions. Yarkol slid his knife from its sheath and found the blade less shiny than he had hoped. Even so, it might serve his purpose. He angled the metal under sunlight, aimed the reflection to penetrate the gloom.

"You don't need that, Ulaansh," cried a voice that startled him. He dropped the knife, heard it fall onto gravel. The stream-polished stones where the weapon lay showed a dizzying rainbow of colors.

So an imp is behind this. He wanted to pick up the blade, but for the moment his fingers remained immobile. The brightness was too much for him. His eyelids closed against the glare.

Yet still he saw the scene! The knife blade had taken on the hue of hot iron; to touch it, he thought, could only bring pain. His gaze shifted back to the opening under the bank.

He had fallen into trance, he realized, this time without need for breathing exercises. What he saw came through spirit eyes, and now the cave appeared filled with a dim blue-green light. He recalled boyhood swimming, deep dives into a lake.

With ease that surprised him, he slipped forward, leaving his body behind. The water-sprite sat in a puddle at the far end of the cave, its thin wet beard dangling to its groin. Its legs were long and spindly, its knees misshapen knobs. "I have waited for you, Ulaansh," the creature said.

"You've closed the trail for everyone," Yarkol replied harshly. "Why must others suffer on my account?"

"How else could I get you to play? Here, look at my gameboard."

"I'll have nothing to do with it." The Hakhan wished to ignore imps and their taunts, yet this one's mischief was more than he could bear. He crawled closer, his gaze averted from his own fleshless limbs. He swung his fist at the sprite but was not surprised to see his spirit bones pass right through the creature. So far as Yarkol knew, only solid matter could push aside an imp. Iron, he recalled from tales, could do more—harm or even destroy a sprite. And sunlight was said to be a most potent scourge . . . "Why do you find me so intriguing?" he demanded of the creature.

"You are special, Ulaansh." The sprite—possibly the same one who had challenged him days earlier—laughed and reached its talons toward the Hakhan's chest.

121

Glancing down, Yarkol gasped. Up to now he'd avoided looking fully at his trance-body, for he had expected to see nothing but bones. His assumption proved correct— or nearly so. The light here gave everything a greenish cast, making the sight far more startling than he'd imagined. And his rib cage was not empty! Within it he saw fluttering what appeared to be a small figure of a bird. "I don't know what you want from me," he said softly.

"A contest. A contest." The imp pointed to a flat rock that lay covered by water.

Reluctantly, Yarkol turned his gaze to the complex pattern of circles inscribed onto the stone. A cluster of water-striders, some colored iridescent blue, some silvery black, floated on the puddle's surface. "A game I know nothing about," the Hakhan said. "But one you surely understand. How could I hope to beat you at it?"

"I have such a tiny brain," the imp answered in a wheedling tone. "Even a blind mole can outwit me."

Yarkol looked with suspicion at the insects, their feet making tiny dimples in the water's surface. They played a part in this game, but he had yet to see how. "Tell me the stakes," he asked warily.

"If you win, I'll solve this little problem outside. I'll whisper soothing words and let the animals cross the stream. If you lose, then I'll take from you what I wish."

Yarkol glanced again at the fluttering bird shape within his chest. This was what the imp wanted, he knew. How could he risk parting with it when he did not know its significance?

"You'll find winning easy," said the imp. "You simply put your piece over any empty circle. Like this." He hissed, and a blue water-strider flitted from the swarm. "Your color is black. Try it."

The Dolmi hesitated before slowly moving his hand toward one of the dark insects. His spirit fingers, he thought, could easily push the small thing into place.

"I am waiting, Newborn."

Yarkol had heard of the tricks that sprites played on men, of ways they deceived with their words. "What did you mean when you promised to let the animals cross?" he asked suddenly. "Will you relent only for a moment? Will you wait until winter to fulfill your bargain?"

"I'll ease their fears at once and never trouble them again, stubborn Ulaansh. They will always cross quickly at this ford. Now play your piece."

Yarkol glanced again at his bone fingers hovering over the water-striders, but he was not ready to start the contest. While the imp danced back and forth impatiently, he turned from the game and crawled to the rear of the cavern. Briefly he searched for an opening there, but found none. When he looked up at the roof, he saw a layer of soil held together by a tangle of roots. The imp might be vulnerable here . . .

The Hakhan gazed once more at the mysterious patterns on the playing surface. The imp had not yet bothered to explain the rules. Why should Yarkol chance a game he did not understand? Instead, he began crawling toward the outside, where his fleshly body still squatted beside the bank.

"I'll make it easy, Ulaansh. I'll play for you." Behind him, Yarkol heard further hisses—instructions to the insect playing-pieces—but refused to look at the results. So long as he did not participate, he was not committed to any agreement. Reaching the cave's mouth, he found the sunlight's intensity almost unbearable, but he forced himself to continue outward. At last he could see the fallen knife glowing as if afire; even the bone handle had a reddish tinge.

"You have nearly won, Ulaansh," called the shrill voice. "Then you'll have what you came for. You shouldn't distrust me."

Yarkol's bones were a blinding white as he stretched

123

his hand toward the weapon. With his spirit-body's feeble strength, he wondered if he could lift such a heavy thing. As he touched the hilt he heard a hiss of steam. A sensation of burning raced up his arm, but he forced his fingers to close. The knife's weight stretched out the bones of his spirit hand.

"One more move and it's over," the creature shrieked. "You must play that one for yourself."

In this form, he had touched coals and felt nothing. But whatever heat lay within the handle seeped out to sear his fingers. Now he understood why sprites feared iron, for in spirit-form he too was vulnerable to its power. Even so, he gathered his strength and pulled. The knife came up, but he thought he could not hold it. Keep it for just a moment, he told himself. He twisted the blade to catch sunlight and reflect a bright beam into the cavern.

"Ulaansh!" screamed the sprite as it leapt away from the brilliance. Yarkol was not certain if the imp could escape. While the creature dodged wildly, he tried to follow it with the burning rays. But at last Yarkol cried out from pain, dropped the weapon, then crawled back into the cool green interior beneath the bank.

"Now we must start over," the sprite whined as it looked with despair into the puddle. Evidently the insects had scattered, though the Hakhan did not care for a closer look. "You're a troublemaker," said the imp. "I should leave you in your fix."

"I am more trouble than you imagine," he replied. "You have no way out of here. I just proved that to myself."

Hunched over his game again, the sprite did not glance up.

"Sunlight will dry you up, destroy you in a moment. All I need do is go back to my body and dig through the ceiling." Yarkol pointed up at the sagging cave roof.

"I'll make it easy for you," said the sprite. "I'll let you choose my moves as well as yours."

"Are you hard of hearing, imp? I leave you to your fate." Yarkol put an arm outside again and began to pull his legs after him. The glare did not seem so dazzling this time. But the sight of his body's deathlike face gave him a chill. Hurriedly he merged back into his flesh.

At once he was seeing with normal eyes again. He stood up slowly, finding his joints slightly stiff. A dull pain throbbed within his right hand though the skin showed no mark or wound. Whatever damage he had inflicted on his spirit-form evidently did not fully affect his body.

He glanced down and saw the knife where it lay on the glittering pebbles. The blade was not where he had first dropped it; he had truly moved it while in trance! Now he reached for the weapon gingerly, half expecting to be burned again, but the metal was merely warm from the sun. He sheathed the knife, then looked around.

The Hakhan saw several tribesmen staring at him from the far bank and wondered if they understood the cause of their troubles. He had no intention of explaining. Already he had wasted too much time here; now he must bring this annoyance to an end. Turning to a fallen tree that lay across the bank, he broke off a stout branch. He pounded the ragged end into the tangle of vines that grew atop the cave, gouging out moist, dark soil. Again and again he lifted the limb, battering the ground until he heard clods of dirt falling within the hollow.

Why were the nomads gaping at him? Perhaps he should have asked someone for a better digging tool. As he raised the branch once more, he heard shouts of surprise and jubilation from the men on the trail. Turning, he saw that goats had surged forward to ford the stream, with sheep following at their heels.

A voice of despair wailed from below. "The game is finished, Ulaansh. You are the victor."

"Pay double," said the Dolmi under his breath. "Your life as well." A few more blows and the imp would face

125

scorching daylight. Yarkol raised the crude weapon, but as he watched the renewed flow of nomads down the trail, his anger suddenly drained out of him, and he lost his will to destroy the creature. He threw the broken branch aside.

It was mid-afternoon before the Hakhan saw a familiar face again. Takijaly caught up with the him as he struggled past a procession of riders. "I heard talk of sorcery back there," the shaman ventured. "Trouble at a crossing. A strange Hakhan who beat the ground."

Yarkol shrugged. "I saw no sorcerers," he answered with a nervous laugh. But the shaman's gaze chilled him and he said no more.

Later they found Etoudoori, who had waited for them where the trail widened again, and the three made camp alone in a narrow gorge. She remained sullen, stirring the cooking pot and saying little. Takijaly leaned back against a log, toying with his bone flute while the fire warmed his boots. Yarkol sighed, for he knew he must put aside his misgivings and ask the nomad's advice. "I am plagued by sprites," he confessed after a time. "Perhaps I told you that already." He winced as he recalled how the boneman had first questioned him.

Takijaly smiled, his face ruddy in the firelight. "I know about your new abilities, and from what I heard, you did well today at the stream crossing. To see sprites as you do is uncommon, even for an ulaansh. I find myself envious."

"I'd be happy if the creatures would leave me in peace."

"But an imp can be an ally as well as a pest. A shaman has no easy time getting favors from one. Your ability may prove useful."

Yarkol shook his head. "Do you know what they want

from me?" He tapped his chest at the place where the bird-shape lived within his spirit body.

"Your gift from the gods, yes. A prize they cannot resist. You must guard it carefully."

"But they will cheat me of it. Today I almost let myself be drawn in."

The mystic tapped the flute against his teeth and seemed deep in thought. "There's no harm in keeping them away awhile," he said finally. "I have some help for you. After the meal, you will see."

They ate a stew cooked from dried meat and a few yellow roots. Yarkol noticed Etou glancing at him, as if about to speak. But the shaman's presence seemed to keep her silent. What a change, Yarkol thought, from her gay chatter of the previous night. He wondered if Takijaly had chided her for her conduct.

"This is for you, Newborn," the shaman said when the pot sat empty. In one hand he held a small pouch, in the other a lump of grease. "First, you coat your face." He rubbed the soft substance over Yarkol's cheeks. Why am I permitting this indignity? the Hakhan asked himself as he grimaced under the application. *Do I now put my faith in a boneman's art?*

Loosening the sack's drawstring, Takijaly poured out a sprinkling of pale powder into his palm. Whether the color was yellow or white, the Dolmi could not judge in firelight. "A little of this is all you need." With his fingertips, the shaman rubbed powder onto Yarkol's oiled skin. The scent was mild, like heated rock.

The Hakhan touched his cheek and felt an annoying stickiness. "Imps are stupid in some ways," explained the shaman. "Now your mark is covered. Your face will confuse them, and they'll seek other victims . . . for a time." He cast a glance toward Etou, and she reacted with a sharp hiss.

127

Takijaly yawned, then complained of weariness. He moved his sleep roll a short distance up the gorge and soon lay snoring. The Hakhan, however, sat wide awake beside the embers, his back resting against a stump. The thick coating on his face irritated him. He was tempted to strip it away, but the promise of freedom from kobolds and hearth-sprites made him want to give the "cure" a try.

Etoudoori had been poking at the coals with a long stick. Now she crept around and sat beside him. "What has happened to my handsome boy?" she asked. Her laughter sounded forced.

"Others suffered today because of me," Yarkol said ruefully. "Maybe this way, I can avoid drawing demons' pranks."

"Do you think you're the only the one the imps torment?"

He felt himself frowning. "I asked you once if you could see them, and you didn't answer. Do they call to you also?"

"They make me foolish in the evening when there's no sun to chase them."

"Last night?"

"All I could think of was the shoy box. An imp was whispering in my ear."

Yarkol smiled skeptically. "Maybe you should smear your face too. Or plug your ears with tallow."

She shook her head. "There's no quick answer. The sprites have reason to dislike me. I need someone to beg forgiveness for my misdeeds."

"From what I see, they're an unforgiving lot." He reached for her hand and gave it a comforting squeeze. Her story did not convince him, yet he felt sympathy for whatever was troubling her.

"If someone . . . perhaps you, Newborn, were to intercede for me—"

128

"The boneman says they'll shun me now."

"But if they don't . . ."

He sighed. "I can try talking to them. Why is it, though, that these imps put so much effort into games and contests?"

"Ah. Hakhan, don't you know anything? Treasure from humans is what really matters to them."

He smiled faintly, recalling the glinting bits of jewelry he'd seen at a cairn. "They get offerings."

"Yes. And they vie against each other for the booty. But if a chance for big stakes comes along, the imps turn their skills directly against men. Someone will be offered a match in his dreams. If he loses, he knows he must pay."

"But why treasure?"

"It gives imps a way to gain souls and be reborn. That is what they most long for."

"A soul!" Yarkol recalled the prize that the water-sprite had sought from him. His fingers strayed to his chest. Here lay treasure worth more to sprites than any heap of trinkets . . .

For the next several days Yarkol measured progress by counting the mountains he had crossed. The air grew colder, and often he looked up at snowy ledges that hung far above the trail. Beyond the closest obstacles always loomed another range, and beyond that another, the mountains' white peaks rising ever higher.

"The Kag is near," whispered the shaman as they stopped one morning to water the mounts at a shallow rock basin. He had just been speaking to a nomad family farther down the path. "We must turn west to catch him." Sunlight glinted at the edges of sharp shadows, but offered little warmth. In sheltered crevices Yarkol saw patches of ice.

129

"I've ridden a long way to see this man," the Hakhan said.

"But now I must ask one favor of you," Takijaly continued. "Let me go on ahead at a quicker pace. I'll reach his camp first and try to sense his mood. Perhaps I can make your arrival less of a surprise to him."

To Yarkol, the boneman's request seemed unnecessary. Etou, not Takijaly, had pledged to be his guide. "Do as you wish, shaman." Takijaly nodded, remounted his spotted mare and immediately rode off down the trail.

Yarkol glanced at Etou, but saw no look of surprise on her face. Evidently, the shaman had told her his plans earlier. "He is a strange one, Ulaansh," she said. "We don't need him to find our way."

"He may yet prove himself a friend," Yarkol answered with a puzzled shake of his head.

The path lay beneath dark overhanging crags and around sharp-edged monoliths that had fallen from the sheer rock face. The high walls bore vertical stains and glistened with moisture where the sun struck. On the stony ground the animals found little to eat; Yarkol knew that they were hungry.

Later, the riders reached a stubbly meadow, a place well-cropped by herds now departed. While the ponies searched for remaining wisps of fodder, Etou made inquiries of almost everyone who passed. "Tomorrow we'll find our Kag," she promised as dusk came on.

Yarkol ate sparingly of the soup she cooked, but Etou emptied the pot. When she was finished, she heated clean water. "Now that *he's* gone," she said, avoiding direct mention of the shaman, "you can wash that silly paste from your face."

The Hakhan smiled. He'd received many stares on the trail, but no more than when his cheek was bare. "I've had peace," he protested. "Not a sprite has come near me."

Etou dipped a scrap of sheepskin into warm water and grasped his chin with one hand. "Your mask keeps me away too, Newborn. The nights are cold." She began to rub his skin briskly. Instead of fighting her, he laughed. Years ago, his mother had scrubbed him this way after his exploits in the muddy yard.

"Enough," he cried when he thought his cheek had been rubbed raw.

"Let me see you." She turned his face one way and another. Her own features were half in shadow, half aglow with firelight. He felt a gentle prickling of gooseflesh as she ran soft fingers over his face. "With a beard, you might be worth looking at."

"I can't oblige you," he said dolefully.

"Sad for us both, but the gods have their reasons. If nothing else, we can keep each other warm." She unrolled the hides and lay down next to him, wrapping blankets around them. She smelled of smoke and horse and dried herbs, a dizzying combination.

At the back of his mind lay a bothersome thought. Was he, as she'd said once, truly a child? Despite her intimate touch, despite his growing feelings for her, he felt no stirring of his manhood. She had hinted at this already, had she not? And days before a boy had called him "man who is no man."

What had he become with his smooth face and scanty appetite? Even Hirchil Zarad had kept silent on this point, though Yarkol could not blame the old man. The Hakhan felt tears trickling from his closed eyes as he clung to Etoudoori. His illness had cheated him of even more than he had guessed.

9

Two tribes disputed possession of a prized winter campsite. "Let us share it," proposed one chief, and the other agreed. But the small valley could not sustain both herds and the animals grew thin; many died.

"Let us alternate," proposed the second chief, and the first agreed. So the good campsite, well-sheltered and with plenty of water, served the two tribes in turn. But the winters away from that site were dismal indeed, and so the two chiefs decided they must settle the matter by force.

After a long series of battles, both tribes were badly weakened and both chiefs were dead. "Let us unite under a new banner," cried the survivors.

Now there was plenty of room for all
at the winter camp.
                    —Chirudak tale (Whitemane tribe)

The shaman kept his gaze
on the trail as he rode through a shadowed pass and began a long descent. Heights made him uneasy; he refused
to look down into the valley that stretched far below. The
time was early morning, and about him he sensed many
creatures stirring—rabbits, ground mice, a circling hawk.
He felt the fleeting touches these souls offered, welcomed
their presence. On the crowded trails he'd been assaulted
without rest by the harsher spirits of men.

Only since leaving the ulaansh had he enjoyed, on
these little-known paths, a brief period of solitude. Now,
after less than a day's steady riding, the Kag's camp lay
directly ahead. The journey of Takijaly was almost at its
end.

The shaman had been traveling since midsummer.
While in Hakhan country he'd heard scanty news from
the north. Not even through divination had he been able
to learn much of the Kag's activities. He was certain, however, that the leader had been busy with his recent obses-
sion—gathering renewed pledges of loyalty from the
tribal chiefs.

The shaman sighed as he thought of the role he must
discard—the guise of a wandering healer. Already he had
donned the full costume of his office, the robe-of-bones
with all its talismans, the peaked cap trimmed by wolf's
fur. To his people he was Dzaminid, shaman of Blood-

133

creek tribe. And the Bloodcreeks were now responsible for the future of all Chirudaks.

The shaman did not relish his current importance. Before the Kag rose from his humble station, Dzaminid's tribe had been a minor one and his life as a shaman pleasingly simple. But the Kag was also a Bloodcreek, and so the fates of these two men remained intertwined.

Perhaps this was Dzaminid's ultimate test, the one that might prove him worthy to commune with the gods. He shook his head. No. He did not think his next life would be as a taawik.

Continuing down the long, rocky path, the shaman sensed a crowd of human souls not far below him. He emerged at the edge of the valley, where morning shadows still darkened much of the ground. Men and animals were milling about a modest campsite. In its center stood a large and familiar yurt.

The group was busy breaking camp, and the chief's women had begun taking apart his round dwelling. Already the dome of bent red poles, and half the sidewalls, had been stripped of their white felt coverings. But the Kag—Nurtaj, as his intimates called him—seemed oblivious to the activity around him. Through the birchwood framework Dzaminid saw him conferring with a tribal chief. Nurtaj's face was covered by a leather mask that exposed only his eyes and mouth.

The Kag's senior wife, supervising the others as they rolled felt into neat bundles, glanced up and noticed the new arrival. "It is you, Dzaminid," she said, smiling suddenly, her weathered cheeks stretched wide. Nimble despite her age, she hurried forward to greet him.

The boneman dismounted to embrace the old woman. He had known Erhen when the Kag was still a herdsman, a humble fellow who counted himself lucky to possess even one wife. "You are thin, shaman," she chided in a

134

merry voice. "You haven't been eating well. I must start fattening you for winter."

Despite her joking words, her face bore worry lines he did not recall. Now that her excitement at his return had calmed, he sensed her anxiety. He'd been gone only since midsummer, yet much had changed.

Erhen glanced quickly in her husband's direction. When she turned back to the shaman, her expression had darkened. "He grows more headstrong every day," she whispered.

Dzaminid nodded, though her warning did not surprise him, and allowed Erhen to return to her work. The last piece of felt came down, leaving the door frame's timbers exposed. Now the lattice of sticks that formed the wall sections stood bare.

An ox waited beside the women, quietly accepting its load of felts. The shaman sensed the beast's shackled spirit, but did not grieve for the animal. What have you done in your past life to deserve this? he might have asked.

His attention turned toward the younger women. To finish their task, they must enter the yurt and remove the roof poles and crown. But the women hung back, reluctant to intrude while the Kag remained with his visitor.

Suddenly the Kag's conversation was over. The visiting chief, mildly agitated, bowed and stepped out backwards through the opening. Nurtaj looked up to see, evidently for the first time, that Dzaminid was watching him. He jumped up from his stool and rushed out to embrace the shaman. "Ah, you've come back to us," Nurtaj said. "I was afraid those southerners might lead you astray."

"They've little to keep a man from home."

The Kag stepped back and studied Dzaminid's face. "What about their women?" Nurtaj asked throatily, his first question no surprise to the shaman. "I hear tales."

The smile that showed beneath his mask, the shaman thought, would chill many a young heart.

"A few beauties. Transplanted northern flowers. The others did not catch my fancy."

"Look at that one," said the Kag, nodding toward a slim girl who stood beside the oxen. The shaman saw a child. "Look once, no more. I've taken her for my own."

Dzaminid nodded, concealing his surprise at the girl's extreme youth. The Kag possessed nearly a dozen wives now; most had borne children, but not of Nurtaj's seed. The true father, in each case, had been strangled by one of Nurtaj's assassins.

"So, shaman," continued the Chief-Among-Chiefs. "I must hear your news. But we're moving on, as you can see. Dine with me tonight, and we'll discuss many things."

"As you say, Chosen One." Dzaminid was mildly troubled by Nurtaj's offhand reply. Why was he not more eager for the shaman's report? Perhaps his spies had already satisfied him about conditions in the south.

The boneman studied the Kag's party, hoping to learn more of the mood that surrounded them. The group was small, consisting mainly of the chief's family and his personal guards. Nurtaj had with him only a handful of soldiers, enough to repel wild animals or make a token show of force. No Chirudak—not even one who resented the Kag's authority—would consider harming Nurtaj.

In addition to the oxen, the livestock included spare riding ponies, mares for milking, and several she-goats. Over all hung a cloud of restlessness, of worry, but the shaman could not discern the reason for such gloom. He watched while riders and beasts found their places and moved out in orderly fashion.

Dzaminid's thoughts turned to Etou and the Hakhan. The shaman had taken shortcuts and had traveled on little sleep, yet in another day or so the two would catch up. Nurtaj made no secret of his whereabouts, so the others had only to keep asking after the Kag. But what reception would they meet at the end of their journey? The shaman hoped soon to have an answer.

The Kag's party arrived before dusk at the confluence of two streams. Here lay a prized winter pasture, one that the Longtail tribe had held for generations. Here the shaman felt the presence of many ghosts. He sensed hints of disembodied souls—some human, some animal—mingling with those of living tribespeople. These spirits had been judged by the gods and now awaited rebirth. If a shade was lucky enough to be present when a child was conceived, then it might find a new fleshly form. Dzaminid smiled at the thought; the Longtails were prosperous, and many souls sought a place among them.

Still mounted, he gazed along the rows of yurts and wondered which would most conveniently accommodate him. He did not mind sleeping in the open, but to do so would be an insult to the tribe. Invitations would come; he must accept what hospitality was offered.

"Revered shaman." Glancing down at an anxious face, Dzaminid knew he had already found his host. "Will you share my poor abode?" the man asked. The petitioner was a short wiry fellow whose dark beard showed streaks of gray.

"I'll be honored," said Dzaminid. "Though I dine with the Kag tonight, I'll share your roof."

The tribesman called a boy to care for the shaman's mount. Then Dzaminid was ushered into the yurt, the first he had entered since the start of his journey. He'd been away from his people far too long.

He savored the simple things first—the scents of hides and wool and cooked meat. This family possessed no great status, he saw at once. Even so, the inside walls were hung with patterned rugs, woven of reds and

137

browns in the Longtail tradition. The cushions by the hearth were clean and neatly bound, especially inviting to one who had ridden so far.

Dzaminid greeted the wife, two sons, and an unmarried daughter. "A blessing on this hearth," he began, reciting the phrases that were expected of him. The hosts were awed by his presence, he sensed, overly anxious to please. And why had they asked him here? His gaze fell on the daughter, plain of face but with a lively smile that caught his attention. She had a part in this, he gleaned, but the father would not say as much. He spoke instead of his obvious troubles, centered on the oldest son, a gangly youth who'd been rebuffed by a high-tempered maiden. Since then he'd grown listless, eating little, taking no interest in his family's affairs.

To present an appearance of thoroughness, Dzaminid examined the youth's dry hands, his dull eyes, his drooping eyelids. He felt the boy's pulse at his throat. "Give him a tonic," the shaman told his mother. "Twice a day till he recovers. I'll recite the ingredients."

His duties completed, the shaman was content to relax and play tunes on his flute. The music helped clear his thoughts so that for a time only one spirit lived within his skull. While the daughter worked by the fire, she glanced at him often as he played, confirming what Dzaminid had suspected from the start. A girl who carried a shaman's child would be much sought after in marriage. To ask such a thing directly was improper; to encourage it subtly was another matter.

Shortly before the women had completed preparing their family's meal, Dzaminid was summoned to the Kag. "Here is your sleeping place, shaman," said the wife before he could leave. She pointed to the place of honor beside the hearth, and he sensed an undercurrent of meaning below her words. "I'll leave you a bear fur for wrap." The guest nodded, avoiding any suggestion that he would do more than sleep.

Within the large yurt Nurtaj sat waiting for him, his face hidden this evening by a mask of beaten copper. Only two women, Erhen and the new child-wife, were present to serve the meal. Dzaminid felt their agitation as their hands moved quickly and their eyes remained lowered. A platter piled high with skewered meat lay beside the women. Two fat trout already hung spitted above a bed of hot coals. The girl poked a sharpened stick at the fire, pierced a wild yam, and plucked it out.

The Kag shifted his legs with evident impatience. "A blessing on this hearth," intoned the shaman, bending slightly at the waist, making the formal bow with finger touching mouth and then forehead. "May your wives be full, your herds fat, your ponies swift."

The Kag muttered the refrain under his breath, exuding relief when Dzaminid sat. "Hear my news first," Nurtaj began. Dzaminid nodded, aware that his earlier surmise had been correct; spies had returned from the south. "We've argued about the Throats over many evenings," the Kag said. "But at last my brother has put our concerns at rest."

"Guzad?" The shaman recalled that the Kag's brother had gone out with many others.

"He is a wily one," Nurtaj said with satisfaction. "He got past the soil-tillers and their lies. Now our plans are set."

"I would hear these plans." Dzaminid sensed what was to come. The realization made him stiffen.

The chief leaned forward. "Listen to what Guzad learned. The soil-tillers have *finished* the Path across the Throats. Finished it—for our benefit." A sharp laugh exploded from his lips. "But the fools are too cautious to use it. They'll send a few families in the spring. Ha. We'll

ride over the wretches and take the entire east for ourselves."

Dzaminid tried to keep his voice calm. "How did your
brother come by this knowledge?"

Nurtaj grinned and leaned forward. "He is wily, as I
told you. A man of tricks, like his father." The Kag's eyes
rolled upward as if paying homage to the recently departed spirit.

"Ah." Of the spies sent south, the Kag's brother was
among the most able. But Guzad's tale contradicted a report that the shaman could not doubt. Yarkol Dolmi had
described the hiatus at Rya Basin and the obstacles to
completing the work. "I am eager to hear more details, if
that suits you," the boneman said. "A full description of
the Path would enlighten me."

"You baffle me, shaman. What is it that you wish to
know?"

"Some sections may be more dangerous than others. If
the way is too narrow—"

"Guzad is my *brother*," the Kag replied, his fingers closing into a fist. "If he says the Path is ready for Hakhans,
then certainly *we* can cross it. Ask nothing more of him,
shaman."

The senior wife's fretting cast a pall over the scene;
Dzaminid tried to calm her with a slight nod of his head.
"Then all is for the best," said the boneman quickly.

"It is settled for me. A few doubters remain, but they
won't hold out long." Nurtaj's voice deepened almost to a
growl. "A chief can be skittish as a fresh foal. The land
waits, yet a few would run another way."

Dzaminid nodded in understanding. Clearly the Kag's
mind was not at rest, despite his assertions. Perhaps a divination might be in order . . . But Nurtaj's mood tonight
seemed unpredictable. Better for now to heed Erhen's
warning and say nothing.

The meal continued with Nurtaj constantly on edge. He

140

spoke disparagingly of men who had scouted the western passes for a route across the Spine-of-Ice. A few had tried to tell him that the way was not so steep as commonly supposed, that the worst places might be cut through with hammers and chisels. "Must I make my horsemen into laborers?" the Kag asked angrily.

Dzaminid gave no reply, for he believed that Chirudak destiny indeed lay beyond the Spine. Chirudaks were walled in—by mountains in three directions and by the Hakhan mound to the south. If the nomads could break through to the west, they would reach vast territories he had seen in visions—lands rich beyond belief. There lay the Chirudaks' best hope, but the way would not be easy. The boneman foresaw much suffering as tribesmen worked to temper the cruel passes, to smooth and widen them so that all could safely cross. Only a rare leader, a man with Nurtaj's energy and determination, could muster the cooperation needed for this effort.

Yet the shaman knew also that men were free—to err or to see truth, to triumph or to fall. The will of the gods had been flouted before, generally with disastrous results. And Nurtaj, disregarding the risks, persisted in looking southward.

At last the bowl of kumiss arrived, and the Chief-Among-Chiefs began to relax. "You'll help me now," he said to Dzaminid. "If others doubt my plans, you'll strengthen my arguments. We move south before the first thaw. As a whole people, we move." Dzaminid grew tired of listening, but the Kag droned on.

Only after Nurtaj had finished most of the drink did he ask about the shaman's travels. Dzaminid gave a quick summary, coming at last to the topic that troubled him. "One odd bit of news," he offered in a casual tone. "I happened to meet an ulaansh. He was headed northward."

"A Hakhan?" The reaction was angry, but lacked surprise. "I have heard a few reports."

"A southerner, yes. He seemed determined to find you."

"Then tell me what this man wants." The Kag's gaze turned fiercely on Dzaminid.

"I understand that he carries a letter for you—from one of his chiefs."

"And is this man genuine?" Nurtaj spread his hand over his masked cheek. "Have you seen his mark?"

The shaman answered shortly. "I have seen it, noble Kag. He bears the mark of the stricken."

"Then he belongs in the south with his own people. We need no soil-tillers here!" Nurtaj swallowed the last of the kumiss and flung the bowl to the far side of the yurt.

After a time the shaman, feeling weary and disillusioned, left the Kag and went out into the biting air. He could scarcely believe how matters had turned against him. This past spring Dzaminid had urged sending many agents south, had followed them to learn for himself what the Dolmi Clan had accomplished. He had expected to find that no eastward crossing was available—even over Hakhan land. Finally, he had found proof. Yet the Kag was preparing to march across the Throat.

Dzaminid looked up into the clear, cold sky. Mother Moon was almost full, her face dimming the other moons. He recalled the tale of how she had gotten up there—the dispute over a fat goat, the bargain between a kobold and a god. But if Nurtaj destroyed the Chirudak people, as Dzaminid feared he might, then who would be left to explain the mysteries of heaven?

The boneman slipped into his host's yurt and found his bedding by the hearth's dying glow. Everyone was asleep, he thought gratefully. But he felt an awakening and

142

turned to see the daughter shyly creeping toward him, her round face ruddy in the coals' dim light. Dzaminid shook his head sadly. "Tonight many troubles weigh me down," he whispered, taking her warm hands in his own. Her gaze fell. She nodded her understanding and returned to her own sleeping place.

He lay back with his face to the roof, breathed deeply, and opened his thoughts to the rugged land around him. What had happened to Etoudoori and the Hakhan? Allowing his senses to range, Dzaminid at last found an answer. The travelers had taken a wrong turn and still remained a day's ride out. But when they arrived they would find cold welcome here.

In the morning at the large yurt's hearth Dzaminid once more sat beside the Kag. They were awaiting Vuotol, the Longtails' chief, a man the shaman had known for many years. Vuotol was sickly, of great age, and with much adventure behind him. He had traveled, it was said, to the Mountain-of-Mountains and had climbed partway up its slope. And he had made his way south through Hakhan territory, forced to stop only by the great marshlands that bordered the sea. Vuotol had once suggested that boats be built, dragged across swamps and launched onto the turbulent waters. The idea had been scoffed at, of course. Not even Hakhans had attempted such a scheme, for the sea was like a wild stallion that would take no rider.

Dzaminid had spent pleasant evenings hearing the old chief's stories. But today, as attendants carried the elder into Nurtaj's abode, the shaman knew he would not enjoy the visit. The Kag gave a cursory welcome. "We speak in privacy here," Nurtaj assured the Longtail after his bearers withdrew. Though the elder had lost his sight, he turned toward Dzaminid.

143

"Honored Vuotol," the mystic announced. "It is I, your humble shaman."

The ancient one's smile and nod of greeting only made the boneman uneasy. Vuotol had a sparse white beard; a few hairs still clung to the crown of his head. "I am glad to be with you again . . . Dzaminid," he replied in a quavering voice. "Maybe . . . you can help me explain my worries."

To the shaman, these concerns were all too evident, but he was in no position to aid the old chief. The Kag cleared his throat and cast a frigid look in the boneman's direction. "We must remember one thing above all," Nurtaj said insistently. "We are Chirudaks, every one of us. That some are Longtails, some Bloodcreeks, means less than our common traditions. We must move together as one people and share the great triumph."

"If triumph there is to be." Vuotol's eyelids trembled, and his hands were constantly aquiver. "But to fight our way south would cost more than we dare lose. Wiser, I say, to starve here slowly and hope for better rains. Wiser still to challenge the Spine as many young men suggest. Take what has been set aside for us. Leave the Hakhans to their demon-plagued Path."

"I'd agree with you, Vuotol," said the Kag, "if we had a few dozen years to spend on it. But how can we survive? Rain alone won't help us. The land is tired, worn out like a she-goat past bearing."

Vuotol shook his head almost imperceptibly. "The grass was good in some places this year," he said. "The land still has life in her. And my grandsons tell me that if all the tribes join in, we can cut a Spine crossing in two years."

"And if we send our men to the passes, who will guard the herds? Who'll protect the children?"

"You speak, honored Kag, as if one tribe still warred against another. Thanks to your leadership, we have

144

peace and unity now. Surely we can spare many men without falling prey to wolves and snow leopards."

"You're correct, Vuotol, to point to our strengths. For too long we have fought each other and let the soil-tillers take what they wanted. But why have I worked to bring the tribes together? So that we can revenge ourselves on our ancient foe! So that we can follow the way of battle as our ancestors did!"

Vuotol licked his lips, but seemed unable to muster a new argument. His head swung slowly as if seeking guidance. "What say you, shaman? Have you roasted bones over this?"

Dzaminid shifted his feet and did not answer at once. He felt the Kag's will piercing him. "The omens are not clear yet," he said hesitantly.

"Tell me," Vuotol persisted, "the time and place of your last augury."

The Kag shot him an inquiring look. Dzaminid pursed his lips, for he preferred informal methods, finding insight in the sparkle of water in a child's palm or the way a leaf fluttered. "Honored Vuotol," said the shaman, "your questions are sharp. I've been traveling in the south for three Risings. I haven't had the resources for a scapula ceremony."

The old one smiled. "Then do me the honor of conducting one here in Longtail camp. At my expense."

Nurtaj's attention was on Dzaminid now, his jaw set, his gaze chilling. The shaman knew how he must answer. "A gracious offer, but I travel with the Chief-Among-Chiefs. I cannot say if his plans permit such an undertaking."

"Ah," replied Vuotol. "The Kag will find time. It is not much to ask."

Later that morning, as Dzaminid rode alone up a steep trail, he thought about the Kag's reaction to Vuotol's re-

145

quest. Nurtaj had been forced to agree to the divination. But he did not disguise his anger, claiming that he'd planned to return to his own tribe for a day or two and was eager to see his other wives. In truth, the Kag was uneasy about how the gods viewed his plans. No one could say how the reading would go.

Diverting his gaze from the steep drop beside the path, the shaman ascended higher. He studied the stones and roots ahead, listening to bird calls, occasionally touched the patient spirit of his mare. Despite these exercises, he did not forget the depths that yawned beside him. The fear within him would never ease, his master had said. At best, he could keep it at bay.

The bright morning was half gone when he reached a suitable stopping place. He led his mount back from the cliff's edge and tethered it beside a spring. Then, gritting his teeth for courage, he crawled onto a ledge that overlooked the broad valley. The view made him dizzy; he imagined rock crumbling, his body falling freely. *As once it had done.*

Sometimes he doubted that such a thing had ever happened, that a pony had stumbled, flinging its young rider into windy depths. He had dropped slowly, scattering hawks, watching shivering pines and jagged rocks and a bright band of water that rose to meet him. All of life was a pole festooned with ribbons. That was the vision he'd had as he fell, as pines reached for him and rocks grew into boulders. Old streamers dropping away as new ones were added above; ribbons in the wind, flying in all directions. He had seen it most clearly just before he struck . . .

Dzaminid could no longer remember the pain, only the astonished look on the old shaman's face when he discovered that the boy was not seriously hurt. A broken leg, bruises, numerous scratches. And a new sense dawning, a hint of what was to come.

146

Now, as he hung over the valley, his fear promised to strengthen that sense. With his eyes he saw goats and sheep milling where the two streams joined. The people who moved among the tiny yurts seemed to call to him, their faint voices drifting on the wind.

The dizziness was too much for him. He gripped a handhold and fell back, his eyelids closing. He was spinning now, twirling as if in a healer's dance. Wind rustled his robe, bringing news of winter, but he barely noticed the chill. Taawiks sang all about him; soon he could not hear their notes.

Then he entered another realm and felt a multitude of souls milling below. He had sensed them weakly before. Now the spirits grew vivid. The light ones belonged to children and to a few fortunate elders. They sparkled in gold and azure like insect wings in a meadow of flowers. Others moved purposefully in well-defined patterns, occasionally taking an upward leap before resuming their somber movements. A miserable few, colored like storm clouds, plodded endlessly in a circle, never deviating from the course.

What must become of these souls, the joyous and the heavy of heart? Many had made progress on the path to ascension. If their lives were cut short, they would be forced to start over, perhaps under far more difficult circumstances.

Dzaminid occasionally posed himself a frightening question. What if the Chirudaks were to suffer great losses? Then many souls must be born Hakhans if they were to live again as human beings. And in Hakhan bodies they would not be properly taught, would not follow the precepts and meditations. They would remain ignorant of the gods and therefore incapable of ascension.

Putting aside such worries for now, the shaman slipped deeper into trance. He sensed the souls of animals—proud spirits of ponies, belligerent spirits of goats. Some

147

of these had lived as humans; soon others would do so. Even the worm and the fly had tiny souls that pulsed in great numbers at the edge of his awareness. He sought to fill himself with all the life that surrounded him. This place held so many spirits . . .

When Dzaminid opened his eyes, the sun was dropping toward distant peaks. He felt both refreshed and burdened by his lengthy communion. To know so much brought a joy that he once had thought reserved for the gods. Yet what future awaited this multitude?

The fortunes of the shaman's people affected not only themselves but the hopes of all other creatures. Even a humble insect might aspire to a human incarnation. But if the Chirudaks were struck down, then all were doomed to misery—not only in the current life but in many lives to come. With this prospect before him, Dzaminid rode grimly back to camp.

His first task was a ritual bathing of hands and feet in the stream. When he returned to the center of camp, the shaman found all preparations completed as he had ordered. The Feather Council, whose members oversaw the tribe's spiritual affairs, had readied the sacrificial animal and the implements. White from muzzle to tail, the chosen stallion was one of the chief's finest. Four councilors, the sturdiest among the graybeards, stood holding the beast as the shaman approached.

Dzaminid put his face to the animal's stout neck and visited with the spirit within. This soul he was about to release would lodge next in a boy-child, he believed. That hope made his task easier. He took the ancient sword that he had entrusted to another councilor and tested its newly honed edge against a hair on the back of his hand. He nodded as the hair parted cleanly. "I am ready."

The sun's disk was still visible as two of Vuotol's granddaughters—young women, apprehensive of what must follow—came forward carrying a silver bowl. The Kag sat

148

beside Vuotol's litter. The remaining councilors, each with a taawik feather hanging from a tether about the neck, had assembled beside the chiefs. A step behind the first rank the rest of the Longtail tribe stood watching.

The shaman held the sword in one hand and faced the setting sun. In the language of the people he shouted a supplication to the spirits of air. Then he repeated the incantation using the ancient tongue. He approached the stallion gently, blew his breath into its nostrils to form a bond he hoped would outlast the creature's fleshly life. With one hand he raised the blade to the white throat; with the other he felt for the pulsing artery.

The blade moved sideways almost imperceptibly, opening a dark seam that at once began to spurt. Dzaminid stood back while the women held up the bowl, their hands trembling so that some drops splattered on the ground or onto their fine jackets. Supported by the councilors, the animal slowly sank to its knees, and the granddaughters bent to catch the thickening flow. At last, Dzaminid signalled the women to step back.

The weapon felt light in his hands, perfectly balanced. It hung down, and his arms briefly relaxed. Then, in an instant, came a whistle of wind as the blade rose and fell.

He barely felt its passage through bone and muscle. The white head trembled. The body, released by the councilors, convulsed several times and lay still. The stallion's soul leapt free, rising to the heavens.

Dzaminid accepted the blood-filled bowl, turned, and carried it to Vuotol's yurt. Behind him, the butchering would begin at once, each family to be given a share of the meat. The shaman wanted only the skin and the right shoulder blade. The rest must be roasted immediately, a portion at every hearthfire.

The shaman waited at the yurt's doorway until the Kag entered, followed by Vuotol and his bearers. Dzaminid took up a position behind the hearth, while the chiefs sat facing him. The Kag's mouth, beneath his jade-studded mask of gold, had hardened into a predatory snarl. Did he think his desires could change the gods' answers?

Dzaminid walled himself from the hopes of his chief. He raised the bowl and chanted in the ancient tongue.

> Grant us a favor, noble spirits,
> You who can speak and be heard.
> For the High Ones do not answer human voices
> Though we honor them with praises.

He handed the bowl to the nearest White-feather, then sank to the floor and immersed himself in meditation. In a short while a rustle from without told him that the flayers were done. Dzaminid stepped to the yurt's door and beckoned the two councilors who stood there to enter. One bore the horse's hide, folded in quarters; the other held the bulky scapula. The third White-feather, who carried the blood bowl, stood behind the shaman. The door flap was pulled down, leaving the men alone inside the yurt.

Dzaminid untied his sashes and belts, ceremoniously put aside his robe, his trousers, and boots, and at last stood bare. He dipped his fingers into the bowl, painting first his chest, then his legs, then his penis with the sticky fluid. He took the reeking skin, still faintly warm, and wrapped it about himself. With a slow, measured tread he approached the fire, circling around four times before stopping at the hearth with his face to the doorway.

"Let all who would be swift share this offering," the shaman called. A White-feather handed the blood bowl to the Kag, who drank deeply. Vuotol took a sip, and then the three other men reddened their lips. Once more, the shaman invoked the spirits in the ancient tongue. Then he spoke to the stallion, to the soul he had released to heaven.

150

You, who will live some day as a man,
Implore the gods to aid us.
You, who would be a Chirudak,
Ask that our future be revealed.

Dzaminid paused, tried with his thoughts to reach above the yurt into the vast night sky and to sense the soul of the beast that had been honored above the others of its kind. Yes, he felt a distant tremor that he took to be an answering promise, an offer of assistance from afar. Then he lifted the heavy bone, still flecked with meat and gristle, and placed it among the flames. A hiss followed and a gout of pungent smoke.

Again, he circled the fire four times. Then he began the chant of divination, whose words no living man understood, a song from the first days of the world. In the clear space beyond the hearth he started his dance—a slow, shuffling movement that kept him turning in tight arcs. At first he felt stiff-legged, but almost at once he was caught up in the flow. His steps became quicker, his melody more compelling, until he lost himself in the rising and falling notes. Now his eyes were closed, but the darkness bloomed with streaks of color—reds of sunsets, gold, and azure. The streaks grew slender, swirling about him in ever brighter hues. Faster and faster he went, until the colors merged into one and he was falling again, plunging into the depths that had once tried to claim him.

When he opened his eyes, he lay sprawled on the carpet beside the hearth. On a large square of bleached felt before him, in accordance with his instructions, lay the cracked and fire-blackened bone. Seizing the cloth, he crumpled it about the scapula with a single frenzied motion.

He lay the bone aside, caring now only for the dark smudges left behind on the felt. His thoughts were still dazed from the chanting and the dance, but he had no

151

wish to clear his head. The sooty markings lay before him; he stared with unfocused eyes, letting the patterns seep into his brain.

What he saw first was the *Impasse*—two monoliths— the opposition of equal forces. Studying this, Dzaminid was drawn into the image. The great boulders on the cloth became real—solid mounds of granite. He began to speak without conscious effort. "Hakhan and Chirudak. They are the great opposites. Two strong men facing each other. They shout and jostle but neither can be moved. The seasons turn, the generations die, yet still they glare at each other." The words had come without pause; he drew a long breath.

He discerned another image overlaid on the first: *Windstorm*, hewer of forests. The scene came alive for him; he could smell the pine scent, hear the thrashing of branches and the cracking of tree trunks before the storm's wrath. Jagged spears of lightning struck, igniting the trees that remained standing. The flames spread. Smoke rose, a thick and suffocating fog. "Now comes a catastrophe that sweeps the land," he said. "All who once stood proudly are fallen; the ground is heaped with corpses. No one is left to mourn the dead. An odor of decay covers all."

He was not finished, he realized, for a third image overlaid the others. *Rebirth*. He saw tendrils growing from the ashes, green shoots struggling toward the sun. "In the end the earth renews herself," he said. "A new people is born from the ruins of the old. Voices rise to honor the gods and placate the spirits. Children dance beneath the sky." Dzaminid remained where he lay, letting the visions fade. His voice fell silent, and for a time he heard nothing but his own slow breathing.

Hands lifted him softly. Someone offered a cup, and he inhaled the rich scent of henga. Gratefully he sipped at

152

the steaming brew, felt the warm liquid soothe his throat. His thoughts began to clear.

"A bold prophecy, shaman," said the Kag. Dzaminid had heard himself speak; now, he strove to remember his words.

"Your reading was profound, honored shaman," Vuotol concurred. "But it leaves me with certain doubts. The first part—the Impasse—we all understand. But this calamity you spoke of. What can it describe but the death of our great people?"

"Not at all," objected the Kag. "The vision is of destruction, but the ones who topple are the soil-tillers. Our march is the storm, the lightning, and fire that destroys them. And this time our victory is final."

"I heard nothing that identifies the doomed ones," countered Vuotol. "Windstorm and forest. Hewer and hewed. Nothing was said to make one Hakhan, another Chirudak. But consider the third section of the prophecy."

"A new people rising." The Kag gave a confident smile, though Dzaminid sensed his inner turmoil. "That is our people, our new nation, as it thrives on the eastern lands."

"Honored Nurtaj, I would not dispute your wisdom," said the old chief. "But I'm told that my memory is still sharp. In the last prophecy, as Dzaminid spoke it, both forest and storm are gone. Only then does the earth start renewing herself. This new race is to grow from the *ruins* of the old. Whose life will it be? Neither Hakhan nor Chirudak but another breed altogether."

Dzaminid's gaze shifted back and forth as the argument continued. He could say nothing more. The gods had guided his eyes and his tongue while he made the pronouncements. If he ventured an interpretation now he was only offering a mortal's opinion.

153

The Kag's face grew dark. "If it pleases you, Vuotol, then I concede two meanings to the third prophecy. After the soil-tillers are destroyed, a people rises to replace them. That's the first meaning. But how can such strangers know how to worship gods and spirits? That portion of the reading describes the strengthened Chirudaks."

"And I say it describes the ones who come after us," Vuotol replied. "This prophecy foretells the end of all we have!" Dzaminid, exercising his right to stay silent, sat and stared woefully at the floor. The Kag had distorted the bone reading, but other men must point this out; the shaman could only discredit himself by speaking now.

"I'll make no decision this night," Vuotol concluded as his voice began to crack. "If my tribe follows you in the spring, then you'll know my answer. And if I do not come south, then you'll also know. But I must discuss this augury with others. The two of us alone cannot settle it."

Dzaminid refused to meet Nurtaj's gaze. The shaman had hoped for a stronger message, one that would force the Kag to see the folly of his plans. Had the sacrifice been inadequate? No, Dzaminid realized. The gods had spoken clearly enough, but had left the Kag free to make his choice.

Still clad in the pungent horse-skin, the shaman strode angrily from the yurt. The gods had done as they must, but he could not conceal his disappointment. Outside, the air's chill was bitter, the wind gusting through the quiet camp. Dropping the sacrificial hide at the stream bank, he lowered himself into the icy flow. Plunging again and again, rubbing his skin with rushes, he cleansed himself until at last he felt renewed. Then he walked, dripping, to his host's yurt where dry clothes lay.

The fire was blazing within. The shaman was not surprised to find the dwelling empty except for the daughter. Lying beneath the bearskin covering, she stared at him, her expression both anxious and eager. Could he

154

forget his troubles for a time, allow himself to be an ordinary man? Letting the cover fall away, she exposed young breasts of such beauty that he halted where he stood. She was not afraid, he knew, merely worried that he might spurn her once again.

The last of his fury was gone, he realized, replaced by an unexpected passion. Was this a gift from the gods, compensation for what had come before? He had failed the Longtails in one way; perhaps he could serve them in another. "A blessing on this hearth," intoned the shaman, as he stepped forward to the waiting girl. He knelt, pressed his lips to her smooth forehead, inhaling the rich scent of her hair, stroking her soft cheek. "May the wives and daughters of this family be fruitful."

10

A ghost sensed a warrior's desire for
his wife and followed him home to
his yurt. The ghost rejoiced as the two
young people lay down together, for if
a child was conceived now the ghost
would at last be reborn. But just at
the moment of bliss, a second ghost
slipped in past the doorflap. "This one
is mine," the first ghost asserted. "It
will be a girl child," the second
replied. "And one most beautiful,"
said the first. "She will be misled by
many men," said the second. "But she
will make her own way in the end,"
insisted the first.

    While they were arguing, a third

ghost slipped past them and entered
the sprouting seed.

—*Greatwing tribe tradition*

W ide awake despite the early hour, Dzaminid followed the Kag's party through the growing dawn light. The souls, human and animal, that moved ahead of him on the trail tugged faintly at his thoughts; he tried to stay free of them. Nurtaj's next stop would be with Bloodcreek tribe, the people who had given both Kag and shaman to the world. Here Dzaminid had many friends and relations. And here he must seek a few crucial answers. For now, however, he wished to ride apart. Of late, he'd had too much of Nurtaj and his affairs.

The trail wound through a narrow gorge, the walls sheer and deeply fractured, the floor littered with scree. The thin slice of visible sky held a few clouds amid deepening blue. Dzaminid let his thoughts roam, allowing his mind to soar with the distant taawiks. What fortunate souls they were to be free at last from earth's bonds.

The passage of time meant nothing to him as Dzaminid rode behind the others. The path climbed, then descended again to another cut, but the shaman remained deep in reverie. When he heard a voice call him and saw that the sun had passed noon, he was mildly startled. "Honored shaman," said one of the Kag's attendants, "the Chosen One calls you."

Everyone had halted along the trickle that followed the ravine. Dzaminid made his way past goats and oxen and impatient riders to the front of the procession. He sensed a newcomer's presence, his note of concern. Then he

157

glimpsed the messenger, his face damp with sweat as he leaned from his mount to confer with the Kag.

"The soil-tiller has come," Nurtaj said darkly when the shaman rode within earshot. "He waits for me at Bloodcreek camp."

Yarkol. Dzaminid's pulse raced, but he tried to conceal his reaction. He turned to the messenger. "Does the Hakhan travel alone?"

"He came with a Greatwing woman, the one who went south with the Kag's cousin, Oron."

"And where is Oron?" Nurtaj demanded.

The messenger frowned. "Taking another route, the woman told me. He should arrive shortly."

"I am waiting for him," Nurtaj snarled. "Maybe he can explain this wanderer. Meanwhile, hold the soil-tiller captive. Go swiftly with my orders." At once the newcomer rode off.

"You know something of this Hakhan," said the Kag. He turned to fix Dzaminid with a piercing stare. "What can you tell me about his letter?"

"Only that it comes from their military leader," replied the shaman, wishing that the Kag would look elsewhere. "I have not read it."

"I want no letter. Whatever the message, its purpose is to mislead us, to make us argue among ourselves. Do you not see this, shaman? The ulaansh has been sent to test our resolve."

Dzaminid chose his words carefully, yet he knew what ire they might provoke. "The man is godstricken. We must treat him with respect. We cannot be sure of his purpose—"

"Purpose? You told me once that the gods touch many, but few prove worthy. This stray Hakhan will wish he'd kept his old face."

"Let us first—"

Nurtaj wheeled his mount. In a moment he was racing

down the trail, leaving the rest of the party to catch up with him as best they could. The shaman stared at the departing chief, then twitched his reins, sending his pony scrambling to follow. What could he do for the Hakhan? Two days of thought had provided no answer. If he supported Yarkol openly, then he risked losing whatever trust the Kag still had in him.

Dzaminid shook his head woefully. The southerner must speak for himself; that was the gods' intent. And somehow, Nurtaj must be made to listen.

Yarkol stood in the center of a nomad camp, but it was not the scene of his nightmares. The earth here remained bare, dark, and sodden, while snow had covered the ground in all his visions of the north. Yet Etou had assured him that this was the Kag's tribe, that the Chief-Among-Chiefs would soon appear.

Four mounted warriors guarded Yarkol as he waited in a clearing before the rows of yurts. He eyed the curved swords slung from their belts, the arrows and short bows in cases hanging from their saddles. Should he lose his resolve and try to escape, he would not get far.

And where had Etou gone, leaving him to be treated like a dangerous beast? The guards' restless mounts and the curious onlookers blocked much of his view. He did not see her in the crowd, nor could he guess what the nomads planned to do with him.

Overhead, the clouds were thickening, the sky growing darker every moment. Might snow be coming after all? Within his pocket, he gripped the letter from Hyar Jornood as if it were a talisman. If the Kag agreed to its proposal, then discussion of the Path might be delayed for some time.

No, he chided himself. He was foolish to hope for a reprieve. The truth must come out at once, to forestall misguided planning. He stamped his boots impatiently, wishing for a sign, a friendly face, a brief distraction.

Then he noticed one guard shifting, turning his attention outward. The crowd parted suddenly, and a gap opened to offer a clear view of the trail. A rider was coming in, his mount a shimmering white, the trappings bright with silvery ornaments. The horseman wore a mask that covered his chin and cheeks.

Yarkol drew in his breath. This mask was of leather instead of the gold of his dreams. But how could he doubt that the approaching figure was the Kag? The stallion halted, blowing heavily, its flanks drenched with sweat. Everyone in the crowd made a bow of reverence.

The stocky rider dismounted, strode forward fiercely, and stopped less than an arm's length from the Hakhan. Behind the mask, Yarkol saw only glaring eyes and lips curled in fury. Reeking strongly of horse, the nomad stepped closer, but still he said nothing. Yarkol held his ground as the Kag reached up to rub his calloused thumb across the Dolmi's cheek.

"So it is true," the Kag said roughly. "You carry the mark. But do you understand what you are, Hakhan?" His voice lifted to become a howl of challenge. "Do you understand what I am?" Suddenly the chief reached behind his head and unhooked his mask, flung it to earth. A chorus of exclamation rose from the crowd, but Yarkol's breath caught in his throat.

How he wished this was a dream he might wake from. But now he saw what his nightmares had concealed—the hairless face, the youthful mien, and above all, the wine-colored sign on the leader's cheek. *Godstricken!* "Then you—suffer as I do," Yarkol whispered.

The Kag tossed his head like a spirited colt. "Suffer? I barely sleep or eat. And I must go on like this until I have what is mine."

"Then we are brothers," the Hakhan managed. Etou's

words. The spirit drum at dawn. Had she known this? Had she understood what the two men had in common?

"Show me this letter you carry," demanded the Kag, thrusting out his hand. Yarkol produced the packet and offered it with trembling fingers. "We are not brothers," the Kag said as he tore the document from Yarkol's grip and flung it aside. "We are enemies, set against each other by the gods. Keep that in mind, and you may live a few days longer."

Dzaminid arrived to find the camp in turmoil, news of the confrontation on everyone's lips. The Kag had made a rare gesture, displaying to all his marked face. And he had taken the other ulaansh his prisoner.

The shaman's thoughts were in disarray as he rode through the busy camp. He needed advice and knew only one man who could help him—his aged mentor, who had healed him after his accident and later introduced him to the mystical arts. As he headed toward Tomuuk's dwelling, men and women rushed up from every side to offer welcome. Dzaminid waved cheerfully, giving no hint of his anguish.

He'd been gone for three Risings, leaving his people with only the sickly old shaman and a youthful assistant to care for their spiritual needs. As he approached Tomuuk's yurt, he wondered how the aged one had fared.

Dzaminid dismounted before a dwelling that had ancient symbols inscribed on its door flap of rabbit skins. Leaving his mount with a youth, he strode forward anxiously, not knowing whether the old one would be able to speak with him. "Tomuuk, my master," he said softly at the entrance. "Do you admit your son-before-heaven?" He sensed two quiet souls within, but heard no answer. He spoke again, louder this time, for the elder's hearing had grown as weak as his body.

161

"Enter," came a faltering voice. "Enter, He-who-seeks-moonbeams."

Dzaminid lifted the flap aside. At once he breathed the familiar rich odors of herbs and hides and talismans. He smiled, for this was the moment of his true homecoming.

The old man lay stretched out beneath a blanket, his one surviving wife seated by his side. Dzaminid greeted her with a warm embrace. "He and I must talk alone," he told her quietly. "There are matters that must not weigh on your spirit."

When the woman was gone, Tomuuk managed a faint nod of welcome. "I feared I—had seen the last of you in this life."

"You may not see me in the next, unless you swoop very low to the ground."

"Such a way to talk!" Tomuuk clasped the visitor's hand in a tremulous grip.

"Ah, things have turned dark. Nurtaj is more stubborn than a hungry goat."

"He is supposed to be stubborn."

"Yes. But only when he's right!" The younger man sat cross-legged and began to explain his predicament.

"Then the Kag's brother becomes important." With leathery fingers Tomuuk pulled his blanket to his chin and closed his eyes.

"I need to get the truth from Guzad, to find out exactly what he learned in the south and what was his source of information. But Nurtaj won't allow his brother to be questioned."

"Yes. Yes." The old one was evidently about to fall asleep.

"This yurt is my only refuge." Dzaminid spoke louder, hoping to keep the man awake a moment longer. "I must speak privately—" A drawn-out snore cut off his words.

"Refuge?" Tomuuk came briefly awake again. "Come

here—stay here—as you wish. This has always been your home."

Dzaminid patted the old one's shoulder and waited until he drifted off again. For now, he must do without his mentor's wisdom. He stood and peered out past the door-flap, considering whether he should go after Etoudoori. But before he could decide what to say to her, he saw Erhen, the Kag's wife, coming toward him.

"Trouble with Nurtaj?" he asked the wife, as he stepped outside.

"He is fuming. He opened the southerner's letter, but of course can't read it."

"I will go to him."

"There is more. I dared not tell you while the others watched. He cries out in the night. His dreams are terrible, but he'll say nothing about them."

"This comes as no surprise." Dzaminid rubbed at his chin and frowned. "He should want an interpretation. But I cannot compel Nurtaj to be frank with me."

"You will ask him?"

"I'll try to catch him when his guard is down. And I beg of you a small thing in return. Find the Greatwing woman, Etoudoori, who came with the southerner. Have her wait for me here—in Tomuuk's yurt."

Erhen nodded. The shaman plunged into the bustle of camp. In a few moments he found a knoll where the Kag watched impatiently while his younger wives assembled his dwelling. The opened letter lay on the ground, its edges stained and torn.

"The soil-tillers think to save themselves with a few scratches of a pen," said Nurtaj contemptuously, acting as if he already knew the contents. "Read it for yourself." He kicked at the crumpled parchment with the toe of his boot.

Dzaminid understood Hakhan writing, but rarely made

use of his skill. "Honored chief," he read aloud, carefully scanning each character. "I would meet with you—to discuss matters—of common interest—"

"Ha. What can talk serve? Will they invite us to graze on their lands or to use their Path?" The Kag ripped the letter from Dzaminid's hand and offered it to a she-goat that had come up beside him. The animal took several bites, chewed vigorously, then took the rest in her mouth and trotted off.

With no great surprise Dzaminid watched the destruction of the letter that had come so far. This overture, after all, was a result of Etou's interference and had no part in the gods' plans. "We still must deal with the messenger," the boneman said cautiously. "I should interview him in Tomuuk's presence. My revered mentor may offer some insights."

"Squeeze what you can from him." Nurtaj scowled as he turned to watch the slow progress of his women. The final red roof pole was just being lashed into place, while within the circle the newest wife was unrolling and arranging his patterned rugs. "Go," he told Dzaminid irritably, waving his hand. "The message means nothing. The Hakhan has come for other reasons."

A short time later Dzaminid found an ill-tempered Etou waiting inside the yurt while Tomuuk continued to doze. "Speak softly," he cautioned, putting a finger to her lips.

"When you rode off, you told us the Kag was nearby," she said in a harsh whisper.

"I thought you would easily catch up with me."

"We took a wrong trail. Then the horses had nothing to eat."

"But you are here." He reached for her hand but she pulled away from him.

"Yes. And I see a different shaman. I took you for a wandering mystic. Now you wear the symbols of Blood-

164

creek tribe." She pointed to a woven talisman on his sleeve.

"I am home. This is my tribe . . . and the Kag's, as you know well." She drew in her breath. "Do not be misled. I am shaman here, but Nurtaj no longer listens to me."

"And the Hakhan—"

"He must finish what he came for. At last I understand why the gods have sent another ulaansh. The Kag has misread his destiny. He is ready to march south and destroy us all."

Etou put her head in her hands. "Then that is why my future looks so poor. The shoy box doesn't lie."

Dzaminid smiled sadly. "You spend too much time thinking about this life."

"With good reason. There's nothing for me in the next."

"You may still change that—"

A guard's voice interrupted, calling from without. "Send the Hakhan in," answered the shaman. He whispered a few words of instruction to Etou.

Yarkol saw the decorated doorflap pulled back, but again the scene failed to match his visions. This dwelling was too small to be the Kag's, and the markings on the doorflap were unlike any he had seen before. Even so, he hesitated at the entrance. The guard escorting him seemed nervous, uncertain of Yarkol's status, reluctant to touch him.

"Come in, Newborn." Etoudoori sounded distressed, but her familiar voice overcame his misgivings. He stepped forward, the flap closed behind him, and for a moment he could see only the column of dim light that filtered in through the smoke hole. "You are with friends, Newborn," she told him quietly. "Join us, but say noth-

165

ing." He could just make out Etou sitting beside . . . *Takijaly!*

Yarkol's mouth fell open, for he barely recognized the shaman beneath his peaked cap. Before this, he had seen the man only in ordinary guise. Now he recalled again the shrine beside the Throats, the dancer's robe with its depiction of breastbone and ribs.

"We must explain a few things, Newborn," the shaman began.

"You offered to help me with the Kag," Yarkol whispered angrily. "He holds me captive. Is that your idea of welcome?" He felt a chill within this yurt, though he'd been standing outside without noticing the cold. The air here carried an odd smell, suggesting dust and great age and things he could not name.

"I had hoped to prepare the way for you," the boneman answered sadly. "I have failed in that."

"He threw my letter in the dirt. Already I see what kind of man leads your people." Yarkol's eyes were adjusting to the gloom. Along the walls hung shapes he could not identify—surely not household implements.

"The letter is nothing. Nurtaj will not talk to your chief in any case."

"Because he heeds a different summons?" Yarkol reached up to touch his cheek.

The shaman frowned. "He was chosen, as you were. But he is free to follow the gods' will or his own." Dzaminid lowered his voice to the faintest whisper. "At present he follows his own."

Yarkol had never heard the shaman in such a dark mood. "I don't understand you. The Kag shares my affliction, but does that make him fit to rule?"

The shaman turned to Etou. "He still knows nothing?"

"I tried to teach him—a few things," the woman answered.

"Listen, Ulaansh." The shaman's voice was hard. "You

166

have not lived among us long, but you can guess the risks we face. Without the herds we are buzzards' meat. A drought can cost us all our sustenance. A harsh winter or a lost battle can do the same. But in times of crisis the gods raise heroes who can surpass the ordinary man. When the need comes, we cannot wait for such a person to be conceived and born, to grow strong and learn wisdom. So the gods provide another way, reshaping someone the way a carver reworks his design. The Kag was so shaped, to lead his people to their new lands."

"And what do you expect of me, a Hakhan? Am I also to be one of your heroes?"

"You alone will decide that."

"But I am treated like an animal here."

"None of these people will harm you, Ulaansh. Only the Kag would dare such an affront to the High Ones, and he'll move cautiously. For now you'll stay here, with Tomuuk and his wife, and keep out of Nurtaj's way."

"I must tell your Kag about the Path."

"That will come, when the time and place are right. Have patience."

"I have ridden this far merely to wait?" Yarkol peered again at the dark hangings around the periphery of the yurt. Memories stirred that he wished to forget. "This is a shaman's dwelling."

"Are you afraid? You traveled with a shaman for several days, and I see no ill effects. Where are your warts?" The boneman seized his hand and turned it over. Yarkol, recalling childish tales, could not help laughing.

"You will be safe here," said the mystic. "But let me warn you on one point. Be careful at night when the Kag is alone in his yurt. He leaves his body as you do. He can prowl through the camp and listen to the faintest of whispers."

*   *   *

That evening, when Dzaminid dined with the Kag again, he sensed Erhen's silent pleas. She glanced frequently in the shaman's direction, her brows knit, her lips tightened. He tried to signal her subtly, to show that he understood. As soon as the kumiss bowl was ready, she and the other wives slipped away to their smaller dwelling.

The drink was well made, but the shaman took only shallow sips; soon the Chief-Among-Chiefs had finished most of the contents. Nurtaj was relaxed now, his spirit soothed by drink. For proof, he stretched out his legs and told a story about two women of Warmbed tribe. No such tribe existed, except in tales men told each other, and mere mention of the name was enough to provoke mirth. Dzaminid did his best to appear amused.

"Nurtaj, your story reminds me of a dream I had recently," ventured the shaman. "There were two women in it; I cannot say they were Warmbeds." The Kag grinned and pushed his boots closer to the fire. "The grass was as high as their knees—"

"You saw their knees?"

"I saw where their leggings bent when they ran." For some reason Nurtaj began bellowing with laughter, lifting his mask so he could wipe away tears. Dzaminid felt a moment of pity for this man whom the gods had both blessed and cursed. He could summon any woman of the tribes, and she would gladly come to him. But for what purpose? Like Yarkol's, his member was useful now only for passing water.

"The grass, as I was saying, grew this high." Dzaminid held up his palm. "And the meadows stretched farther than I could see. No mountains loomed in the distance, so vast was that plain."

"Eastern land," said Nurtaj.

168

"Country unknown to me. But the women were laughing. I saw fat herds and many rows of yurts."

"A dream of prophecy, shaman." His lips pursed briefly as a worry seemed to cross his thoughts.

"If it matches your own dreams," the shaman suggested, "then there may be truth in it. I would like to think so."

Nurtaj's frown deepened and an air of suspicion surrounded his spirit. "Does Erhen tell you I sleep badly?" he asked with a sudden bitter tone. "Is that why your talk turns so?" He spread fingers across his stomach. "It's the meat she cooks for me. Too gristly. I get pains in the night."

Dzaminid sighed. Did the man not realize how transparent his lies were? "I've heard of a shaman who made a point of eating too much gristle and fat. He woke frequently, suffering, and each time recalled vivid scenes. He became a renowned prophet."

"I'm no prophet." Nurtaj continued to massage his stomach. "I do what I think is right. Only the gods know how it will turn out."

"Even so, your dreams are of value."

"Then I'll relate some for you. But not tonight. No, not with such good drink inside me."

I have tried, Erhen. Dzaminid allowed the conversation to drift elsewhere and was relieved that the Kag said nothing about Yarkol Dolmi. Nurtaj was brooding on the matter and for now must be left with his thoughts.

But suddenly Dzaminid sensed a commotion outside and realized that the Hakhan's fate might well be decided this night. The shaman waited tensely for the messenger who approached.

"Your cousin, Chosen One," said the voice of the guard beyond the door. "Oron has just reached camp."

"Bring him," said Nurtaj, jumping up from his stool.

169

"Now! And tell the women I need them. Drag them from sleep if you must."

The shaman gritted his teeth as he felt Oron's angry spirit nearby. Moments later the disheveled traveler entered the yurt, his face grimy, his chin unshaved, his coat spattered with mud. Despite his rough appearance, he gave the ritual bow with dignity. The Kag embraced his cousin, then led him to a seat before the hearth. The fire had burned down, and the kumiss bowl stood dry. "Ten wives!" the Kag fumed. "And not one here when you need her."

The shaman received a curt greeting from Oron. Dzaminid had seen the warrior just once while in the south, but he believed that Oron knew nothing about that encounter. Now he saw heavy pouches beneath the warrior's eyes; evidently he'd been riding for days and nights to make up lost time. "I've startling news, noble one," he said in a rasping voice.

The Kag held up his hand. "You must drink something first." He found the long kumiss sack, upended it, and managed to half-fill the bowl. As he passed the drink to his cousin, a young wife peered sleepily in at the doorway.

"Build up the fire. Brew henga. Roast meat." He barked the orders almost too quickly to be followed, then sat down and looked expectantly at Oron.

"I should have been here days ago," complained the cousin. "It was sorcery that stopped me." He cast a cold glance at the shaman, as if he suspected Dzaminid's part. But Oron had already been snoring when the shaman used a reed to blow powder into his mouth. After that, his sleep had been sounder yet!

"Sorcery in the south?" Nurtaj glanced from Dzaminid to his cousin.

"No matter about that now," said Oron. "I had companions who should have reached you ahead of me. Baatibi.

170

Etou. They bore news of the Hakhan I found—the ulaansh."

"The soil-tiller is here," replied the Kag coldly. "He threatens all that I've achieved."

Oron frowned. "I did not see him as a threat, noble cousin. The man is a Dolmi. His clan is charged with building the Path, and he has ridden it more than once. He knows its turnings."

Nurtaj snorted. "Do I need a guide to find such a well-used trail? The markings will be plain as the hairs on your belly."

"There may be tricks—false branchings, spurs that lead to boiling pools."

"We'll find those easily enough." The Kag fell thoughtful, and his stirrings within troubled Dzaminid. "Ah," said Nurtaj after a moment of silence. "I see a use for this southerner now. He can help us with such weak-hearts as Vuotol. How can they deny our ability to cross, if I show them a guide who knows the way?"

Oron smiled faintly and nodded. "The gods gave him to you. They plucked him from his home and sent him here. What else could their purpose be?"

Nurtaj's head came up. He looked to the shaman as if he'd been granted a revelation. "What do you say to that?" he demanded with a grin. "My cousin's a sharp thinker!"

Dzaminid cleared his throat. Oron, he thought, had inadvertently become his ally. "We must question the ulaansh," Dzaminid said vigorously. "As a Dolmi, his knowledge of the Path is indisputable."

"Question him we shall." The Kag, his grin broadening, hastened to the doorway and shouted orders to a guard.

171

11

> *Pupil: Why is the ulaansh marked across his cheek?*
>
> *Teacher: Because his belly is hidden beneath his coat.*
> —*Chirudak tradition (varies with tribe)*

Y arkol, roused from sleep, could see nothing but the torch that blazed painfully close to his face. "Up!" said a harsh voice. He turned his head, but the flame followed, permitting him no relief.

Groggily he pulled on his boots and stood. Out of habit he felt for his knife, but remembered suddenly that the guards had taken it. Now other soldiers clustered about him; in the confusion he could not count them.

"Quickly!" the guards said. Yarkol glanced aside as he was leaving and saw the old shaman and his wife

172

stretched out on the far side of the yurt. He didn't know whether they had slept through this commotion, or now lay awake, rigid with fear. But the woman had tried to make Yarkol welcome, and for this she was receiving poor reward.

In the cold outside Yarkol's head began to clear. Despite Mouchin's hospitality, he realized now, the shaman's yurt had oppressed him. After the hearthfire had been lit, he'd glimpsed ceremonial weapons, painted hides, toothy masks that brought back unwanted memories of the cavern near the Throat. He had tried to keep his eyes away from the shaman's implements, but their presence seemed to suffuse the stale air. Now, as the guards urged him on, he breathed deeply of the bracing wind.

Though the warriors avoided touching him, the sight of their unsheathed swords prompted him to obey. The men led him toward a knoll that he hadn't seen before; under moonlight he could just discern the outlines of the large yurt that stood in its center. He hadn't dreamed this scene precisely, but he knew where he was heading.

From the doorway came several voices, and Yarkol was relieved to learn that the Kag was not alone. The Hakhan thought he heard Takijaly—Dzaminid he called himself now. Yarkol remained wary of the shaman, but he could count on no one else to aid his cause.

As he stepped through the opening, he saw the silver-masked Kag seated on his stool. The chief's felt trousers and hide coat matched exactly the garb of Yarkol's dreams. Some furnishings also looked familiar—the cups of beaten gold and the ancient, cracked table. But these other visitors had played no part in his visions . . .

Suddenly Yarkol noticed Oron. Etou had warned that her former companion would catch up with them. Even so, the Hakhan drew in his breath as he studied the warrior's disheveled appearance.

"So, Newborn," Oron said. "You arrived without me. In

good health, it seems." He spoke with the same nomad dialect he had used at their first meeting, yet now his speech sounded proper to Yarkol's ears.

"You sent me on my way," the Dolmi answered.

"Ah, but I followed you," the tall man continued, his confession no surprise to Yarkol. "I watched you ride up to Jornood House and come down. Trailed you to a forest camp. Then, through trickery, you left me behind."

Trying to ignore the accusation, Yarkol returned his attention to the Kag. The chief's silver mask glinted in the firelight as his eyes held steady on Yarkol's face. The Dolmi began to perspire, for the shaman's sake as well as his own. "Enough banter," said the Kag after a moment. "I called you for one reason. I want to hear of the Path across the Throats."

"The Path is no use to you," Yarkol said at once.

"No use?" The Kag stood and pointed at Dzaminid. "Pull the truth from him," he demanded. "Now!"

The Hakhan felt suddenly alarmed. He had one escape route—through the doorway—and six guards stood out there waiting for him. Yet, what had he to fear? Truth was what he had come to speak.

He watched the shaman draw something from a pouch. "Show me your tongue, Ulaansh," sad Dzaminid calmly. The voice hinted that Yarkol was in no danger, but the Hakhan felt prickles of gooseflesh on his neck and shoulders. The shaman held a thumb-sized wooden tube that was decorated with a crisscross pattern. From the tube he pulled a slender wand; a thick yellow droplet glistened at the bottom of the stick. Involuntarily, Yarkol stepped away.

"If I harm you, Newborn, my soul will suffer for many lives."

"I am worried about *this* life!"

"Then permit me to question you."

The Hakhan heard a subtle emphasis on "me" and

174

guessed at Dzaminid's meaning. Surely the issue of Oron's delay must not be raised, for then the shaman would have to explain his part in it. Yarkol glanced from the Kag's mask to Oron's haggard countenance. Beside the fire sat an old woman and a girl, both also watching him intently. *Five witnesses. But to what?* The shaman approached, his ugly droplet rising toward Yarkol's mouth. A voice of warning rose from the physician he had been, yet he allowed the wand between his lips.

The taste was bitter and unlike any herb he knew. A mild numbing sensation raced from tongue to palate to cheek. His legs weakened, and he clutched at the shaman's outstretched hand as he slid down to an awkward sitting position.

Yarkol tried to turn his head but found the motion extremely sluggish. The shaman's movements too seemed oddly slowed. When Dzaminid spoke his tones were deep, each syllable greatly extended.

"Now . . . we . . . must . . . be . . . sure . . . the . . . binding . . . is . . . firm," came the voice from the boneman's lips. Waiting for each word became an exercise in patience. Yarkol could do nothing but listen to the sounds emerge at their own drowsy pace. "Look . . . Newborn. Gaze at the women . . . who serve the Kag. Tell us . . . what you think of them."

Yarkol's thoughts were racing before the shaman's words finished. He was obliged to flatter his host, he understood, and a dozen pompous phrases came to mind. But when he began to speak, he found his own voice issuing with the same maddening slowness as had Dzaminid's. Once he began, it was as if he had started a heavy cart rolling and could not change its course. "I see . . . a child . . . possibly the Kag's daughter. I see . . . a crone, who may be his mother."

Why was Oron smiling? Had Yarkol forgotten the obvious, that the Kag too had been made young again? "The old one may be . . . his wife, the other his grand-daughter," he added. Once the words began flowing, he felt like a listener who could only wait for them to end. He'd spoken too frankly, he realized. What had happened to the compliments he'd meant to bestow?

"Tell us this, Newborn," the shaman continued. "What would you do if no guards stood outside, if you were free of all restraint?"

Once more, polite phrases tantalized Yarkol, but they refused to move his tongue. "I came to confront . . . the Kag as an equal . . . not as a prisoner. I would challenge him to face me in fair argument. And in combat . . . if there is no other way to settle our differences."

"You see," said the boneman, "now he can only speak truth."

"That will be seen," replied the Kag, his body leaning forward, his fists tightening. "Tell me about the Path," he demanded of Yarkol. "How narrow is it at the thinnest part?"

The Dolmi had been mildly amused by the start of the questioning, but now his indignation rose. The shaman had promised to direct the interview, but the Kag had taken charge. Let this Chief-Among-Chiefs meet Yarkol's challenge if he wished to learn of the Path.

"How narrow?" asked the Kag again.

"A horseman or a cart can pass easily at the narrowest point," Yarkol's voice answered, seemingly of its own accord.

"I am told that the Path is complete," the chief continued. "Can you give any reason to doubt that report?"

Yarkol had time to frame an evasive answer, but he heard other words flowing before he could stop himself. "It extends to the edge of Rya Basin."

"And what is this Basin?"

"A treacherous landscape of fumaroles and mudpots and boiling pools."

"Then tell me how you cross the final stretch."

"We've had accidents, lost many men. The work teams are still searching for a way."

"*Still searching?* Then what is your route to the east?"

"We have none yet. The last barrier appears the most difficult of all."

The Kag rose to his feet, his movements so gradual that Yarkol could examine every change in the muscles of his jaw. The Chief-Among-Chiefs turned on the shaman. "Is this your idea of truth?"

"We should compare his testimony with that of others," replied Dzaminid. "What of the discoveries of our own people in the south?"

"I have heard the others," said Nurtaj. "I needed no tricks to make them speak." He shouted for his guards to remove the Hakhan.

Yarkol felt both relief and anger at his sudden dismissal. He wanted to defend himself, but to do so in this drugged state was impossible. He glanced up at the oncoming warriors, who entered in such a ponderous manner that Yarkol was almost moved to laughter. If his own limbs were not similarly slowed, how easily he could dodge these oafs!

The guards did not seize him at once; only after they heard the shaman's assurances did they dare touch the visitor. The Hakhan offered no struggle as they lifted him and carried him out of the yurt. Floating like a tufted seed pod, he drifted down the slope toward the rows of smaller dwellings.

He had plenty of time for observations, but what was there to see at this late hour? On the ground, a small figure looked up at him and waved its long arms in greeting. Then another joined it and another. He had encountered few imps of late, even after removing the shaman's covering from his cheek. Now he saw the creatures arriving from all directions.

"Ulaansh," they shouted in shrill chorus. "We have sport for you." They danced between the guards' boots, but the nomads did not seem to notice. One imp playfully leaped up, scaling leggings and jacket as a man might scale a cliff. An ugly face thrust itself into the Hakhan's, and he thought he smelled a musty odor.

Yarkol noted that the imps moved and spoke at what he perceived as normal rates. His thoughts followed the rhythms of these creatures, though his body remained sluggish. For a moment he was tempted to slip from his constraining flesh, poisoned as it was by the shaman's medicine, and dance with the small ones under Mother Moon. He felt himself loosening, slipping free. But where were the guards taking his body? What if he should lose track of it? The prospect so frightened him that he dismissed the temptation, clinging fiercely to his logy form as the men bore him on.

Again the spirits shouted to him. "Join us, Ulaansh." Despite Yarkol's triumph over the water-sprite, these hobs had not given up on him. Perhaps they were seeking revenge for their cousin's disgrace. Wishing for the protection of the paste mask again, he closed his eyes and waited for the slow ride to end. He could not block the sounds of the imps' shrill calls.

The guards lowered Yarkol onto his bedding, then withdrew. The only sound now was Tomuuk's labored breathing. For a long while the Hakhan stared into darkness, but at last he slept. When next he opened his eyes, morning sunlight was seeping into the yurt. He heard lowered voices, possibly a conversation that he was not meant to hear.

Dzaminid and Etou! Recalling their intimacy of earlier days, the Hakhan felt gnawing envy. But he realized that their current talk was of serious matters. And since their voices possessed proper cadence and tone, he knew also that the effect of the drug had worn off.

178

"The Kag's brother is wary," the shaman was saying.

"But there's no way to question him openly," she replied.

"In time, there may be."

"By then will be too late. Give me something to use on him. I can be subtle. You should have seen me with a pack of southern soldiers."

"Guzad is too important—"

"Give me something to make him talk," she insisted. "If I'm caught, I can say that I stole it from you."

Dzaminid began to laugh. "Stole? Don't you think a shaman can protect his goods? More likely, I *gave* you this." Cloth rustled. "In exchange for a favor."

"*Favor?* Takijaly was one man, you another. Sometimes I wish I could find that other shaman."

"He is gone," Dzaminid sighed. "But he has not forgotten you. Here. Take this, and be careful." A shuffling sound. The door flap opening and closing. Who had stayed behind?

"I know you are awake, Newborn," said the deeper voice. Yarkol turned with chagrin and finally sat up. "No harm is done," continued the shaman. "I do not keep secrets from you."

"Nor did I keep any last night," Yarkol replied coldly. "Though the Kag ignored my warnings."

Dzaminid frowned. "So long as the Kag accepts Guzad's report, he can put aside yours. And Nurtaj won't let me question his brother." He nodded toward the far side of the yurt. "I hoped Tomuuk might offer advice. Otherwise I have only Etou's risky plan."

The Hakhan saw that Mouchin was gone, leaving her husband in Dzaminid's care. But in his time here Yarkol had heard nothing from the old man but his snoring. He had known many similar cases . . .

"Honored Tomuuk," the younger shaman said softly. Yarkol was surprised to see eyelids fluttering. "This morning, I am the one to bring your bowl of yohourt. Can you receive it from these rough hands?" He propped a pillow behind the elder's head.

"Seeker-of-moonbeams, you are full of trouble today. Your questions dance on your tongue." Tomuuk's rasping voice made Yarkol stiffen. Hairs rose on his nape, but he could not say why. He watched as the old man sipped from the bowl. "The Kag is dissatisfied," Tomuuk said between tastes. "He will visit me. I don't like the set of his mind."

"I know his intent," said Dzaminid. "He'll ask you to examine our Hakhan. To prove that the words uttered last night are false."

"And how shall I accommodate him?" Tomuuk, his lips smeared with white, motioned for the bowl to be withdrawn. "The answer is obvious. I'll be too ill for any work." He waved a hand feebly. "What would be gained by forcing the ulaansh to repeat what he has said?"

Dzaminid nodded. "But to make Nurtaj understand—"

"Is beyond your power, Seeker. Let him live the whole winter with his dreams. Do you think I do not know his anguish? But you must stop meddling, my son, for you only harden his resolve."

"I have already meddled, honored father."

"Then your soul must suffer for it." Tomuuk flailed at the pillow. "You have just had a full day's talking from me," he complained, his voice trailing off. "I must save some breath for your Hakhan. Bring him when I am rested." Dzaminid lowered the old man's head and allowed him to sleep again.

Etou rode her mare toward Guzad's yurt. She found the Kag's brother outside, unloading firewood from a restless pack ox. A young boy held the beast's nose rope while Guzad carried the logs in. When he emerged again, the

180

man stared at her with deeply set eyes that seemed to probe her intents. He was not so tall as Oron, but possessed his cousin's good looks, his wide cheekbones and broad mouth. The gray at the tip of his beard gave him an air of distinction.

"I've had trouble with the horse herd—while you were on watch," she said hesitantly, her tongue faltering as she studied his gray eyes.

"I know who you are," he answered. "You're the woman the wives speak of when they think I'm not listening!"

For a moment, Etou could not respond. She had come here to get his attention, to encourage him subtly so that later he would seek her out. But already she had aroused his suspicions. "I—I am a visitor to the camp," she managed. "I pastured my roan with the others—"

"And the lead mare gave challenge. Should that surprise anyone?"

Etou dismounted. "That animal is dangerous. Look where she nipped the flanks of my mount."

Guzad laughed and made no move to examine the wound. "Tell me if you recognize the tooth marks."

"I'm not the first one with this problem. The others may not dare complain to you."

"And why should they be afraid? I'm no one special." Etou bit her lip to keep from crying out. *The Kag's brother is surely no one special.* He returned to the ox, loosening ropes to let another pile of logs rumble to the ground. He picked up an armload just as a slender woman, somewhat older than Etou, emerged from the yurt. One of Guzad's wives?

"Are you still here?" he asked Etou after making another trip inside. "What is it you want?" He approached angrily, bent to look at the place she showed him. Etou fingered the red hide, brushing back hairs, pointing to several faint marks. "I see no sign of an attack," he

181

grumbled, finally making his own examination. "Those are flea bites. Where do you come from that you don't know the difference?"

"Maybe our Greatwing fleas are smaller," she said with a forced laugh. "But I saw your mare nip my animal."

"Her foals are widely sought. Should we swap her for a meekling?"

Etou tossed her head. "I've wasted time for both of us." Angrily remounting, she noticed that the wife was still watching from beside the doorway.

Guzad put a hand on her bridle. "Is it true," he asked in a low voice, "that Oron spurned you? I would have thought him easy prey."

She smiled but did not reply. He turned, laughing, and she rode off with tears starting to brim.

In the afternoon Yarkol was sent outside with six mounted guards to watch him. The horsemen directed him away from Tomuuk's yurt, allowing him to sit by the stream while the flocks were watered. The Kag was visiting the old shaman, he knew. And the Chief-Among-Chiefs would not easily be put off.

Catching stares from the passing youngsters, Yarkol lingered by the stream bank, his fingers dabbling in mud. Perhaps he was a child again in mind as well as body. For a moment he longed for a life of tending sheep, with no other cares.

Nurtaj did not wish to hear the truth, and no persuasion would change his plans. Yarkol recalled his own early dreams, his knife blade lodged in the nomad leader's chest. A Chirudak would never raise a hand against the Kag—the Chosen One. Only an outsider could stop him.

The Kag knew that, of course. Why else was the Hakhan deprived of his weapon and kept under constant guard? When Yarkol's usefulness was over, Nurtaj would dispose of him secretly. Slow strangulation, the Dolmi had heard, was the Kag's preferred technique.

Perhaps escape remained an alternative. If Yarkol could reach the south and warn Jornood, then the Hakhan forces might prepare a trap. But Jornood already expected a nomad advance, so the Hakhan would have little new to tell him. At best, Yarkol might report his observations in the camps.

As the day wore on, the guards allowed him to stroll downstream, to a place where craftsmen sat tooling leather. The low-legged stools and workbenches were designed for ease of transport, Yarkol noted, though they exacted a toll from their users' backs. Farther on, he watched a smith quickening his fire with a pair of bellows. In the coals the Hakhan thought he saw a tiny imp grinning.

When the sun began to redden the western clouds, the guards returned Yarkol to Tomuuk's yurt. Mouchin glanced up as he entered. The old shaman was snoring quietly.

"I'm to blame for your husband's troubles," the Hakhan said penitently.

"Nurtaj is a blusterer," she replied. "But he stayed here only for a moment. When my husband told him that you spoke truthfully, he stormed away."

Yarkol shook his head. "He will find someone else to give him the answer he wants."

Evening came quietly, bringing no further developments. Yarkol knew only that the Kag would leave tomorrow, taking him to another encampment. And Guzad was to join them, perhaps to give his testimony to other tribal chiefs. The prospect of the journey gave the Hakhan a small hope. The Kag had dismissed his report, but the other chiefs might prove more open-minded. If only he could confront the Kag's brother . . .

Mouchin, as was her habit, fell asleep soon after the meal was done. Yarkol lay awake, hoping for a visit from Etoudoori. The fire burned down to embers, and still he lay awake. Through the walls of the yurt he heard shrill voices calling. "Ulaansh, come out. The moons are bright."

Etou did not come. Yarkol stared up into the darkness and felt again the chill of this shaman's dwelling. How pleasant, he thought, to escape for a few moments from the guards who constantly surrounded him.

"Ulaansh! Come dance with us." The cries were too tempting to ignore. He stared at the hearth, picking out a bright coal—the remains of a forked branch that shimmered in the heat. He recalled how the sight of glittering pebbles had put him into trance. Now, as he studied one particular ember, he felt his flesh softening like warmed wax. He broke away from his body, at once seeing with new eyes that made the room brighter. In skeletal form, he crawled to the doorway, pushed against the flap.

Too heavy! He'd forgotten the limitations of his trance-body. Furious that even now he remained trapped, he beat the hide with his fist. The flap moved slightly, but not enough to let him pass.

From without came the imps' cries of encouragement. Yarkol pushed again, but accomplished no more than on his first try. Suddenly he remembered the water-sprite from the ravine. The creature had followed him as he walked, flattening itself when the water grew shallow. Perhaps his own spirit-form might flex in a similar way.

He recalled seeing his spirit bones bend and flow. Once more he pounded at the covering and this time thrust his hand into the gap. His fingers and wrist thinned out, and he pushed them through the narrow opening. He wedged a toe in near the doorway's bottom, and quickly followed with his leg. Making a final determined shove he squeezed the rest of his body outside. His guards did not turn as he strode past them.

So bright! Above, the moons were dazzling, the stars aglow with colors he had never noticed before. And on the bare ground a dozen imps frolicked—one flipping backwards to land on its feet, another walking on its outsized hands. Several hobs joined in a circle to dance about Yarkol's knees.

"We found your knife," said the imp with the longest beard. "It's in the Kag's yurt. We can help you get it back."

"In return for what?"

The sprite laughed, his pointed tongue waggling.

"I'll make no bargains with your kind," said Yarkol.

"We can bring your mount."

"For what purpose? My body is constantly guarded."

"Then die here," the hob retorted. "The masked one won't change. Your journey was wasted."

"How can you know about these things? You are wisps. When the sun rises, you'll melt away like hoarfrost."

"When dawn comes, we'll be safe in our dens. We can hear everything from down there."

"Then tell me, since you're so free with advice, what I should do."

"Simple. Help the Kag across. Finish your Path to the east so he can use it."

"Fine advice. After years of labor, you tell me to throw away the Hakhan hopes and offer them instead to your friends."

"The nomads are no friends of ours," the longbeard countered. "Their offerings grow stingier every year. If we didn't whip up a plague now and then—to shock them into piety—our storehouses would be empty."

"Plague?"

"It takes three years to prepare one. With the proper arrangements, we could start work tonight."

Arrangements. The Hakhan was taken aback; he had almost forgotten his physician's oath! "What can you do," he asked cautiously, "that won't take three years?"

"That depends on what you offer."

The Hakhan forced himself to look down into his rib cage, at the graceful form that fluttered within. "For this?" he asked. "What is it worth to you?"

At those words, the sprites ceased their games and clustered about him. "We can put out all the cookfires," shouted one. "Bring a swarm of gnats," offered another.

"Can you keep the whole Chirudak nation from moving south?"

They looked at each other and shrugged. "There are only so many of us."

"Then no use haggling." He glanced down through white ribs at his prize once again. If he was to risk that, then he must find the proper stakes.

Evidently sensing his mood, the crowd dispersed. The imps returned to their stunts—one riding another's shoulders, others tumbling. Yarkol derived no amusement from the sight.

"Go back inside now," the longbeard told him suddenly, his voice carrying a note of warning.

"First you invite me out here. Then you tell me I'm not welcome."

"Fool! There's danger afoot!"

Yarkol had almost forgotten his body. Had something happened to it within the yurt? He hurried to the entrance and squeezed through a gap.

Within, all appeared as he had left it; his body lay undisturbed. But it pained him to look at the lifeless eyes and rigid face. At once he returned to his flesh, grateful for the rhythm of his breathing, for the taste of smoky air. To his human vision, the room was almost dark.

186

"Newborn!" The voice was Tomuuk's, its deep resonances as startling as when he'd first heard them. "*He* is coming. Lie still and say nothing till he's gone."

He? Yarkol pulled up the blanket, feeling like a child who huddles beneath a cover to keep safe from night's evils. Realizing what he was doing, he could not help laughing at himself. He exposed his eyes, but found nothing to see in the gloom. From the doorway came a sound of flapping, a cold rush of air.

Was that a faint glow in front of the entrance? He squinted, thinking for a moment that he saw an animal figure, an image of a huge white bear. The creature's lips pulled back in a snarl as the head turned slowly, surveying the room with ruddy eyes. The jaw opened, displaying huge curved canines that gleamed with an inner fire. The paws twitched, showing needle claws, as if the beast sought something to shred. Then the bear circled with a shambling gait and used its head to push its way out.

"He is looking for someone else," whispered Tomuuk. "We are safe now."

"That was the Kag?" Yarkol refused to believe what he'd seen.

"Out of his body. Prowling in spirit form, as you have done."

"But his strength—I could barely move the doorflap. He pushed right through." Yarkol crept closer to the shaman.

The elder stirred. When he spoke again his voice was firmer, his breathing less labored. "Each one the gods choose has somewhat different powers," he said. "In your earlier days you were a healer. Had you been born a Chirudak you would surely have become a mystic instead—a boneman like myself."

Yarkol shook his head. "I would not choose such a life. To be constantly taunted by imps—"

Tomuuk sighed. "It is not the same with us. We

187

shamans cannot see spirits clearly, as you do, but we sense their presence. We can sometimes force one to our bidding, but you have a vaster power. If you deal fairly—"

"As they've been fair to men? Their tricks are known to every child."

Tomuuk gave a dry cackle. "They are fond of games, for they have little else. To best an ulaansh is their greatest hope."

"And what do they offer to tempt me? You called me a healer. But the imps talked of loosing a plague . . . and I listened."

The old one smiled faintly. "You have not yet betrayed your former self. And when the time comes, you will do what you must." He yawned, his brief spurt of energy apparently waning. "Here is my advice. Listen to the sprites, but be cautious. I suspect they have plans of their own— even a conspiracy against the gods. Yet you may find a way to make them your allies. Try . . ." His voice faded, and he seemed asleep again.

12

*What do we sing when our husband is
away?*

*"The cauldrons are simmering;
We keep each other warm."*

*What do we sing when our husband
comes home?*

*"The cauldrons need stirring;
We must share one stick."*

                 —Women's chant (Pinebole tribe)

Etoudoori watched from a
distance as the Kag's party prepared to leave camp. Already astride her mount, she was planning to follow,
though the Kag had not asked for her presence. Her roan

189

pawed the hard ground, and Etou understood the mount's impatience.

The sky had grown overcast. Etou felt snow in the air. She wished she could ride with Yarkol, but guards surrounded him on every side. And the man she wanted most to avoid—Oron—had just noticed her.

She'd heard of his recent arrival, but this was her first sight of him in the Kag's camp. Glancing at Oron now, she noted that he'd grown leaner and bore a haggard look. "You've been hiding from me," he said as he rode up to her.

"People say you've been sleeping since you came here. Should I have wakened you?"

"We've something to settle."

"For that old cart? I could have given you its value in a night."

"I care nothing for the cart, though it was worth a lifetime of your favors. What did you do to me while I slept near Jornood House?" He pointed to her mount's forefeet. "I found tracks on a nearby hillside. You were there."

"I was many places. I followed the Hakhan as you did. Is it strange that I passed you?"

"The soil-tiller was also on that hillside. But what of the third rider? His tracks I didn't recognize. The third one was the sorcerer who bound me in sleep. You three plotted together."

"I saw no sorcerer," she answered evenly.

"I'll find him. Then all your smiles and lies won't save you."

"If you find a sorcerer, I may have use for him." She sat straight in the saddle, staring at Oron until he snarled and turned away. Then she noticed Guzad, astride a bay gelding. He was watching her, she knew, though his gaze seemed directed elsewhere. *Ah, Guzad. You are my challenge.* Studying him, she considered a plan. In the past she had benefitted by setting one man against another . . .

190

*   *   *

Yarkol's mood remained bleak as the procession moved out onto the pebbled trail. Today, the shaman had told him, the Kag's retinue was headed for a far larger camp. Around a sheltered lake lay the traditional winter quarters for three tribes: Mossbend, Leatherhead, and Whitemane. If the leaders of these tribes agreed with the Kag's plan, then Dzaminid expected all other opposition to cease. Even poor Vuotol would be forced to join the invasion.

Yarkol now understood how the shaman's situation had altered, his once-powerful influence largely eroded. Dzaminid had been Nurtaj's spiritual advisor from the first days of his illness and had stood by him while his hairs fell away and his body grew youthful. While Tomuuk—sickly even then—languished in his yurt, the younger shaman listened to Nurtaj's dreams and helped him learn that he must unite his people. Nurtaj had spent three years riding from camp to camp, meeting with elders and mystics, showing the face beneath his mask. He had been accepted by every tribe as the gods' appointed Chief-Among-Chiefs. Old rivalries had been put aside until the new Kag could lead everyone to the pastures of legend.

But the issue of where those lands lay became a subject of dispute, sending the Kag to seek fresh assurances from the chiefs. As pressure on the Kag increased, he became more rigid, less willing to hear advice. He no longer put his trust even in the shaman who had nurtured him.

These thoughts kept Yarkol occupied while the procession followed a deeply-worn trail, then took a series of switchbacks, ascending to a bare and stony ridge. The sky remained cloudy as a few white flakes began to fall. Feeling an icy sting on his neck, the Hakhan pulled up his fur collar and turned his face from the wind.

The snowfall grew heavier, leaving a drift of white across the trail. With the sky clouded, he could not gauge the passing of time. He had only the steady jouncing of the pony and the swirling dance of snowflakes to mark the day's progress.

At long last, by the dimming light, he knew that afternoon was waning. The storm ceased, and the air grew clear, though the sky remained overcast. Then the party crossed another ridge, and suddenly he gazed down onto a startling sight. Below lay a round lake, dark and wind-blown, surrounded by whiteness. All about the shore stood clustered yurts, made tiny by distance. Farther out, on a vast snow-covered plain, moved miniature herds— sheep, goats, horses. He felt that a single leap might take him down to them.

Descending by the trail, however, proved a tedious chore, and the travelers did not reach bottom until shortly before dusk. A welcoming party of riders waited on the plain. Yarkol saw a swath of tracks in the snow leading back toward the lake.

After the waiting riders made their bows of respect to the Kag, one man turned to the nearest yurts and began to whistle a series of warbling notes. In a few moments a faint answering whistle returned. Then the welcoming party and the Kag galloped ahead, leaving the others to follow at a slower pace.

Soon Yarkol was watching the Kag's women use stiff hides to scrape snow from a circular patch of ground. They began to erect the yurt's framework, but even as they worked, more snow began falling through the open roof. The Dolmi's guards looked in another direction, as if the mere sight of women's work might corrupt them. Yarkol would have helped with the labor, but he knew that if he dared dismount his warders would draw their swords. Soon other women from the tribe came, a few carrying torches, and the task proceeded more quickly.

Four guards came to lead the Hakhan away. After beating snow from his coat and boots, he entered a sparsely furnished yurt that was far smaller than the Kag's. The sputtering fire was burning dung that had not dried fully; the odor made him gasp. He glanced about, noting the few old hides that barely covered the dirt floor, and the tattered furs provided for bedding. Poor comfort indeed! Was this how an ulaansh was welcomed?

The guards, Bloodcreek men he had seen for the first time this morning, entered with him, one remaining by the doorway while the others pulled off hide gloves and held their hands to the meager warmth. On the trail Yarkol had taken little interest in these four, but now he studied their faces. Three were youths, large-framed and bristling with strength. The fourth had the appearance of a hardened warrior, with an old scar across his nose and cheek.

Yarkol managed to draw the older man into sporadic conversation. Raz, as he was called, seemed to be waiting for someone and frequently glanced outside. Each time he pulled back the felt doorflap, a whirl of snowflakes blew in. At last a woman arrived carrying a deep wooden bowl and a handful of wooden skewers; behind her another woman bore a sooty pot. Finally a young girl entered holding a parcel of cheese.

The bowl contained gutted fish, the pot, henga brew. The women departed at once, leaving the guests to fend for themselves. Raz added more dung pats to the fire and set the pot on hearth stones in the center of the blaze. The soldiers skewered fish and set them to cook at the fire's edge. Yarkol followed their example.

One guard went out for more fuel and came back with an armload of thin logs. The four nomads consumed the remaining food, but evidently were still hungry. Another youth left the yurt, returning shortly with a cold leg of goat and a shoy box. Yarkol, content with a single fish, smiled in surprise at the others' appetites.

Raz sliced up the meat, which the men quickly

193

devoured. They licked greasy fingers, then wiped their hands on their trouser legs. While one youth sat by the door again, the other two placed the heavily worn shoy box between them.

Yarkol had no great interest in this pastime. He stared into the fire and let his thoughts drift to home. Soon snow would be falling on Dolmi fields, though warm air from the Throats would melt it quickly. And within the thick walls of Hakhan houses nobody would suffer winter's sting. He imagined his children as they sat by the huge stone fireplaces. Did any of them give him a thought? Perhaps they had already forgotten him. He shook his head, wishing he could ease his bitterness. Etoudoori's presence sometimes soothed his pain, but lately he had seen far too little of her . . .

His musings were disturbed by Raz's voice. "Newborn, they ask me to challenge you," said the warrior with a faint smile. He held out the box while the others looked on eagerly.

Unwilling to offend these warriors, who seemed to bear him no ill will, the Hakhan shrugged. A game would pass the time. "You go first," he suggested.

"Gladly." Raz rattled the box, then shook out the pieces, all smudged and grimy, onto the horsehide that lay before him. Yarkol paid scant attention as the nomad arranged and rearranged the tokens into pairs. Suddenly the Hakhan noticed Raz frowning, for a bad omen— Drought's withered stalk of grass—stood alone. Beyond that, Yarkol could not interpret the results. "Your turn, southerner," the warrior sighed.

The Hakhan nodded, collected the pieces and returned them to the box. Why this game fascinated Chirudaks he had yet to understand. Shamans disapproved of it, perhaps because its use diminished their special role in divination. Nonetheless, even the humblest nomad possessed a shoy set. And this one, Yarkol thought, as he shook the box, was the poorest he had seen. The bone slabs clattered against their shabby container so noisily that he feared the thin wood might split. Hastily he let the pieces drop in a long line that crossed the hide.

At once the guards bent over to study the results. No one, he realized, was watching the door. He might escape now, dash out into the snowstorm, see how far he could run before riders caught him. He smiled sadly at the foolish notion.

Raz took charge of interpreting the toss. Yarkol recalled his first experience with this game, when he had come up even with the fates while fat Baatibi's future had looked woeful. At that memory he stiffened, for he had almost forgotten Etou's companion. Baatibi had seemingly vanished on his way north, so perhaps the bones correctly foretold his demise.

"Look, Newborn." Raz showed him the reckoning. Yarkol leaned forward, no longer certain he could dismiss this practice. He felt a chill as he realized that his balance had fallen to the negative side, worse than what Raz had drawn. "That is the Imp," said the scarred one, pointing to a piece that stood by itself. Yarkol could see the hint of a laughing mouth in the lines scratched on its surface. "And that is the Wounded Warrior. Those are the tokens that follow you."

Raz, having come out with better prospects, went to rummage through his saddlebags for a suitable forfeit. "Here, Newborn," he said, offering a thick animal tooth, a molar that had been pierced and strung on a tether. "Wear this for luck. It comes from a chief's stallion."

"In old age, you can grind it up," said one youth, laughing. "It'll help you with your wives."

The others joined the merriment, but Raz quickly cuffed the outspoken one. "Brain of a sheep!" he shouted. The young men grew sober and exchanged glances with one another. They knew, evidently, that Yarkol was beyond such help. *What must they think of the Kag?* Surely no one was fooled by the number of women surrounding him.

"I thank you for the gift," said the Hakhan, pretending he hadn't heard the last remark. He knotted the tether in a loop and slipped the talisman into his shirt. But his eyes stung as the guards' laughter echoed in memory.

Later he had a revenge of sorts, when all but the man on watch were preparing for sleep. Etoudoori arrived, evoking stares of interest from every side. She took off her fur cap, letting her braids fall free. Then, saying nothing, she lay down beside Yarkol and shared his cover. "Oron is suspicious," she whispered, her warm breath moist against his ear. "He found our tracks at the Jornood campsite. But the shaman used horsehide shoes to disguise his mount's prints. He says Oron won't recognize them. I hope he's right."

"I have a charm," said Yarkol, retreating from the new problems that Etou had raised. He showed her his prize. "A tooth from a chief's mount. If I grind it up and swallow it all, do you think it will help me?"

She laughed and threw her arms around him.

The next morning, Dzaminid woke to find himself alone in the yurt of his host—Shaman Sagond of Mossbend tribe. He heard faint animal bleatings and sensed the strivings of many busy human souls. Daylight diffused through the smokehole, brightening the red lines of the roof poles, reaching down to touch feathered staffs and ornate spirit drums. Why, he wondered, had he slept so late?

The events of the previous night came back to him. The young shaman had invited him to share his quarters. Here, attended by Sagond's sisters—for he had no wife—they had feasted and talked far past midnight. Among the

196

delicacies that the Mossbends had pressed on him was a preserved duck egg, highly seasoned. Dzaminid suspected that a soporific had been added, its taste masked by spices. Even now he felt a lingering grogginess.

He pulled aside the doorflap, a piece of white felt decorated on both sides. The sunlight, reflecting from new snow, dazzled him. Squinting into the glare, he turned for relief toward the waters of the lake. Closer to shore the drifts had already melted, exposing mud and brown stubble; on the far side he saw sheep grazing with their tails to the wind. He stepped outside, stretched, inhaled the crisp air.

Then he heard a rider and turned to watch Sagond's hurried approach. The spirit of the young shaman carried a dark aura that puzzled his guest. Dzaminid greeted Sagond politely, all the while seeking to probe his thoughts. The Mossbend's beard was a thin curl on his cheeks, his moustache a smudge above his lips. Though his youthful face showed a smile, it was not one of friendship.

"Our tribe has its share of troubles this morning," Sagond said. "A difficult birth in one yurt, a man with the coughing sickness in another."

Dzaminid nodded in sympathy. Mossbend had only one shaman since the death of Sagond's mentor, and the young man sometimes could not provide for all his tribe's needs. As a guest who had accepted hospitality, the Kag's shaman was obliged to offer assistance.

Sagond accepted at once. "The mother is a kinswoman, so I must go to her. The sick man will be glad to receive your aid."

The older shaman nodded. Deceit lay behind this, he sensed, but its nature and purpose eluded him. He would do as he was asked for now, until he uncovered Sagond's intent.

Soon he was arrayed in his full ceremonial garb,

197

carrying his healer's bundle and staff as he followed Sagond along the shore. Odd, he thought, that his leg should trouble him today when the air was so clear. Dzaminid was limping noticeably by the time he reached his destination.

Asleep in his bed, the sick man was coughing badly. Dzaminid touched his cheek, his temple, his throat. On the far side of the yurt two women and a child sat watching, their faces dark with concern. "I leave my tribesman in your care," said Sagond, who made a hasty exit.

Dzaminid frowned as studied his patient. He sensed an evil thing in this man's lungs. But to draw it out, he saw, would prove no easy task. The problem should have been caught earlier, when a simple chant would have served.

The shaman turned to the wives, who were trembling, and spoke in a reassuring tone. "I am not so fearsome as I look," he said. "But you'll be better off staying elsewhere. Do one thing for me before you leave. Boil a big pot of water to fill the air with steam."

The boneman sat cross-legged before the victim and opened his healer's bundle. The sick man's face was slick with sweat; his lips were covered with spittle. When he coughed, his whole body heaved from the effort, each spasm weaker than the last, until the sound from his throat resembled a death rattle. The dark thing within him already had a grip on his soul. In a day or so, unless help came, that soul would be paying its respects to the gods.

As the shaman became engrossed in sorting through his talismans, a troubling thought intruded. This evening, after discussions with the tribal chiefs, Nurtaj planned to call the Hakhan for questioning. Dzaminid had intended to preside over the interview, for he did not wish Yarkol to face the chiefs alone. Yet the shaman could not abandon his duty; he must finish here before the meeting with Yarkol began.

From the bearhide sack he took three objects: a snake's rattle, a dried up embryo of a wolf cub, and a thin black cone from the sacred god-pine that grows at the foot of the Mount-of-Mounts. The pine cone he slipped under the sick man's heavy shirt, placing it at the center of his chest. The embryo he lay at the man's feet. He touched the rattle to the pale lips and whispered the start of a chant. This was but a simple conjuration, a warning to the offending demon that worse was to come.

After a time Dzaminid felt the air grow thick with steam from the cauldron. The women had set the pot boiling, then left him to finish his task alone. Raising his voice, he brought the chant to its strident conclusion.

Had he made any progress? Probing with his mind, he recognized that the dark thing clutching this hapless soul had not loosened its grip. He felt it hunkering within, preparing to withstand a stronger siege.

The boneman took a strip of beaten copper and wrapped it around the sick man's right ankle. On this strip he had incised, under Mother Moon's full light, the symbols from an ancient carving. For the patient's left wrist Dzaminid chose a narrow strip of gold. Only a single figure decorated the piece, but one so powerful that ordinary eyes must not see it. About the left ankle he tied the preserved navel cord of a chief. And the right wrist he encircled with twisted web from the deadliest of spiders.

Dzaminid began to dance, spinning around and around, scarcely noticing the pain that throbbed in his leg. His voice carried a new chant, far more powerful than the first. Each time he shook his rattle he felt the enemy stir, extending cautious feelers one way and then another. The dark thing seemed to sense the charms that surrounded it, for it retreated into itself. One escape route was left— out through the victim's mouth—but the demon did not move in that direction.

At last the boneman tumbled to the floor. He could no

longer feel his material body. Though he remained within the confines of his flesh, his spirit grew long arms that emerged from his temples and reached toward the troubled soul. The demon, like a tick half-buried in its prey, tightened its grip.

Dzaminid's spirit hands reached closer. Suddenly he lunged, grasping the shapeless thing, squeezing it with all his strength. What sort of creature was this that neither struggled nor weakened under his attack? He wrenched one way and another, unable to loosen it from the sick man's soul.

The demon hung on as a tick would even after its body had been broiled by a hot iron. Dzaminid now recognized the difficulty of his task and began to doubt that he could handle the problem on his own. He called to the spirits of the yurt for aid, but none seemed to hear him. To the hearth-sprite cowering in the coals—a creature invisible to his eyes but whose presence he felt strongly—he spoke in an angry voice. "Have they skimped on your ration of fat?" he asked. "Think how much poorer you'll be if this man dies." The creature remained silent, and the shaman thought enviously of Yarkol's abilities with sprites.

Knowing he had only his own strengths for this task, Dzaminid considered his experiences as a healer. He had lost battles with bringers of illness, usually because he reached the victim too late. But until this man expired, hope of a cure remained. He resolved to withdraw from the struggle awhile and to meditate on the teachings of the wise.

But he found that he could not relax his grip. His spirit hands clutched the strange creature, and he could not pull them free. Now the shaman understood that sorcery had been used against him. No ordinary demon infected the sick man's soul. Sagond had conjured a foul thing and planted it here to trap him.

Dzaminid knew only one explanation for this outrage. The Kag had influenced the young shaman, gaining his collusion in sorcery. The purpose was surely to keep Dzaminid away from the Hakhan's questioning . . .

Time passed, and the shaman remained in trance. He tested his enemy, but with every attempt at breaking free he merely weakened himself further. Through his spirit eyes he saw movements in the light that poured down the smokehole and crossed the yurt's rugs. Dusk was approaching, and the man's illness was growing worse.

Dzaminid contemplated the dark thing, which to him was the embodiment of death. One could not exhort or cajole such a being. It possessed no intellect, only the fierce will to survive by destroying others.

The shaman's thoughts raced back over all he knew, dwelling on the lessons in his mentor's yurt. Tomuuk had mentioned such spiritual vermin, rare as they were, but had offered no suggestions for combating them. "Be wary in strange places," the old one had warned. But today his pupil had forgotten that advice.

Was there nothing he could do but wait for Sagond to release him? Dzaminid had not quite used up the ability to alter his spirit form. Just as he had grown arms to grapple with the beast, he might try one more projection. If the creature represented death, then he must counter it with life.

As soon as he started the change, he felt the dark thing shudder. From the shaman's groin sprouted a phallus such as no woman had ever taken into her loins. Stout as a young tree it grew, its sides sleek, its head throbbing. It arched aross the room to where the beast lay.

Here was the bringer of new life, come to undo the destroyer. But the dark thing did not wait to suffer the shaman's touch. Without warning it released Dzaminid, flung him backward so fiercely that his fleshly body rolled

201

toward the burnt-out fire. At once he broke from his trance and crawled from the yurt.

Outside, the sun was almost gone. Dzaminid shouted to the waiting wives, told them to bring a torch, a cur, a pinch of salt. Then he stood up and moved warily away from the yurt. Sagond's beast was dangerous—perhaps more so than the youthful sorcerer had imagined.

The trembling women returned almost at once. He grabbed the small dog under one arm, took the salt in the other hand. "Follow me," he said to the one holding the torch.

He sprinkled the sick man's lips, then dropped the cur onto his chest. At once the animal began to lick the husband's mouth. With a single motion, Dzaminid pulled the man's garment away to expose his belly. Then he shoved the torch's flame against naked flesh.

The screams came from the women; the man had lost consciousness. Dzaminid grabbed the cur by the nape and tossed it out into the snow. A moment later a piteous yelping cleaved the air, but the shaman stood by the doorway and would not let the women peer outside. The dark thing, startled by the man's sudden pain, had fled by its only exit and lodged within the animal. The dog's soul was no match for this destroyer. In an instant the demon finished its work and returned to its home within the earth.

The shaman carried firewood outside and lit a blaze from the torch. When the flames were high, he tossed on the cur's mangled body. Then he rejoined the women beside their husband, the man now cured of his cough. The tribesman lay quietly, his breathing steady, his fever gone. His burns were not severe; the flames had only touched him for a moment. Dzaminid smeared on ointment, packed his talismans, and staggered out into the night.

"Let me borrow a mount," he called to the wives, as he realized how far he must travel. He still had time, he thought, to ride around the lake and confront Sagond. But the ground felt unsteady, and he recalled that he had not eaten since the previous night. "A horse," he begged again.

Taking a step back toward the doorway, he lost his balance. He swung out an arm but could not keep from toppling. The ground came up. He felt a thin, cold layer of snow against his face . . .

Etoudoori had spent the morning with a kinswoman, a grandmother now, who had long ago married into Whitemane tribe. In the afternoon, unaware of Dzaminid's predicament, Etou went riding, circling the lake. The brown grass was damp where the snow had melted, and the herd animals had crowded onto this narrow strip. She bypassed the sheep, crossing lingering drifts.

For a while she watched a group of men at the shore pull in a broad fishing net. The men shouted in high-pitched voices while the captured fish glimmered in sunlight. This was as fine a winter camp as she had ever seen, with ample food and water and good shelter on all sides; she envied the people who lived here.

But her own lot, she had discovered long ago, was to be a wanderer. In that respect she was like Yarkol, doomed never to have a home. Yet it pleased her to imagine that the gods might release him and allow him to be an ordinary man again. If that should happen, perhaps she also might find release; the thought made her sigh. She turned to the southern edge of the lake, where the horses were grazing.

"Are you looking for fleas again?"

The voice surprised her. She had not seen Guzad since leaving Bloodcreek camp. Now she eyed him with interest as he approached on his bay, for she had hoped she might find him vulnerable here, away from the scrutiny of his wives. "I'd like to let my mare graze with the others," she said, trying to explain her presence near the pasture. "But I don't want more trouble."

He gave an ugly laugh, light dancing on his broad face. "Maybe she's just not welcome." His mount began nuzzling snow to reach the grass beneath.

"I suppose you also find me unwelcome." She tossed her head and gazed past him to the boisterous fishermen.

"I don't know what you're doing in this camp. You're not in the Kag's party, yet you travel with us."

"Ask Oron why he took me south. Certainly not to warm his blanket."

"Oron and I have never agreed on much."

She pretended to ignore his hint. "Do you want to know why I'm here? Because I guided the Hakhan in his moment of need. When the gods called him, I helped him find his way. He's my charge now, just as your brother's fate is tied up with his shaman."

"So you intend to follow your soil-tiller?" Guzad spat to the side. "I'm obliged to travel with Nurtaj for other reasons. But it's a hardship to be away from home."

Etou felt a cold smile form on her lips. "You were in the south for some time and returned looking no worse for it."

"Weedchewer women are like their soups. Satisfying— for a short while. Not very nourishing."

"And what of the tales those women whispered to you? Did they also lack substance?"

His eyes narrowed. "I speak of one thing, you another."

"Or perhaps we share a common interest."

The Kag's brother turned, his chin raised, his eyes seeming to sweep the circular valley. To the south rose low hills; in all other directions high cliffs walled in the plain. "Ride with me," he said bluntly, nodding toward the hills. "Then we'll see what we have to talk about."

They discovered a trail at the far end of the valley and

followed it up to a secluded spot surrounded by high rocks. Here the snow was gone, the sunlight warm, the dry, dead grass thick. Guzad dismounted and lay on his back with his face to the sky.

"I have something for you," said Etou, still astride her roan. She opened a saddle pouch and brought out a long cheroot. *Dzaminid's gift.* Its vapors would make Guzad speak.

"Are we to build a cookfire?" he asked with a laugh. "So I can smoke after the meal."

"This is no ordinary smoke," she retorted. "It will double your enjoyment of being a man."

"Now I understand why they talk about you." He reached up for her gift, held it to his nose and sniffed curiously. Then, with a snort, he tossed the cheroot over his shoulder to land in a tangle of thorns. "I need no sorcerer's tricks," he said angrily. "And I'm not so stupid as to think you came here for pleasure. What do you want from me?"

She could not meet his gaze. What point, she asked herself, in further coyness? "I only wish to hear your news from the south," she confessed in a quiet voice.

"Ha. Now this begins to make sense. You're looking after your soil-tiller again."

"I need to know the truth. Exactly what you learned."

"I've told it already. To repeat it is a waste of breath." He paused with a sneer on his lips. "Even so, a man sometimes can be cajoled."

"I am listening," she said in a tone of impatience. "Afterwards, you'll have your reward."

Guzad grinned but narrowed his eyes. "How do I know you won't run off?"

Etou frowned. "Here. Take this as my pledge." She pulled from about her neck the sachet of rare pollens, from which she made offerings to the spirits, and flung it past him. Guzad retrieved the leather pouch and opened

205

it carefully, pouring out a few grains into his grimy palm. He rubbed the pollen into the sweat of his face and laughed.

"I am listening," she prompted.

The Kag's brother lay back, put his hands behind his head, closed his eyes. "There's little to tell. Don't complain that it's not enough for you. I was traveling with my uncle by the edge of the Throats. You know what we were seeking."

"I was there too. I might have passed you on the road."

"I'd never have mistaken you for a weedchewer. No, I didn't see you there. But after too many days in the saddle, my uncle and I fell in with a Hakhan, a laborer who'd been working on the Dolmi Path. He liked wine, and we had a good skin of it. We spent half the night filling him with grape."

"And what did he tell you?"

"That the work was done, the great Path open to the east. He boasted of his part in it. Don't tell me that surprises you."

"You believed the drunken lout? The word of one soil-tiller?"

"We asked him to swear. We held his hand over the fire and made him repeat what he'd said."

"And? What were his words?"

"Come down and I'll tell you."

"First let me see what I have waiting for me."

Guzad laughed and loosened his trousers.

"Are you ashamed to show yourself, brother-of-the-Kag?"

He undid the lacings, sat with his bottom bare, his stiff member pointing at the sky. "Did the man swear on the Great Horse?" she insisted.

Guzad drew his knees together. "He passed out first. We left him there."

"*Left* him? And with no oath? A drunken soil-tiller's word is enough to sway the Kag?"

Guzad shrugged. "I reported my news and how I got it. I've no control over my brother's moves. But enough talk. I've done my part." He picked up the sachet and tossed it from hand to hand. "Come down now, before the air turns cold." He squinted at the lowered sun. "Hurry. Otherwise, I'll pour this out."

"It is cold already," she shouted, turning her mare sharply and plunging across the clearing. "Wait 'til summer. Then maybe I'll oblige you!" All the way back his parting insults echoed in her ears.

13

A shaman's drum knows many tales.
—*Chirudak saying*

Flanked by several guards, Yarkol stood inside the large yurt's doorway and watched the men who would question him. Seated by the hearth he saw only one shaman—Sagond, whose youthful, brooding face offered no comfort. Where was Dzaminid? Yarkol wondered. Why was this meeting proceeding without him?

The Kag and three tribal chiefs talked among themselves for some time, and the Hakhan thought they might be waiting for Dzaminid to appear. But at last young Sagond stood up and strode toward Yarkol. The mystic was dressed in the traditional peaked cap and bone-robe, with many talismans of bone or fur or copper dangling from his clothing. The sight of his drum, with its skin covered by arcane symbols, made Yarkol shiver.

The guards moved away, leaving the Hakhan alone with Sagond. "Listen to my song," chanted the shaman. He began to circle the captive, drumming softly as he sang. His body writhed, twisting so abruptly that the Hakhan thought his joints must break. His legs jerked one way, his torso another, and then reversed. The sight made Yarkol dizzy.

As the chant continued, its insistent rhythm seemed to be affecting Yarkol's thoughts. He wanted to shut his eyes and block his ears, but he could not force his muscles to obey. The dancer's image blurred, and his melody became a steady drone. Then, suddenly, distinct words whispered within the Hakhan's ear. He heard phrases clearly from a disembodied voice, yet failed to grasp their meanings.

Meekly, he allowed himself to be led toward the hearth. Sagond pushed him down to sit on the floor, then began asking questions. At once, Yarkol realized that something within him was not right. He felt a barrier that held back certain thoughts while letting others flow.

Sagond began with simple queries about Yarkol's home and past life. He answered freely, unable to consider deceit. "What drives the men of Dolmi?" the shaman asked. Yarkol responded by telling of worn-out lands, of diseases attacking the crops, of towns nervously dependent on the harvests.

Hakhan woes interested the shaman only briefly. "Describe the Path, with all its turnings," Sagond demanded, and Yarkol at once began to speak. He told of Boiled-Meat Spring and Kobold Lake, of the Pinched Worm and the Bridge of Summer. He warned about Hot Pan Clearing and the Spouting Baths. But when his account touched Rya Basin, he found himself out of words.

"Is that the end?" Sagond asked.

Yarkol could only nod agreement. He had more to tell, but certain thoughts lay just beyond reach. The shaman had blocked him from saying all he knew.

The chiefs appeared impressed by Yarkol's answers, and for a time their conversation passed to other topics. He wondered if they were still waiting for Dzaminid before ending the interrogation. Remaining by the fire, the Hakhan raged within, convinced that Sagond had cheated him. Yarkol had told no untruths, yet he'd omitted something of great import, something that even now he could not recall.

Staring into the coals, he saw a small figure reclining on a hearthstone. The sprite beckoned with a fiery hand, its tiny face grinning, its ears aglow. At that moment Yarkol saw the imp as a possible ally.

Sagond and the chiefs continued talking, paying him no heed. Though the Hakhan's thoughts had been tampered with, he still recalled how to slip from his body. He focused his eyes on one yellow flame, controlled his breathing into a steady rhythm, felt himself flowing out. He took a single step toward the imp and realized that he'd already broken Sagond's spell.

Now he remembered the crucial message he carried. The image of Rya Basin, with its treacherous, thin crust and yellow fumes, stood vividly before him. He must describe the dangers that awaited anyone who attempted the crossing.

Ignoring the sprite for now, he hastened back into his body, bent forward to speak, and felt dumbfounded. The urgent message was gone! The shaman's spell still lay on his flesh and he could not get by it.

He grew so angry that he had difficulty breaking loose

again. Soon, he knew, the guards would come for him and his chance to speak would be lost. He forced himself into regular breathing, a slow and deep rhythm. Sagond lay in his thoughts, and only with great will could he push that cold face aside. The air smelled of burnt meat and incense and sweat—more distractions. At last Yarkol felt his spirit slipping its bonds.

"You should have stayed with me," said the hearth-sprite from its seat amid the coals.

"Going back did me no good," Yarkol replied angrily. "Now I must find a way to get clear of that sorcerer."

"He is tricky."

"Even so, I am not helpless." The Hakhan thought he might startle Sagond, throw him off balance. A blow to the boneman's confidence might weaken his sorcerous grip. Surveying the area, Yarkol discovered the shaman's drum hanging from a roof pole. He crossed the floor cautiously, looking back once at his own rigid body beside the hearth.

If he could budge a door flap, then why not make sounds on the drumhead? But he hesitated when he saw the figures drawn on the skin—squares and zigzags and long serpentine figures. Such markings had decorated the underground shrine of long ago.

Time was running short. Yarkol forced back the old memory and began to tap on the drum with his bone fingers. An eerie sound emerged, at once causing everyone to turn. Seeing the surprised faces, the Hakhan struck harder, wishing he could knock the instrument to the ground.

Sagond reacted mildly. "A harmless ghost," he said, laughing. "Someone must oblige it by conceiving a child." The other men glanced at each other with raised eyebrows while Sagond took down the drum and put a heavy cushion across its face. Yarkol pushed and squeezed, but

211

could neither budge the cushion nor make any more sounds on the membrane.

"What have we here?" asked the shaman, as he returned to the fire and stood before Yarkol's motionless form. "Now I understand. He thinks he has escaped us. A childish mistake."

The spirit-Yarkol hastened back toward his body, but did not reenter it. He was free for now, safe from whatever spells were applied to his flesh. If he could find some other ruse . . . He turned and saw the hearth-sprite grinning. "Can you do anything for me?" the Hakhan asked in desperation.

"I have a few tricks of my own. Perhaps a deal—"

"Yes?" Yarkol had never felt so willing to listen to an imp.

"You may choose the game and rules, I the stakes."

"Let me hear the stakes." The Dolmi was trying to watch both sprite and shaman at once. Sagond was removing something from a pouch.

"First, as a token of faith," said the imp, "I'll set the shaman's braids and robe on fire. That will frighten everyone away, and we can have our contest in peace."

Sagond held up a bulky, black talisman, seemingly made of skins fitted to a frame. Yarkol could not imagine its purpose. "The stakes?" he asked insistently.

"If you win, I am yours to command until morning. If you lose, then you go with my friends to meet the Small One, our chief."

"How far to this chief? What does he want of me?"

"Less than half a night's journey will bring you to his hall. The Small One wishes merely to have a talk with you. But you must leave before dawn, and I advise you take your body of flesh."

"My body is not free. Also, I've matters to settle here. The chiefs must hear me out—"

"I can help you escape. And I promise that you'll return to the Kag when you're done. But why fear losing when I offer you such an advantage?"

The Dolmi did not answer. He watched with alarm as Sagond began to wave the talisman before his body's lifeless face. Something was drawing him back to his flesh; he felt a huge hand clutching him, dragging him across the floor. Once he was imprisoned again, the sorcerer could do what he wished . . . "I agree!" Yarkol shouted, though he was not certain he understood the bargain. The part about choosing the game sounded fair.

At once the imp jumped up and began to dance on the shaman's head. Sagond's cap burst into flame. His braids began to sizzle. The shaman stood firm and spoke words that made the imp tremble, but the blaze remained lit. He spoke again, this time sending the hearth-sprite tumbling across the room. But the sorcerer's words did not damp the fires. With a yelp Sagond turned, streaming smoke and ash, and raced from the yurt. The lake was close, Yarkol recalled ruefully. Soon he heard a splash.

Meanwhile, the guards had fled; the chiefs could not leave the yurt quickly enough. Only the Kag remained, staring with a puzzled look at Yarkol's rigid body. Then he too abandoned the yurt.

"Now we can begin," the sprite said with glee. Yarkol's delight in the victory was quickly fading. He was safe now, but soon the Kag would find new guards to watch over him. "Tell me your game and rules," the sprite insisted.

"Give me a moment to think." Suddenly Yarkol recalled a contest he could not lose, a game that his children played with unwary friends. "Here are the rules," Yarkol said, concealing his confidence. "This won't take long. We each name in turn one of the Great Horse's foals. Whoever speaks last is the winner. And I'll go first."

The hob sat on the hearthstone, its beard and eyebrows aglow, its feet twitching in a dance. "The foals . . . A good choice, Ulaansh. I am listening. Please begin."

"Blackmane," said Yarkol. He had a momentary fear that he might forget one of the seven stars in the familiar cluster—seven foals trailing the Great Horse. But no, he knew them as well the names of the seasons.

"Windeater," replied the imp.

"Spanglehide."

"Redjaw."

Seven foals. By starting first, the Hakhan would name the last one as well. When his final turn came, he calmly finished the sequence.

"Windeater," said the sprite.

"You used that one already. There are no more."

"I spoke last," the imp pointed out.

"But the rules—"

"Where were they broken?" Fiery eyebrows waggled.

Yarkol's thoughts raced back. *We each name in turn* . . . It was understood that names were not repeated, yet he had not explained the rules precisely. *Whoever speaks last is the winner.* "Then I'll continue," he replied angrily, and repeated another foal's name.

The imp responded in kind. Clearly the game would not end until exhaustion forced one or the other to quit.

"Sagond is coming back from his bath," warned the sprite. "And you're still here."

Now Yarkol knew he had lost. He fumed at the trickery, but could blame no one but himself. Even so, he still might obtain a concession. "Keep Sagond and the guards away from me for the entire night," he offered, "and I'll give you the victory."

"Done," said the sprite, who then named one last star. Yarkol rejoined his body and found, to his relief, that his thoughts remained his own; the sorcerous spell was gone.

As he hurried from the yurt into the night's chill, he saw
Sagond's distant figure running clumsily away along the
shore. That sight alone made Yarkol's defeat seem worth-
while.

"Newborn?"

"Etou!" He turned in astonishment to see her ride out
from beneath a shadow.

"Dzaminid's vanished," she said in a troubled voice.
"Something has happened to him. He should have been
here with the others."

"He might have helped me. Now I must pay a debt. I'm
obliged to leave here tonight."

"But I must find him. I've talked to Guzad—"

"Can you locate my mount?" Recalling his agreement
with the sprite, Yarkol glanced at the sky and estimated
the time before dawn. "I may have a way to help you.
Find my mare and come to the yurt where we slept." She
nodded and quickly rode off.

Yarkol followed the shoreline away from where Sagond
had gone. Looking about for signs of pursuit, he found
none. Even so, he wondered if he should trust the sprite's
promise. The guards, anticipating Yarkol's moves, might
be waiting for him where he had left his tack.

When he reached the dwelling, he circled to the rear
and sat cross-legged where he would not be seen. Leaving
his body, he crept in spirit form to the doorway and
squeezed past the flap. The guards hadn't returned; the
embers from their cookfire still glowed faintly.

"Ulaansh!" A familiar voice.

He heard the imp but could not see it. "You can do
something else for me," Yarkol suggested as he neared
the hearth. "If you want me to leave soon, find Dzaminid
the shaman."

"We have an agreement," the sprite reminded him.

"There is time," Yarkol countered, now glimpsing the

215

small figure astride the coals. Hobs seemed to shrink and expand at will; this tiny being he recognized as the one he'd just dealt with. "I'm in no hurry. You promised to protect me until morning."

"But the other task was not in our bargain."

"Then I'll wait. Until just before first light. Then I'll see which imp leads me to your Small One." As the sun rose, his guide would be forced to leap from shadow to shadow and finally to take refuge within a cave or hollow log.

The sprite jumped from the embers and danced maliciously on the nearest scrap of horsehide. Dark smoke rose. "If you burn my tack, I can't ride," the Dolmi said. The hob shrieked and plunged back between the hearthstones; in a moment it was gone. Tunnels must connect one fire to another, Yarkol realized. If Dzaminid was near a hearth, then the imp would find him quickly.

Yarkol turned to the smoking skin and dragged it with skeletal fingers toward the doorway. The hanging flap felt wooden to him, yet he thrust what force he had against it. He pushed past, dropped the singed hide in the snow, then hurried back to his body.

In a few moments Yarkol returned to the yurt and used muscles of flesh to carry the saddle and the rest outside. Overhead, the Wolfpack chased the Great Horse across the sky. But Etou had not returned. He heard a voice and went back to the hearth, where the sprite stood waiting for him.

"Go to the yurts of the Mossbends," the imp told him in a surly voice. "Look up at the smoke holes. I'll dance on the one you want." The Hakhan nodded and hurried out again. He was not sure where he was headed, but Etou would know.

Where had the woman gone? At any moment someone might come looking for him. He envied the sprite with its ability to travel quickly or to shrink itself small enough to fit into a tiny hole. Glancing at the sky, he thought about the oncoming dawn.

Then he heard two horses, their steps falling softly on snow-covered ground. "Etou!" She had used a neck rope to lead his animal, he saw. In a moment she was beside him, helping with cheekstrap and bit. The saddle seemed to fly into place. "To the Mossbend camp," he whispered. His mount sprang forward eagerly as Etou led him along rows of quiet dwellings.

Scanning the tops of the yurts, Yarkol spotted one capped by a dancing flame. "That way," he whispered. They halted, and he approached the doorway. Cautiously, he lifted the flap and peered in. He heard slow breathing; everyone was asleep. And the sprite was standing in the hearth, pointing its long finger.

Yarkol slipped inside to the figure that lay beside the embers. The light was dim, but he made out the shaman's cap and robe. "Dzaminid!" he called softly. He shook the man's shoulders and heard an answering groan.

"Throw water on him," suggested the sprite.

Yarkol saw no bucket but the imp stretched its arm out from the fire until the Hakhan noticed a small leather pail near the wall. Stepping carefully over sleepers, he poured a little of the contents onto Dzaminid's face. Another groan.

"Shaman!" Yarkol hissed. The robed figure stirred and slowly sat up. "I waited for you."

"I could not come, Newborn." Dzaminid crawled to the door and staggered out into moonlight. Etou jumped down to help him, and Yarkol was just behind. "Sagond trapped me," he said weakly. "But you have escaped. A good sign."

"I must go," Yarkol said. "I've a bargain to keep with a

217

sprite. But my imp friend has given Sagond repayment in kind."

Dzaminid shook his head sadly. "A man such as Sagond, who betrays his people, has far worse coming."

"Will you stay here?" the Hakhan asked.

"My place is with the Kag. Even now, when he sends sorcerers to waylay me, I must remain."

"I've something to finish here as well. The chiefs have not heard the last from me."

Dzaminid nodded. "I did not think you would desert us." Then, as if sensing Etou's impatience to speak, he turned to her with a quizzical stare.

"I had some luck with Guzad," she said quickly. "He told me the source of his news from the south. It came from a single soil-tiller, and that one full of wine."

Dzaminid sighed. "I expected as much. But Nurtaj is more than willing to believe a tale that pleases him."

"Is there nothing you can do?"

The shaman gave a weak smile. "Guzad thinks no one will dare doubt his story. I must try to prove him wrong." He put his hand on Etou's shoulder. "You have done well, She-who-shatters. And now your duty is to stay with the newborn. Help him follow his instincts. See where they lead."

"May the Great Horse watch over you!" She embraced the shaman, and when she turned away, Yarkol saw a glimmer of tears on her cheek. Hurriedly she mounted and began to ride.

Yarkol took the lead as they galloped across the snowy plain. Ahead pranced a small figure, an imp he did not recognize, its short legs carrying it in huge bounds as quickly as the horses could follow. They reached the valley's end and began to climb a trail that showed faintly in moonlight. Near the top they rounded a rockfall, then passed a line of leafless bushes. The Dolmi heard running water, a creek descending into a cleft. And then he heard a roar that set his hairs on end.

An albino bear stood blocking the trail above, its head huge, it's lips drawn back to show curved, glimmering fangs. The horses seemed not to notice the creature, and Yarkol heard no shout of surprise from Etou. But the sprite trotted up to the Kag's spirit-form and waved a small fist at its head. The bear growled in answer. Yarkol thought he heard words exchanged between the two.

The Hakhan realized that he was the only one Nurtaj wanted. "Ride on without me," he told Etou sharply. "Go a short way and stop. Don't ask questions." She stiffened, but said nothing. A moment later she passed through the bear as if it were a puff of dust.

The beast came no closer. It was waiting, Yarkol realized, not for his fleshly form but for the spirit that lay within. The Hakhan halted, stepped down onto the muddy trail, secured the mare. He saw that his guide had come back. The tiny bright figure stood beside his boots, its hands on its hips in a belligerent pose. "I'll have to fight him," the Hakhan said firmly. "I know that now. It's the reason my dreams called me northward."

"But the Small One is waiting."

"And he'll wait awhile longer." Yarkol had not asked what would happen if he failed to keep his pledge. But if the Kag destroyed him, then what would it matter?

"I'll face him," he said firmly. "Don't distract me from what I must do. Watch over Etou, if you want to be useful, and take care of my mount." He sat atop a fallen tree trunk, closed his eyes and began his deep breathing. The sprite continued to protest, until Yarkol shouted in anguish: "Tell me how to rid myself of this bear!" When the imp did not answer, Yarkol resumed his exercise.

At last the Hakhan had silence. He focused on the inrush and outflow of breath until, for a moment, he was

219

alone in the space of the world. Then he eased from his flesh and saw his ribs shimmering in moonlight. The bear's red eyes glinted harshly. With a roar of defiance, it loped toward him from the top of the rise.

The spirit-beast possessed teeth and claws, but Yarkol had no weapon. A bark-covered stick lay on the ground; he knew how heavy such a thing would feel to him now. Kneeling, he grasped the makeshift club in two hands, straining as a man would in lifting a weighty branch. The bear was almost on him . . .

Yarkol dodged and swung his weapon, felt a satisfying shock of contact with the creature's head. The Kag's spirit form hurtled past him, but when it spun around it seemed unhurt.

The Hakhan's anger exploded in words. "You are more stubborn than a hundred billygoats," he shouted. "Guzad reports a boastful lie, and you risk your entire people."

The beast snarled an answer. From deep within its throat came sounds that were nearly human. "The east will be mine, soil-tiller." Then the creature rose on its shaggy hindlegs.

Yarkol dropped the useless club, retreated a dozen steps, and reached for a sharp stone the size of his fist. *Too heavy.* As he struggled to lift the dense object, he felt the bones of his spirit hand flowing around it. The bear was almost on him. He rolled aside, felt one leg dangling in midair. Turning hastily, he realized that he lay at the edge of a ravine. What if he could throw Nurtaj into the depths?

But before he could plan, the bear fell on top of him, began to chew and claw at his bones. He felt no pain, only sensations of being squeezed and stretched. Yet he could not get free of the frenzied animal. The two rolled one way and then another while Yarkol tried to beat back the huge paws.

One of his old dreams flashed before him. He and the Kag were wrestling at the edge of a precipice. The nightmare's setting had differed from this one, but none of Yarkol's visions ever quite matched real events.

Now the heavy jaws were mauling his rib cage, trying, he suspected, to reach the fluttering shape within. Yarkol grew alarmed, for he did not know what would happen if the beast succeeded. He made a desperate lunge, breaking free and scrambling aside, but realized that he had misjudged the distance. His legs slid over the cliff's edge, and when he reached out to catch himself, the bear leaned over to knock his hand away. The Kag too lost his balance . . .

At that moment Yarkol remembered the end of the dream—both men plummeting. And now rock walls rushed past him in a blur. The Hakhan flailed at a few passing shrubs but could not slow his descent.

They landed with a concussion that seemed to flatten Yarkol for a moment. This time he felt pain, a node of fire in the small of his back. The Kag appeared stunned, lying motionless in shallow water while Yarkol pulled himself to his feet. As soon as he rose, the pain vanished.

Turning, Yarkol knelt in the shallow pool where he had fallen. A rough, pitted stone underwater glowed red-orange like heated metal. It was hot to the touch! Then he recalled the knife he'd used to probe a water-sprite's den. His skeletal fingers had been seared by the mere touch of its handle. And the stone he had just found evidently contained iron.

The bear was stirring. Yarkol did not know how to attack it with the ironstone without equally harming himself. He tried lifting the pebble gingerly between two fingers and cried out from pain. The creature roared and swung its huge forepaw.

Yarkol sprawled headlong, dropping the stone as he

221

fell. The bear may have been dazed briefly, but now its strength seemed doubled. Its spirit body was stronger than his, more rigid. The Hakhan felt its paws fiercely pushing his ribs aside. It was breaking through!

He flailed in the water, but could not loosen the bear's grip. Then, once more, he felt a nodule of fire beneath his fingers. The stone had not gone far, he realized, and suddenly an idea came. He forced his hand to lift the searing pebble. With a scream of agony he brought it up and shoved it deep inside the beast's ear.

At once the claws left Yarkol and began scrabbling frantically at the creature's head. While the bear writhed and hissed, the Hakhan leaped onto the wall of the gorge. A man, he realized, would be trapped in such a place. Even the Kag, with his less flexible form, would not easily get out.

But Yarkol's spirit fingers flowed into crevices and his toes found holds where only birds could perch. A few strands of moss sustained his light body as he scrambled ever higher. When he was halfway up, he looked back to see the bear vainly dunking its head underwater, as if that might quench the burning in its ear.

"Go home to your sorcerer!" Yarkol shouted. "Maybe he can cure you." Looking up toward the top of the cliff, he saw his imp guide peering down at him. How long had this struggle gone on? he wondered. Only a short while had seemed to pass, but in trance one might be deluded about time.

At last, grabbing roots and dangling vines, he arrived at the rim. "Come," the imp insisted, as if nothing unusual had happened. Yarkol felt weary, but did not pause. His body still sat beside the trail, its face staring eerily. Hastily, he reclaimed what was his.

In the moonlight Etou's expression appeared distraught as he rode up to her. "I watched," she confessed.

"What was there to see?" His fingers still felt singed where he had touched the pebble.

"A newborn in trance. Like a shaman."

Yarkol smiled sadly. "You may see such things again." But he wondered as he rode on whether he could survive another bout with Nurtaj. He touched his hand to his chest and imagined the bird-figure trembling within.

14

> *Pupil: How high is the Mount-of-Mounts?*
>
> *Teacher: High enough to hold up the sky.*
>
> *Pupil: And how deep are the kobolds' caves?*
>
> *Teacher: Deep enough to hold all their treasure.*
>
> —*Chirudak tradition*

T he stars were fading as Yarkol's guide led the riders through a rugged pass and down into a narrow valley. Soon the imp swerved onto a side trail that wound back and forth along the edge of a steep drop. The horses descended slowly; at every turning the sky grew brighter and the sprite more agitated.

As the party neared bottom, the guide darted off the trail and suddenly vanished. "This way!" his muffled voice called. Yarkol saw a tangle of withered vines clinging to the sheer slope, and behind the snarl he made out the imp's glowing face. The Hakhan dismounted, stepped closer, and found that a sizable cavern was hidden by the vines.

"Walk through, walk through," the sprite urged.

Yarkol found the dead stems surprisingly tough. He ripped a few away, then attempted to lead his mare inside. The usually bold horse balked, planting her legs firmly.

"Ah, human, you are so helpless!" The sprite emerged for an instant, though sunlight already was touching the top of the ridge. The imp leaped to the horse's mane and whispered into her ear. At once, the animal lowered her head and squeezed through the tangle. Yarkol hurried after. A moment later, Etou followed, leading her mount into the dimly-lit cavern.

"This place is full of kobolds," Etou said, as she sniffed the air.

"Is that what they smell like?" Yarkol noticed only scents of wet earth and decayed vegetation. He frowned, however, when he saw strange symbols marked in red ochre on the walls. "If kobolds are here," he said cautiously, "they want nothing from you. I'm the one they've called, and I must go on alone."

Yarkol followed Etou's gaze as she took in the leaf-littered floor and the low ceiling with its patches of yellow mineral deposits. While she too scowled at the markings, Yarkol surmised their purpose—to keep unwanted visitors away. He saw no gnawed bones or other indications that predators entered this place. "You'll be safe," he said uneasily. "Maybe you can sleep while I'm gone."

"In this imps' den?"

"I won't be long," he promised, as he helped her settle the ponies. He glanced at his guide and wondered if the sprite might charm Etou and the animals into drowsiness. With evident misgivings, she began unrolling a blanket. How he wished he could stay with her.

But a moment later he was following the dancing imp, feeling his way as the light faded and the ceiling grew lower. The passage narrowed until he barely had room to turn around. "Your body stays here," said the hob, already out of sight. "We will look after it."

Yarkol sighed, seated himself in as comfortable a position as he could manage, and entered his trance. As soon as he was out of his body, he felt more at ease. With his spirit-eyes he could see clearly despite the gloom. And the tight confines were no longer a hindrance; he could squeeze through the narrowest of openings.

The sprite kept him moving, pausing only when Yarkol fell far behind. One tunnel followed another, some twisting sharply, others angling straight into the depths. The Hakhan soon lost track of the branchings, continuing until the passage opened into a high gallery, with many small alcoves carved into the walls.

Within these spaces sat hobs of several kinds, some with dark, woolly hair, others with pendulous lips and noses. Now he realized that he'd been taken to one of the deep realms, where imps were said to go when they tired of troubling humans. Out of curiosity Yarkol paused to examine a few dwellings. Within the niches he saw bits of human treasure: jewelry, scraps of weaving, tiny carvings. Here lay the offerings that Chirudaks buried to placate sprites. But he wondered how the imps, who possessed no physical strength, could carry the trinkets to their dens.

226

A short while later he had his answer. A rat scurried past and Yarkol caught a glimmer of something bright dangling from its mouth. A kobold was following the creature, directing it by squeaks and whistles. Using their power over animals, the Hakhan realized, the hobs could move any object they wished.

Most of the inhabitants that Yarkol passed were busy in one contest or another, and none bothered to glance at him. He saw imps standing face-to-face as they shouted riddles in high-pitched voices. He saw others hovering over stone surfaces marked for play, with beetles, either red or black, serving as game pieces. These imps, evidently, were constantly practicing their skills. He understood why they were so eager to challenge humans.

The Hakhan glanced down to find his impatient guide dancing about his ankles. "The Small One waits," the creature insisted. Yarkol put aside his curiosity, for he wanted only to fulfill his bargain and get back to his body. He continued through the gallery until it opened suddenly into a cavernous chamber.

Yarkol's jaw dropped in astonishment. The ceiling rose so high that he could not see its peak. From its center, a cascade of water fell into a pool that was alive with glinting fish. Along every wall of the chamber, niches filled with busy imps rose tier upon tier. And the main floor glowed with color, its surface a patchwork of luminescent squares and stars and circles. For the games played here he saw that the "pieces" were small animals—moles, toads, newts. In one arena dozens of imps stood about a complex playing surface shouting instructions that moved their tokens from one bright triangle to another.

The activity was dizzying. If he'd been called here to match wits with hobs, Yarkol knew he had no chance of victory. But he continued, threading his way past one group and then another, reaching at last a stairway that

227

rose steeply. To ascend such a construction might have daunted him in human form; now, he took the narrow steps two at a time.

After a lengthy climb he still could not see the top of the stair. Looking down, he glimpsed the colorful floor in its entirety, its tiny inhabitants darting from match to match. At last he reached a high niche cut deeply into the wall. A pair of unusually ugly hobs stood blocking the way, but these sentries stepped aside to let him pass. He found himself before a pedestal of gold on which perched a tiny figure at the level of his chin. "Pay your respects, Ulaansh," said the guide harshly.

Yarkol did not know what was expected of him, so he imitated the bow that the Kag's followers used. Then he peered at the miniature imp to see its reaction.

This creature, evidently the Small One who had summoned him, possessed a face so wrinkled that Yarkol could scarcely make out its features. The eyes were pinpoints, almost hidden deep in the tiny skull. From the chin dangled a wispy beard that reached halfway down the pedestal. The Small One seemed to smile at the visitor's greeting. When it opened its mouth to speak, Yarkol leaned forward, afraid he might miss its words.

"You are welcome to my domain," boomed the imp, in a voice deeper than that of most men. After granting Yarkol a moment's attention, however, the hob turned to a spiderweb that hung beside it and hissed an order. Clearly the Small One too was engaged in a match, though the playing surface was unconventional. Five green spiders and five yellow ones were arrayed on the web. At the imp's command a green crawled to a new position. Another imp, standing at the base of the pedestal, called his response and a yellow spider moved.

The Small One grinned as it turned back to Yarkol. "This is a child's game. Would you care to try it?"

Yarkol shook his head slowly. "You sprites are too clever for me. Even when I chose the contest, I lost."

The Small One made another spider-move before resuming his conversation. "Clever? Not really. I heard about Kuuli Burntknee getting the better of you. Naming the foals—what an idea! If you hadn't been so rushed, you'd have stated the rules clearly."

"Perhaps—"

"Let me offer stakes to tempt you." The Small One paused to move another green spider so that now a yellow was surrounded on four sides. At a signal the greens advanced and pounced. The hapless yellow struggled for only a moment; then the attackers wrapped its body in threads before returning to their places. "I have many loyal subjects," continued the imp. "Together we can solve your problem."

"Can you keep Chirudaks off Hakhan land?"

"That is precisely what I offer." The imp turned back to finish his game, and shortly all the yellow spiders were dead. The green ones began to feed but Yarkol did not care to watch.

"Listen, Ulaansh. Here's how it can be done. The nomads won't go anywhere without their herds. And we have ways with beasts, as you must know."

"Tell me what you offer."

"To keep the herds north of your great wall—the place you call Barrier."

"*All* of them?" Yarkol had seen hobs control a modest number of animals.

"You see how many we are. And there are more of us in deeper caves."

"Even so, you couldn't hold the herds for long."

"Surely not forever. We have our amusements to get on

229

with. But ten years should be enough. By then your own people will be across the Path and settling the eastern lands."

"Ten years . . ." Yarkol said thoughtfully. "That should suffice."

"Done!" cried the sprite.

"But I've agreed to nothing."

"You'll be surprised at how little we ask. Not what you think."

Yarkol refrained from glancing into his rib cage. "What then?"

"A day's labor."

"As a man?"

"As you are now. Look." It stretched an arm that was thin as a twig. "See how poor a flow we have." Yarkol realized that the tiny creature was pointing to the waterfall. "Once that was a sight to draw kobolds from the other side of the mountains."

"I find it—attractive," the Hakhan offered.

"Ah, this is but a trickle now. A rockfall some years ago diverted water from the source."

"And you want someone to fix the problem?" He looked down at his bone fingers. "In this form I can pick up a pebble or a light stick. You need hard muscle."

"No body of flesh can reach the place," the imp said. "Only with your present . . . abilities can you aid us. And so long as you're with us we can channel strength to you. We are helpless in ourselves. But by combining your hands and our energies, much can be done."

"And that's my penalty if I lose? One day's labor?"

"Exactly."

"And if I win, the Chirudak herds will stay north of the Barrier." Remembering how careful one must be with imps, he rephrased his statement. "North of where the Barrier now stands. For a time of ten years. And the

230

period we speak of begins at once—as soon as the game is over." The Small One hesitated this time, and Yarkol felt satisfied when he agreed.

"Then all is settled except the contest. I've seen enough of those already—and too many skillful players. How can you offer me a fair match?"

"You deserve an honest chance, Ulaansh. To pit you against one of us will not do. Instead, I let you challenge yourself. Call it a test of courage." Yarkol looked around, half expecting a monster to spring at him. "Jump to the floor," said the sprite. "If you can do that, you win our aid."

"Jump?" Yarkol glanced down, recalling how he'd fallen into a ravine with mild discomfort but no lasting ill effects. This was possibly a deeper drop.

"From the top step. Up there."

The Hakhan craned his neck. He hadn't realized that the stairway continued above this niche.

The Small One shouted an order, and five imps suddenly swarmed up toward the heights. Yarkol watched their luminous figures shrink until they reached a point far above him. Then they halted—five firefly glows. "Jump from there to the floor," ordered the chief-of-the-realm. "That's all I ask."

"Agreed," said the visitor, though he wished immediately afterwards that he had considered the matter further. Now he could not retract what he'd offered. Best to do it quickly, he thought, as he began to take the steps two at a time. He tried not to look down.

He was unlike Dzaminid, whose fear of high places he had observed on the trail. Even so, the Hakhan found daunting the prospect of such a fall. While wrestling with the Kag he had learned how his spirit body could plummet helplessly. He did not look forward to repeating the experience.

231

The stairway grew increasingly steep, until he was forced to use his hands to aid the ascent. Each time he glanced up, he saw the row of waiting imps still far out of reach. Finally he pulled himself onto the topmost step, a platform just large enough for his feet.

He recalled standing above an icy pool once, summoning courage for a plunge. No, this was far worse. The floor lay so far below him that he could scarcely make out any details. The color patches ran together and the individual gamers were no longer discernible. Behind him, he heard his guides wagering, one offering heavy odds against his taking the leap.

"Come along with me!" he suggested to the imps. When the five turned him down, he laughed, bent his knees, and sprang. He fell only for an instant.

In the gloom, he wasn't certain what had stopped him. Spider webs? Hanging in midair, he felt a network of filaments under him. By thrashing he found that he could tear free an arm or a leg. But beneath one layer hung another and then another. For all he knew, the entire space was filled with webs.

Jump to the floor. Recalling the Small One's challenge, he began to struggle more violently, hoping to break through. With persistence, he thought, he might still accomplish his task. But then he noticed the spiders, a hairy dark variety whose silhouettes were visible as they crawled over the white of his bones. They were spinning anew faster than he could rip away their strands. "Unfair!" he shouted. "I jumped, but I can't get to the bottom."

The deep voice of the Small One reached him even at that height. "Concede the match, and I'll free you."

"I concede nothing, you grandson-of-a-slug." Yarkol had learned to force his spirit-body through narrow crevices and into the smallest of openings. Why not flow through

232

this woven barrier? He squeezed his head forward, hit another strand, then had to change direction once again. Even if the spiders left him alone, he realized, he'd be years at getting down.

"We can be patient," said the deep voice. "But the Kag won't wait."

Yarkol vented his anger by struggling a while longer. If anything, he was working his way higher. Almost at his eye level he saw the five imps still watching him from the high platform. He must get free at any price, he realized, or lose his chance to return to the Kag. "You win," he shouted at last to their chief. "And may spirit-fleas plague your beard to the end of your days." As soon as he finished speaking, the webbing fell away.

He dropped, this time without hindrance. The wall niches became a blur of lights. Below him, patches of color grew. And the dots became figures with arms and heads.

The impact shot through him, making him feel as though a giant foot had stepped on his back. For a few moments he did not move. Then he heard high-pitched, angry voices. He'd landed in the middle of a match, he realized, squashing several playing pieces. Muttering oaths, he pulled himself up and staggered away. He had gotten what he deserved, had he not? Everyone knew about sprites and their tricks.

That he hadn't risked much was his sole consolation. He followed his guide, who had somehow come down ahead of him, to a low passageway at the side of the great hall. They began to climb through the narrowing tunnel, the hob setting a moderate pace. Luminescent mosses clung to the walls, casting a green glow over all. Underfoot, many small animals—moles, lizards, toads—came and went in a steady stream. The floor was caked with their droppings.

Ascending ever higher, Yarkol was at last forced to crawl. For the final length, which seemed to go on interminably, he squeezed through a tunnel no thicker than a man's arm. The sound of running water grew, and suddenly he came out into an open chamber.

The place was filled with sprites—hundreds, perhaps thousands of grinning figures. He tried not to look at them, but focused instead on what he took to be the waterfall's source, a spring emerging from clefts higher up. He saw, as the Small One had indicated, that rocks from the ceiling had fallen, diverting much water to another path. "This must be the opening to the great hall," he said, pointing to a hole where water flowed into the chamber's floor.

His guide agreed, leaping up onto a rough chunk of granite that rose as high as Yarkol's chest. "Move this, Ul-aansh, and you are done. But be careful of the water."

The Hakhan gazed at the swirling current. He had almost forgotten how light he was in this form. Were he to fall into the flow, he'd be swept down into the cavern.

Placing his feet carefully, he leaned into the obstacle. The offending rock was jagged, offering many handholds. If he truly could push it aside . . .

"We'll help," said the sprite. "Ready your hands."

Yarkol gave a tentative tug and felt his spirit-bones bending. He pushed harder, but managed only to stretch his pliant fingers across the grainy surface. Why had the Small One sent him on this fool's errand? Two men of flesh with a prybar might succeed, but not a spirit like himself.

"Our power will flow to you," the imp insisted. Yarkol, to show good faith, tugged again. Then he felt an odd tingling as a low hum rose from all sides. The sprites, standing rank on rank, were making the sound. And something was happening to his strength.

234

"Push," shouted the imps. "Lean your body into it."

The humming grew louder. His bones seemed to stiffen, and he thought he felt something shift beneath his hands. "Again!" He was growing dizzy from the effort.

"Push!"

The hum became a roar that echoed through the chamber. Now his bones felt charged with power that converged from every direction. He heard a scraping of rock, a hiss of water. But his vision was clouding; he could barely see what he'd accomplished.

"Again!"

He gave a last great shove and was astonished to feel the stone tumble aside. But then he was off balance, falling forward, unable to stop himself. His foot slipped into the surging water that came rushing through the opened channel. His leg shot out from under him, and then he flipped onto his back. What of his new strength? Before he could think to use it he dropped into blackness.

Etoudoori slept and soon found herself among the kobolds of the cave. Before her stood three wizened figures with enormous earlobes and pointed, beardless chins. "I am dreaming," she said, for she knew that ordinary eyes could not see such creatures. The stakes must be high indeed if imps had entered her dreams.

"Yes, you are asleep. More than asleep," the shortest imp agreed. "But this is no dream, for all of it's true. Our cousins have bested your ulaansh again. Now he does their labor and gets nothing in return."

"What else would you expect? He has little experience with rogues."

"And you?"

She laughed. "I've seen every type. And been under a blanket with most of them."

"Then game with us. If you win, we'll credit your Hakhan with the victory."

"You told me he has lost already."

"Lost this match, yes. But the ulaansh will not abandon his fight. He must come to us again, and here is what you can gain for him. We'll waive all his forfeits. He can try our next contest with no risk to himself."

"And if I fail?"

The imp stepped forward and ran his taloned finger over her cheek. She felt only a mild tingle. "Your face, of course, is what you must wager."

Etou, alarmed suddenly, put her own hand to her smooth skin.

"We'll give you another face in exchange. Older, not so pretty. You'll get used to it."

She laughed nervously. "When I wake I'll be myself again."

"How long do you think you've been here?" asked the tallest sprite. "Half the night?" She nodded. "In fact," the creature continued, "many days have passed. If you don't believe us, look outside."

Etou turned toward the entrance and saw snowdrifts partially blocking the opening. Daylight was streaming in. She climbed over the drifts and looked out to see that winter had settled in, filling the small valley with snow to the level of the cavern's mouth. Realizing that the sprites had spoken truly, she grew concerned for the ponies. At the back of the cave, she found both mounts lying on the ground as if in trance.

"We can do what we want with you," said the first imp. "You can sleep your life away here and wake up a crone. If you wager with us, believe that the contest is in earnest."

"Tell me your challenge," she countered.

"You must come underground."

"But Yarkol—"

"He'll be busy until you get back."

She glanced once again at her roan, which showed no signs of waking. "If you keep us until spring, we'll have nothing to go back to," she said quietly as she entered the tunnel.

The way was long, through passageways faintly lit by sources she couldn't see. As she walked, her size seemed to change. Where the tunnel narrowed, she shrank; where the ceiling was high, she sprang back to her normal height. But with no standard for comparison, she could not know what size anything was. At last she reached a bustling hall, full of imps so involved in play that they did not glance at her. She noticed that the kobolds who had brought her here were different in appearance from the others, possibly a separate breed. The more common variety had small ears, but their lips were thick and their hair wild.

Etou's guides halted at a small arena ringed by stones. Two speckled salamanders were penned within, one spindly and missing a foreleg, the other showing more energy than she had ever seen in such a creature. The larger one pranced about briskly, testing the wall and then turning back. "We'll race these two against each other," said the tall imp. "You can pick your beast."

Etou laughed, for the trick here was obvious; the spindly one must be the better racer. But as she was about to announce her choice, a worry rose. If the imps were clever, they would anticipate her thinking and plan to use it against her. She must select the large salamander after all.

Now she found herself increasingly confused. Perhaps they would credit her with enough insight to catch even this subtle trick. There was no end to how far such arguing could go. "This is not for me," she told the hobs. "Find something else."

The three muttered together, then beckoned her to the

side of the hall where a stream of rats poured from a small opening near the floor. Most of the creatures were dull brown in color, but occasionally a larger, white rat emerged. "We'll count how many of each kind comes out," said the shortest sprite. "Whoever sees ten of their chosen color first is the winner. Do you want brown or white?"

"Neither," said Etou. Again, choosing brown was too obvious. "Give me a fair match, or none at all."

The three argued among themselves awhile. "We'll try a game so old that even the gods have played it," one told her at last. They walked a short way, stopping where the floor was marked in a pattern of crisscrossed lines:

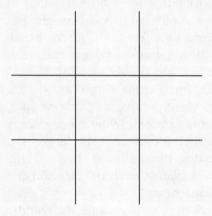

"You may take red or black beetles for markers," said the hob who seemed to be the trio's leader. "At each turn you move another of your color into place. Whoever first gets three in a row is the victor."

"Do I begin?" she asked.

"As you wish. But if there is no winner, we go back to counting rats."

Etou was no stranger to this game. "I want red. And I start in the middle."

The sprite clicked a command with its tongue, and one of the nearby beetles crawled into place. At once the kobold followed with his own move, sending a black insect into the corner.

	B	
R		

"Mine to the upper left corner," said Etou nervously. If she merely tied, she could not hope to win the other contest. But she would not have started without a plan for victory. The imp quickly countered with its own play.

R		B
	R	
	B	

"Move a red one to the right lower corner," said Etou in an even voice.

239

"But mine is already there," shrieked the hob.

"Did you tell me that only one was allowed in a space?"

"Everyone knows how this is played." He looked at his companions for agreement.

"I win, by the rules you stated," Etou insisted. "Three in a row." She bent down to push another red beetle into the square, but found that it slipped past her fingers. "Move it for me," she said firmly. "Otherwise, call a judge or a wise man. You must have someone who handles disputes." Turning to scan the huge room, she saw nearby a sprite wearing a long tasseled cap. He was standing between two larger imps who were shouting and waving fists. In a few moments, arguing first with one and then the other, he appeared to settle their quarrel.

Etou hurried over and told the capped one her problem. He smiled and followed her. "Welcome to our domain, southerners," he said when he saw Etou's kobolds. "And remember that we have a reputation for fairness here."

Southerners? She wondered what they were doing so far from home, but had no time to press the matter. She explained what had happened and then let her challenger speak. He insisted that she'd made an improper play.

"Recite the rules as you gave them," said the referee.

The short kobold bowed his head and spoke in a low voice. Was that really a look of dismay on his face? Etou thought she saw a smirk at the corner of his mouth.

"Then she has defeated you," declared the sprite-judge. "And you deserve worse for being so careless. Perhaps I should report the three of you to the Small One."

When Yarkol woke, he was stretched out on the great hall's floor, lying at the edge of the vastly expanded pool. He heard the new cascade of water, but did not care to

240

look up at it, nor to think about how he'd come down. Wearily, he pulled himself to his feet and began to walk back toward the passageways.

"Follow me, Ulaansh," said a familiar voice, "if you wish to find your body again." The sprite who had guided him earlier leaped down from a niche and beckoned him onward. Yarkol followed silently, paying no attention to the other kobolds or their caches of treasure. But when he glanced ahead he saw an impossible sight. The figure walking between two imps, though small, had the shape and dress of a nomad woman. Etoudoori? How could she be here? He tried to catch up with her, but she was moving too quickly. If he persisted, he feared, he would lose his guide.

"She has risked much for you," his sprite said, nodding toward where Etou had vanished.

"I don't understand."

"My cousins were careless. She beat them at a match."

"But how is she here? And what did she win?" He couldn't ask questions quickly enough.

"She's here the only way an ordinary person can be— through her dreams. And you'll know what she's gained for you when the time comes. But let me give you this bit of advice. She deceived you once. Now she's not the same woman."

Yarkol laughed. "Do I need a hob to tell me that?"

"With humans, one can never be certain."

They left the gallery, and Yarkol had to revert to crawling for a time. The way seemed longer and more complicated than he recalled; the sprite kept pressing on ahead of him. The Hakhan was baffled by the route, certain that he'd never seen this ragged cleft, that trickle of water. But at last he was relieved to glimpse his familiar leather coat and his dead eyes staring.

Then he noticed the posture of his body, the legs oddly

241

angled, one arm askew. Surely he had not left himself in such a state. Hurriedly he slipped back into his flesh. The initial sensations startled him. He'd almost forgotten what it was to smell damp air, to feel cloth against skin. His muscles felt stiff, as if unused for days.

He stood up cautiously, keeping his head low because of the ceiling. The guide was still there, beckoning him onward. Nothing here was quite as he remembered it— the passageway, the opening into the outermost cavern. When he reached the end, he found a candle burning and Etou saddling her mount. She stared at him with a strange expression, a mixture of relief and dismay. "I talked to kobolds while I slept," she said. "They told me you were defeated."

He shook his head ruefully. "They challenged me and I was fool enough to accept. I lost through trickery, but I didn't lose much."

"More than you know. Half the winter's gone, maybe more."

"Half? I was down there for only a day." *Or so it had seemed while in spirit form.* At the cave's entrance he noted snowdrifts lit by moonlight. Glancing outside he saw a few flakes still falling. Had the weather changed so quickly? And the landscape too was not what he recalled. "We must find the Kag," he said nervously. "There's time before he marches. There must be."

"You'll find him, as we promised," said the sprite, who remained in deep shadows. "At dawn, which is almost here, look out and you'll know where you are. The Kag is not far south of you."

Yarkol's mount appeared thinner than when he'd last seen it, but otherwise seemed well. He saddled the mare and slipped the bridle on. Unable to hold back his growing suspicions, he hurried outside onto what looked to be a gentle slope. Where was the fiendish trail that had

242

brought him here? Where was the steep-sided gorge? He dug into the snow with his boot and found solid soil beneath the covering of white.

The sky was brightening. Ahead loomed a high obstacle he could not identify, something that stretched across his entire field of vision. Suddenly he began to shout in disbelief, forgetting his horse, running without care over treacherous ground. "The Wall!" he shouted. "The Barrier! Come look and tell me I've gone mad."

15

The world is vast; we have seen only
one small part of it.
—Chief Vuotol (Longtail tribe)

Staring up at spikes bristling
from the snow-dusted earthen mound, Yarkol wondered
what monstrous prank had been played to bring him
here. To reach the Barrier from the Kag's camp took a
journey of at least ten days. He stamped his feet, feeling
the solid thump of ground beneath his boots. He was neither dreaming nor still in trance.

The imps had moved four bodies of flesh—two human,
two animal. How? The answer so sickened him that he
wished to put it aside. He had heard that hobs might enter a dormant body and animate the limbs . . .

At once his concern turned toward his physical well-being. He had raced from the cave without noticing anything amiss. Now he flexed elbows and knees, patted his arms and chest and legs through the thick clothing. If an imp's spirit had occupied his flesh, he found no obvious signs of abuse. Even so, he shuddered at the thought of hob-possessed horses and riders.

He needed desperately to know how much time had passed while his body remained in trance. Breathing deeply of the morning air, he thought he smelled hints of spring. *Spring?* Glancing down, he saw green shoots where his boots had scuffed through the snow.

"Etou!" he bellowed. The kobold had told him to seek the Kag *south* of here, but only Hakhan territory lay in that direction. If the Kag had crossed the Barrier, then surely his tribes had gone with him! Yarkol managed to climb into his saddle, tears of defeat already rolling down his cheeks. The animal trotted along the base of the wall while the Hakhan clung numbly to its back.

He heard hoofbeats behind him, but did not turn. "Ul-aansh," came Etou's voice, "they made us sleep through the entire winter."

"Worse than that," he answered hoarsely. Suddenly he reined in his mount. Ahead, the smooth course of the wall gave way to a shadowy rift. He proceeded cautiously and with dread. What had happened to the Barrier? Mounds of dirt lay scattered about the edges of a narrow, ragged cut.

Yarkol shook his head with disbelief as he gazed past heaps of rock and earth to the forest on the Barrier's far side. He felt as if his own flesh had been torn. "Do you see what's been done to us?" he groaned. While kobolds had kept Yarkol busy, Chirudaks had broken through the mound. He imagined the nomad force moving now, pouring over Hakhan lands, a river of animals and riders.

With his head bowed, he stared at the path that the tribes had taken. Despite a dusting of new snow, he saw how the ground was littered with animal droppings and beaten down by the passage of many hoofs. One explanation pounded through his thoughts. *The imps are behind it! This is what they planned all along!*

He recalled Nurtaj in his spirit-form on the night that the two had fought. The Kag and Yarkol's guide had argued briefly. But if Nurtaj could see and converse with imps, then why could he not make a pact with them?

Yarkol thought first of returning to the cave, of venting his wrath on any kobolds he could find. But he knew he could not manage their maze of passageways. Even if he got through to their great hall, he had no weapon to use against the creatures. What he needed was an army of men with picks and shovels, an army to break open the caverns and let sunlight destroy all who lived within. For a moment he imagined such a scene. The shrieks he heard in his mind gave him a glimmer of satisfaction.

"A day old," said Etoudoori. Yarkol roused himself from his daydream and saw her kneeling on the ravaged path. She was poking with a stick at a pile of horse droppings. "They're a day ahead of us," she said. "And traveling slowly."

"Then ride!" he shouted. Without waiting for her to remount, he raced his own mare through the gap. The trail beyond was all too easy to read.

First he followed the wall's southern face, then reached a track that headed down into a larchwood forest. In a blur he saw the branches whipping past, the logs and tree stumps, the startled hares that ran from his path. A murky pond forced the trail to bend, but his gaze was only on the way ahead as his mare galloped into the turn. A range of hills, pine-covered, loomed in the near distance. He plunged on, up a stony rise, hearing the labored breathing of his horse as it strove to maintain the pace.

At the hill's brow he looked down onto a panorama of lakes, five strung in a row with white-tipped pines all

246

around them. He paused to scan the horizon, but found no Chirudaks.

He slapped the reins and the mare sped down the slope. Had he heard a voice behind him? He could think of nothing but clinging to his mount, watching the valley rise up and the trees grow large. The horse's whistling breath came louder, but he pressed on toward the first shimmering lake.

The animal waited for no signal from Yarkol, but headed directly for water. *Don't kill your horse!* Was that the warning he'd heard from Etou? At the last moment he managed to turn the mare, to keep her from drinking while overheated. He slid from saddle to ground, grasping the halter firmly. The mare's chest and flanks were foamed with sweat.

"Walk her!" shouted Etou as she rode up behind him.

Feeling like a chastised youngster, Yarkol began to lead the animal around the lake. As he went, he noted grimly that Chirudaks had camped here the previous night. Piles of fresh dung lay wherever he glanced. All new vegetation had been cropped to the roots and the low-hanging branches stripped of their buds.

His head cleared, and he asked himself one question after another. What had happened to Jornood's men? The Barrier clans had been preparing for this assault, so why had they failed to hold it back? When he thought of a possible answer, his face burned and blood pulsed in his ears. The imps, of course. They had boasted of their power over animals, and Yarkol could imagine the result—horses in panic, men thrown from their saddles long before they reached the site of battle. Against such an enemy, the Hakhans had no chance.

"Take it slowly, Newborn." Etou came up behind him, her mare in tow. "Your pony is doing well. And the tribes are not so far ahead of us."

"Our mounts must eat," Yarkol replied, wondering how and what their hob-masters had fed them. "And here the ground is stripped bare."

"After they cool down, we'll ride west. Away from the line of march. The Kag will take days to reach your precious Throat."

The Dolmi sighed. He must choke back his impulses or lose his mare altogether. Yet what could he accomplish in a handful of days? Ahead, protected by secret allies, moved a torrent of riders and beasts. Without the imps' help, he saw now, Nurtaj would not have attempted such a march. "I need to find Dzaminid," Yarkol said, his voice full of despair.

"He must be traveling with the Kag. At the head of the column. But that is no place for you."

Yarkol nodded gloomily. "I don't dare show myself in the camps."

"But I can go. I can bring him to you."

The shadows had grown long by the time Etou took her first look at the marchers. Cresting a ridge, she gazed down onto ragged fields bordered by woodlands. Just below her, the last herds were moving slowly, black dogs bouncing from one sheep to the next to keep them all in line. A few warriors rode behind, but no Hakhan army challenged the procession. She shook her head in astonishment, willing now to believe, as Yarkol did, that kobolds had joined with the Kag.

From the distance, she heard the bleating of goats and the deep lowing of cattle. She tried to imagine the entire Chirudak nation strung out in a line, but could not grasp such an immensity. She turned to see Yarkol's brooding face. The mark on his cheek, darker than usual, was almost as black as his mood. Nothing could be done now,

248

she thought, to halt what the Kag had begun. Yet she was compelled to see this through.

They turned westward, skirting the long, thin column. She feared outriders, but saw none. Was the Kag so confident that he ignored all precautions? Pressing on, taking sightings from the brow of every hill, she saw no end to the marchers.

Dusk arrived but still she and Yarkol continued. "They've stopped for the night," Etou announced shortly, pointing to flickering lights and a few plumes of smoke. Soon, when darkness fell, the cookfires would serve as her beacons.

The night sky was clear, lit by the Fish Moons and by all the spring stars. Above the southern horizon the Shaman's Mask hung, a dazzling array of brights. But Etou's attention turned always to the east, following the string of fires that marked the encampments of her people. "There!" she said at last, noting the final cluster of lights in the distance. Beyond that point, a vast darkness stretched across the plain. "Look. It must be the head of the column."

She left Yarkol camped in a hollow and rode toward the nearest fire. The cooking smells made her stomach growl and her mouth fill with water. Today she had tasted only some dry biscuit. Before that, when had she eaten?

But tribes on the march would have little enough for themselves. Undoubtedly they had spent the winter slaughtering their weaker animals and smoking the meat. Most families would be content with cold fare tonight.

In the gloom she saw shapes of mounted horsemen and wondered how she would face their challenges. She wished she could approach her own tribe instead, but Greatwing might be anywhere behind her. Bloodcreek must lead this journey, and here she would find her shaman.

249

"You!" came a shout. "What are you doing?" A torch rose high, red light showing the gaunt face of a guard.

"Looking for fodder for my mare."

"Don't you listen? Pasture on the other side—if you can find any."

She attempted to ride casually past him, but he reached out and snatched her mare's halter. "You don't belong here," he said.

"I've lost Greatwing tribe."

"You've a long way back to find them." He glared, his expression a half-snarl. What if he remembered her from the Kag's camp? She'd tried to keep out of sight there, but she knew how men pointed at her when she passed.

"Must I ride on the outside?" she asked in an even tone. "Soil-tillers are nearby."

"Soil-tillers?" He began to laugh. "They want to get close to us, they have to walk." His broken teeth showed again, but then his brow furrowed. Was he remembering something?

"I've a message for shaman Dzaminid," she blurted out.

"The shaman's got no business with your kind. No business with anyone now."

"And if you are wrong?"

"Then the Kag hears it first. Come on, if you want to see his guards. Maybe they'll believe you. If not, they'll have fun with you anyway."

She tossed her head. "Lead me to them." When the sentry sneered and turned, she let him go on a few paces. Her mare was well-trained and took her silent signals. In a moment Etou was galloping in the opposite direction, seemingly toward Greatwing's camp. The man swore a few oaths, but did not bother to pursue.

After a brief run she changed course and returned to

find the Hakhan standing beside his mount. "Where is Dzaminid?" Yarkol asked in an agitated voice.

"We'll have to wait," she replied angrily. "I cannot go to the shaman unless the Kag agrees. But later—"

"Then Nurtaj has control of him. And if he's under guard—"

"I know how to slip past guards."

Yarkol shook his head. "I won't send you back alone. But I have another idea. Come, eat some more biscuit, and I'll explain."

Yarkol watched Etou dozing, her breathing slow and quiet, the moonlight playing across her face. He wished he could sit the whole night beside her, but now the nomad camp had grown still. Reluctantly, he woke her with a gentle touch to her cheek. "I am going into trance," he whispered. In front of him on the ground lay a white quill that had fallen from a passing bird. "To follow my spirit form, you must watch this feather."

"A sacred token," she said. "From a taawik's wing."

"All the better. In my hands it will lead you to Dzaminid." He needed to say no more, for she understood his plans. Yarkol focused on the feather and quickly slipped from his body. A vague worry rose as he reached bony fingers toward the quill. If imps were nearby then they might easily steal his flesh, moving it once again to some place of their choosing. But the imps were busy tonight, he thought bitterly. Busy keeping Hakhan mounts away.

The quill felt as light to his spirit fingers as a stick to human touch. When he tried to move forward, however, he found himself fighting air with the vane. He paused, turned the feather, and saw that by pointing its edge in the direction he was going, he could handle it more

251

easily. At last he began to advance while Etou crouched behind him like a rabbit, scampering from one shadow to the next.

They soon reached the edge of the encampment. A mounted guard saw Yarkol's quill and tried to snatch it from the air. The Hakhan teased him, drawing back in time to send the man off balance. Before the nomad could right himself in the saddle, feather and Etou were past him.

From the far side of camp came the sporadic bleating of livestock. Yarkol saw that few yurts had been erected; most people huddled in the open under blankets and furs. He stepped carefully around the sleepers—wrapped bundles with only noses exposed—while behind him Etou moved almost soundlessly.

Then he saw the Kag's large yurt, its perimeter guarded by a dozen men. A sudden thought startled Yarkol. Was this the moment his early dreams had shown? His own knife was gone, but surely he could find another. Nervously, he set the feather down outside the dwelling so that Etou would not follow him. Then he crept forward and slipped through the doorway's gap.

With his spirit eyes, the interior appeared brightly lit. Nurtaj lay asleep, or possibly in trance, a wife close at each side. A sword lay within easy reach . . .

"Ulaansh, you'll not touch him this night."

The Hakhan shouted with angry surprise as a dozen kobolds tumbled out of the bedding. "And how will you stop me, imps?" his spirit-voice challenged.

"Have you forgotten our allies?" From the back of the yurt scurried a mass of dark spiders. Yarkol kicked a few creatures aside, but others clambered up the bones of his legs, reached his arms and shoulder blades, and began to spin. "Your shaman is in the next yurt, if you want him," advised one of the imps.

"And I want you broiled in the morning sun. All of

you." Yarkol tore his arm loose from the first threads, but other spiders were swarming between his ribs. He felt cords wrapped about his ankles and thighs.

Demon sprites! They would not let him harm the Kag. He must focus his hopes on whatever the shaman could offer.

He broke free, retreated back outside, and was relieved that the hairy things did not follow. He sighed, picked up the feather, and saw Etou's slight movement as he started forward again. The next yurt was smaller, with only a single guard on watch. Yarkol squeezed his head past the doorway, saw Dzaminid dozing, pulled the feather inside after him as a signal to Etou. Then he went back out to deal with the guard.

A pebble lay on the ground. The Hakhan raised it with surprising ease and dropped it into the top of the guard's boot. The man seemed not to notice, so Yarkol gave him another. This time the soldier squirmed and lifted his foot.

What next? The Hakhan reached down for a pinch of dust and flung it at the guard's nostrils. The nomad doubled over sneezing. Yarkol nodded in satisfaction as he watched Etou dart silently past and into the yurt. When he was certain that the soldier had not seen her, the Dolmi hurried inside.

She was kneeling by the boneman's side, shaking him cautiously. Yarkol noticed at once the gaunt appearance of Dzaminid's face, the deepening of lines about his eyes and mouth. His eyelids opened, and he stared briefly with no reaction, then put a finger to Etou's lips. "I sense the newborn . . . here too," he whispered, his speech halting. "I'll need his help . . . and yours."

"We'll get you out," she replied, mouthing the words almost silently.

"They weakened me . . . with poison," he gasped. "To keep me quiet. They took . . . all my things." Yarkol saw

253

that Dzaminid now wore the coat and trousers of a herdsman. "But I need only the antidote." The shaman spread his hand over his stomach. "The remedy is in my bearhide sack," he whispered. "Seeds within a small, black gourd."

But where was the sack? Yarkol puzzled.

"Guarded. Outside." He waved toward the doorflap. "Etou, hide under that heap of furs until the newborn comes back."

The Dolmi crept out and quickly found a pile of saddlebags and equipment. A sentry stood on watch, but after the long day's ride, the man's eyelids were drooping. To Yarkol's spirit vision the scene was brightly lit, and he recognized at once the shaman's medicine sack. His major obstacle would be loosening the drawstring.

Yarkol poked a finger into the sack's opening and tried to widen it. He wiggled with all his strength and jerked the entire heavy bag toward him, but this accomplished nothing. The drawstring had been pulled tight, he realized. No matter how he tried, he only stretched his spirit-bones without loosening the cord.

The guard shifted his stance, turning his head toward the shaman's belongings. Perhaps the Chirudak heard a noise . . . Yarkol kept still until the warrior turned away. Then he recalled the constricted passageways he'd traveled and saw how he might reach his prize.

Holding the sack steady with one hand, he forced the other against the small opening. His spirit bones thinned and began to flow. His fingers wriggled through the hole until, at last, even his wrist lay inside. Within the sack, he felt objects of fur, others of bone or hair.

Was this wrinkled thing the gourd? With a difficult twist, he pulled it away from the other implements and up to the sack's narrow mouth. Glancing through the hole, he saw that the gourd's color was black, the end sealed with beeswax. He worked his finger through the plug, shook several long seeds into his palm. Carefully, without losing a precious grain, he withdrew his stretched white hand.

A moment later he was back in the yurt, holding his prize out to the shaman. Dzaminid took the seeds onto his tongue, chewed them thoroughly, swallowed water. From his herdsman's pouch he took a bit of henga root, offering some to Etou; but she insisted that he keep it for himself. After Dzaminid had eaten the henga, Yarkol saw color returning to his pallid complexion.

"My tack," said the shaman quietly, nodding to the rear of the yurt. "Etou, you are the only one of us who can carry that out of here. Take it to your camp. Go that way." He pointed to the left of the doorway.

"But the guards!"

The shaman smiled. "Several are dozing now. If you're quiet, you'll have no trouble." He rose, beckoned her to follow, pushed back the doorflap and showed her the safe route again. Yarkol slipped past them and saw the closest sentry standing with his mouth open, his snores rumbling softly. In a moment Etou was gone.

Saying nothing further, Dzaminid headed east, bypassing the clusters of wrapped sleepers. Yarkol followed his limping progress, wary for challengers at every step. "Don't desert me yet, Newborn," he heard the shaman say under his breath.

They walked steadily, leaving behind the main encampment. Ahead, Yarkol saw horses grazing on last year's stubble and this year's first shoots. The shaman whistled an odd sequence of notes; a few moments later his mount cantered up to him.

Would Dzaminid ride bareback? It seemed impossible for one in his weak condition. Yet a mounted guard was already approaching; the shaman could escape in no other way. Dzaminid grunted, swung up his leg, and managed to straddle the mare. Yarkol raced to intercept the sentry.

"Who goes at this hour?" shouted the guard as he unsheathed his curved sword. Yarkol, leaping from the ground, grabbed the soldier's coat and pulled his spirit body up onto the mount. He perched behind the guard's saddle as the horseman wheeled to challenge Dzaminid. "Answer, or I cut you down."

Yarkol tugged and prodded but could not budge the warrior from his seat. The shaman, only a few strides ahead, seemed barely able to keep himself from falling. "I treat you as a thief, then," the sentry concluded. The Dolmi battered at the heavy arm, but the guard lifted the blade and plunged forward.

Suddenly Yarkol reached around to the warrior's face and jabbed a finger into each nostril, cutting off the air. The nomad's hand came up to claw away the obstruction, but the Hakhan lunged deeper, pushing his spirit bones through the nasal passages and on into the back of the guard's throat. What a marvelous ability for a physician, he thought, imagining he might explore the man's windpipe, his gullet, even his stomach. But violent gagging threw the sentry from his mount. The Hakhan stayed with him, riding out the spasms, until he was certain that Dzaminid was safely away.

"They'll be searching for you soon, shaman," said Yarkol when he was back in his body at Etou's campsite. He rubbed his hands together, enjoying the sensation of having solid bones again. Dzaminid lay with his head propped up by the saddle Etou had brought for him. His eyelids were shut, and Yarkol feared he had fallen asleep.

"No, Ulaansh," the shaman replied wearily. "The Kag

256

does not want me back. Otherwise, his imps would have kept me from leaving."

Yarkol beat his fist against the ground. "Then we can do only what Nurtaj allows."

"So far, he has gotten his way. With a few exceptions."

"And what were those?" Etou, seated beside the shaman, leaned over to brush dust from his jacket.

The shaman sighed. "I challenged Guzad's story. Vuotol and his friends listened to me. The old man kept his tribe out of this march, and a few others stayed with him. Both of you take credit for that."

"Then all the rest are doomed?" Etou asked.

"Our newborn will tell us."

"I'm as helpless as you. The imps—"

"They have schemed against the gods' will," the shaman interrupted. "Perhaps the High Ones knew this might happen when they shaped you."

"Then they made a poor choice," Yarkol said angrily. "I was a quiet man, not meant for great deeds."

"Perhaps you are mistaken. You told me a tale once." The shaman turned to stare into Yarkol's eyes. "That first night beneath the stars you spoke of entering a buried shrine beside the Throats."

Yarkol knew he had said much that night, with his thoughts numbed and his tongue loosened by the shaman's trickery. But he did not realize that he had described his youthful misadventure.

"The gods judged you then," Dzaminid insisted. "We must go back to that place and learn if they still find you worthy."

"Go back?" The Hakhan had almost managed to stop puzzling over the mysteries that lay buried. "A priest told me he'd have the cavern filled in."

"Then we'll get good exercise digging." The shaman smiled faintly, resettled himself, and closed his eyes again.

257

16

*A sprite stood beneath the Mount-of-
Mounts and begged the gods for a
soul. After a time a voice called down
to him. "Your wish is granted. You
will be reborn as a fly. But if you
trouble any animal or man, then
again you must return as a fly." The
imp was overjoyed. Once in his
winged body, however, he found the
temptations impossible to resist. The
odor of horses intoxicated him. He
buzzed ceaselessly about the herds.*

*Each time he was reborn, he heard
the same warning, but always he
succumbed to his nature. At last, after
a hundred cycles, he shouted to the
gods. "A fly is a living thing and must
eat. A horse is its proper feeding
ground."*

"That is your problem," the god-
voice answered.
—*tradition of Whitemane tribe*

Y arkol watched the shaman
doze briefly, then wake and reach toward the one saddlebag that Etou had brought out with his tack. "Open it,"
said Dzaminid. "Provisions for us all." Etou willingly took
out cheese and biscuit and dried meat, but the shaman
swallowed only a few morsels. "My stomach needs time
to recover," he said, nibbling on a bit of goats' milk
cheese. "Enough for me. But you must eat. Both of you."

Etou began to chew hungrily, but Yarkol was content
with a few bites. His appetite had been meager since the
time of his illness; now, even after the long trance, he did
not feel famished. Perhaps his body had been fed by its
hob-master on its forced journey south. In any case, he
was far more concerned about Dzaminid's health than his
own. "Tell me about the poison, shaman," he asked.

Dzaminid murmured a word that Yarkol did not know.
"Made from herbs that grow only in the far north. Each
morning they held me down and blew the potion in
through my nostrils. After that I was so sleepy that I could
barely open my eyes, much less work against Nurtaj."

"And your antidote—"

"Gave me strength to get free. But now I must wait for
my body to purge itself of the drug."

"Will you be able to ride?"

The shaman smiled. "If not, then you will tie me to my
mount." He closed his eyes, and for a time he slept again.

Well before dawn, however, Dzaminid climbed into his
saddle unaided. Yarkol led the party southward, leaving

behind the sluggish nomad column. "The others are still stretching and yawning," said Etou with a laugh.

"They'll be on the march soon enough," Yarkol replied. "And farther south, the Hakhans must be waiting for them."

"What the Hakhans plan is not so certain," said the shaman. "Their chiefs know that they can't attack on horseback. They've tried several times, but their mounts always panicked and ran."

"Then they'll defend their territory on foot."

"Perhaps. But not right away." The shaman swept his gaze across the landscape, as if seeking distant riders. "Chirudaks are marching in narrow file, not swarming over Hakhan lands. Once your armies realize where Nurtaj is heading, they'll fall back and let him pass."

Yarkol scowled. *Let Nurtaj find his own doom.* Yes, Jornood would embrace that strategy. But the nomads would soon learn that death awaited them on the unfinished Path. "When the tribes are forced back," he replied, "Dolmi land will become a battleground. All that my ancestors built will be destroyed."

"*If* the tribes are forced back . . ."

"Do you suddenly doubt me, shaman?" Yarkol had seen the demon's land of Rya Basin too many times; he knew what would happen if the tribes marched that far. For the sake of both peoples, the nomads must be turned around before they neared the Throat.

"The Path is not finished," Dzaminid agreed, his voice growing weary. "But I must keep my mind open. When we reach the shrine, we will see things more clearly."

As travel continued, Yarkol noticed Dzaminid slumping in the saddle; despite his protests, the shaman was still weak from his ordeal. At noon the Dolmi called a halt at the edge of an unplowed field. Etou gathered brush, built a small fire, and made watery soup.

"Better," Dzaminid said, rubbing his stomach when he

was finished. "A quick nap for me, and then we ride again."

Resuming the southward trek, the travelers skirted settlements and an occasional high-perched stone keep. Yarkol saw no smoke rising from any chimney; not a single rider passed him on the road. The land felt abandoned.

That night, the travelers rested well. Next morning they set out again early, avoiding towns, though they'd seen no evidence of habitation. Yarkol tried to imagine the people hastily packing their belongings and moving out, heading west or south to escape the oncoming nomads. Perhaps the farmers had left everything behind, with a few men to care for the livestock. But Yarkol did not even hear the lowing of cattle.

The unplowed fields went by, one like another. The snow had melted here, and the dark, moist smell of earth rose on every breeze. Soon the land must be planted, Yarkol knew, but the farmers had fled with everyone else. Famine would come this year for certain if the people did not return soon.

That day the three rode until dark, with only enough rest for the horses. "The shaman recovers quickly," Yarkol whispered to Etou, but still he kept Dzaminid under careful watch. They camped by a stand of birches, then rose early and sped over deserted roads, aiming now toward the southeast. The Throat of Sorrows lay less than a day ahead. Yarkol kept sniffing the wind, imagining he smelled the first hints of sulfur.

In late afternoon they approached at last the borders of Dolmi Land. As they crested a hill, Dzaminid hissed a warning. Etou stayed back with the horses while Yarkol and the shaman dismounted and crept up the last stretch of road. "There are your defenders," the boneman said softly.

Crouching behind the cover of a thorn bush, Yarkol

261

gazed out at a curious scene. The eastward road lay open, inviting the nomads to march onto the Path. But the rudiments of a barricade stretched along the road's southern side. Along a broad front laborers and soldiers were noisily digging holes, dragging palings into place, erecting crude earthen ramparts. Shouts and sounds of hammering rang through the air.

Yarkol surmised the purpose of this effort. The hasty construction was to be Jornood's shield after the nomads discovered their predicament. Here the Hakhans would make their stand. But whether the barrier would be finished in time, whether it would hold against the furious onslaught to come, Yarkol could not say. And on the hill not far behind sat the towers of Dolmi House. For a moment he gazed at the familiar walls.

"No oxen," whispered the shaman. "Look. No horses either."

Yarkol brought his focus back to the construction site and narrowed his eyes. The work was proceeding entirely by human efforts. Then the kobolds were here, he concluded, lurking underground, whispering words that made Hakhan beasts intractable.

"Our mounts—" Yarkol began.

"Are mountain ponies. But that's not what saves them from imps." The shaman, keeping his head down, retreated back toward the bottom of the hill. Yarkol followed, relieved to see his mare standing calmly beside Etou. "The kobolds aren't finished with you, Newborn," said the shaman. "That's why we rode here so easily."

The words made Yarkol's face burn, for he was not done with the imps either. But unless the shaman found some new way to deal with them . . .

"Have patience, Yarkol. Soon we will know why we came here."

The journey was almost done. Yarkol led his party on a roundabout route, heading northward, away from the

262

sounds of hammering. The wind shifted, bringing an acrid scent. He glimpsed mineral-encrusted ground, saw yellow steam rising. Then, on a rise above a field of fumaroles, he sighted a familiar copse of stunted trees. "That is where I fell into your shrine," he said, feeling gooseflesh growing.

Sunset was approaching. The Hakhan dismounted in the grove and led Dzaminid down a steep slope that edged the harsh landscape of the Throat. He heard soft bubblings of mud pots, hisses of escaping steam. "Here." He recognized an overhang, a stained outcrop of stone above the place he had entered long before. "Someone has filled it in." He could not hide the sound of relief in his voice.

Dzaminid picked up a sharp stick and began to probe. An old, dank smell rose from the exposed earth. *Urine.* Yarkol grimaced, recalling the priest's pledge to desecrate the site. *Murtok, you filthy goat.*

"Look, Newborn." The shaman had already broken through the thin wall of dirt. He attacked with renewed vigor, opening a fist-sized hole. "The defilers were in a hurry, it seems. This place may yet serve us."

With little effort, Dzaminid enlarged the hole further, but Yarkol could not will himself to assist. The Hakhan stood watching until the shaman clambered down through the opening, then mustered his courage to peer inside. He found the scene less terrifying than he remembered. A few skulls lay scattered about the bottom, but not the heaps of bones he recalled. His youthful imagination may have supplied the rest.

Even so, he heard blood pulsing in his ears as he slid down after Dzaminid. In the gloom he made out the shaman's dark figure standing beside a wall, his fingers tracing carved runes. "This is an ancient place," the Chirudak said softly. "A place for shamans of a different age. The ones who came here did not suffer from our limitations. They spoke directly to the gods."

"And what of a Hakhan youth who stumbled here by chance? Why should the gods take an interest in him?"

"Perhaps they foresaw what was to come." Dzaminid moved closer to the row of masks carved into the longest wall. Yarkol remembered how the eye sockets had seemed to glow with fire. Now he saw only shadowy images in dark stone.

The shaman turned. "I have looked into your soul, Newborn. Long ago, you chose the arduous lot of a healer. Have you ever asked yourself the reason?" Uncomfortable under the nomad's stare, Yarkol lowered his gaze. "Let me tell you, then. I am also a healer, driven as you were. My calling began with a fall and the fear that experience left in me. Yours began here."

The Dolmi could not recall when he'd first started following his grandfather's physician on his rounds. "Think back, Ulaansh. This place changed you in ways you found frightening. The memories would not let go. You hoped that by healing others, you might someday find the cure for your own troubled spirit."

"And where is my cure?"

"It lies in your heritage. Your people and mine were once the same, but our ways diverged. Born in the south, you became a physician, using Hakhan skills. But now you are one of us as well—a true boneman, thanks to the gods. Your cure lies in accepting this truth."

Yarkol shook his head. "I am neither Hakhan nor Chirudak. I am the man who is no man."

"You are beyond such distinctions, Newborn. Listen to me. It is time for you to dance. Leave your body and let your spirit become what it must." Dzaminid began to chant a series of long, warbling notes. At once Yarkol felt hairs rising on his nape.

The Dolmi took a few steps backward. He felt a torpor creeping over him and sank onto a stone ledge that projected from the wall. He had sat here during his earlier

264

visit, he recalled, gripped by a power he could not fathom. Now a similar force held him to the hard seat. The shaman's droning voice made Yarkol's eyelids heavy.

Night was approaching, the Dolmi realized. He did not wish to remain here after dark. But his body would not serve him, and he felt his spirit straining to break free.

Suddenly, without effort he slipped from his flesh. He glanced at the shimmering ribs of his trance-body and heard Dzaminid's words repeated in his mind. *You are a true boneman now.* The chant caught him, and he found himself turning in a dance he did not know. His feet took on a life of their own, twirling him around and around in the chamber. His spirit eyes pierced the darkness, and he saw whirling past him the runes and masks, the skulls, the rigid features of the Hakhan who seemed to be watching.

The dance slowed gradually, until at last he stopped spinning and approached the wall of masks. One of these was meant for him, he realized. One stood out, seemingly larger than the others, and drew him closer. The features were his, but subtly altered, suggesting the frenzy of a madman. His pale fingers hesitated, trembled as they reached up. The mask seemed suddenly alive, pliant as living flesh. Without thinking, he plucked it free and slapped it into place over his cheekbones.

He began to dance once more, but this time lost track of everything around him. The mask was transforming him, he suspected, into a mindless creature that could only keep turning. He heard no sounds, not even Dzaminid's chant. He no longer felt the floor beneath his bone feet. His vision blurred the scene into colorless haze, and still he whirled on, entering at last a realm that no sense could illuminate.

"Newborn!"

Yarkol heard a voice, though all remained dark. He had

been on a journey, he realized hazily. He had come back
filled with a strange sense of elation. But what had passed?
He knew only that he had communed with a presence
both vast and dazzling, a source of wisdom and hope.

"You danced well, Ulaansh."

The Dolmi opened his eyes and found himself still in
his skeletal trance-body, now stretched out on the floor of
the shrine. He reached up cautiously to feel his face, and
discovered that the mask had vanished. "I have known
the madness," he said.

The shaman sat beside him in trance, an iridescent light
bathing his features. "And?" The voice that spoke was a
spirit-voice, for the shaman's lips did not move.

Yarkol sat up slowly, but did not try at once to stand.
He had lost the final moments of his experience, but the
rest—the unpleasant parts—came back to him. "Nightmares," he complained. He pressed his bony hand to his
temple, as if he might wipe out the recollections.
"Dreams of what we know is to come."

In his stupor, he had seen Jornood's barricade attacked
by every force the imps could bring to bear. Now he recalled vivid details—palings, a stamping ground for
hearth-sprites, burning in a smoky blaze; earthworks tumbling, undermined by armies of burrowing animals. Suddenly the nomads broke through, rode over the Hakhan
foot soldiers. Dolmi House lay undefended . . .

"If the tribes cross safely," the shaman said, "the disas-
ter you saw will be averted. It is not the solution we
wished—"

Yarkol groaned, for he had glimpsed the shaman's alternative as well. Through some means he did not understand, the Path was made whole from one end to the
other. The nomads passed safely into the coveted lands
and left the Hakhans in peace. "Not possible."

"That is for you to determine."

"I can do nothing about the Path."

266

"Do not forget the kobolds, Ulaansh. They are the heart of the problem. And you alone have the means to deal with them."

"I would rather deal with the most treacherous of men."

"You are beyond help of men. Even so, I have not lost hope for you."

Yarkol turned warily and saw a dozen small faces peering out from crevices. As if at the shaman's signal, the hobs emerged from hiding to cluster around him. He could scarcely restrain himself from swinging his fist at their ugly heads. But his spirit-bones could not harm these creatures. Perhaps he might have his revenge by some other means . . .

He glanced at them angrily, noting how they differed from the ones he'd seen up north. Their beardless chins were long, scaly masses that resembled the nearby encrusted rocks. Their huge earlobes dangled like pendants. "Etoudoori beat us at a game of wits," said one. "Because of that, you risk nothing to try our contest. It is the last thing we'll ask of you."

"Tell me what you want," Yarkol growled.

"To see you in a test of strength—a fair one. If you win, the Hakhans will be preserved. Lands and people will be safe from these invaders."

"And how will you achieve such a feat?"

"Come with us and learn."

Yarkol glanced at the shaman's still form. Dzaminid's spirit-voice did not speak, but the Dolmi sensed his silent urging. *What more can be lost by going on?*

He considered his only other course—to return to the makeshift barrier and offer his services to Hyar Jornood. Yarkol was no soldier, but his spirit-body had tripped up a nomad or two.

Hopeless. With the imps against them, the Hakhans could not stand. The Dolmi shook his head sadly, wishing

267

to recall what had happened just before he woke. He wondered if the gods had reached down to this place and touched him. If he could capture the feeling that was lost . . .

"Shaman, make me one promise," he asked. "If I don't return, send word of my death to Hirchil Zarad."

The shaman whispered agreement. At last Yarkol took his leave and followed the kobolds to a narrow rift in the wall. The gap proved no obstacle for his spirit-form. He plunged through, with only a quick glance back at the empty body that sat waiting for him.

The imps led him on a path that dipped sharply. Yarkol realized that he was being led eastward, to the unknown realms beneath the Throat of Sorrows. Mists rose ahead, dimming but not obscuring his view. A steady trickle of water pooled under his feet. The ceiling and walls glowed with yellow phosphorescence, sulfur coating everything.

Even this dismal region was inhabited, he learned, as he glimpsed half-hidden faces, tiny bright eyes within crevices. He paused briefly, peering into a ragged, steamy hole. Two hobs sat watching a pair of glow-worms race along a track. Their store of treasure, heaped in a corner, included Hakhan belongings—a bronze ring, a writing quill, polished blue beads from a woman's necklace. These had come as offerings, Yarkol believed, for many Hakhans still secretly followed the old practices. It no longer surprised him that workers tried to appease the spirits that lived beneath the Throat.

This thought amused Yarkol, for he knew how the priests railed against what they dubbed "superstition." He wished that Murtok could be dragged down here, his hairy face shoved into a kobold den. What a treat to see imps swarming up the old one's beard!

The Dolmi's attention returned to the zigzag route he was following. He realized that he had lost all sense of direction. But the imps guiding him pressed on, while all around him murmured the voices of the Throat.

After crawling through a winding tunnel, Yarkol came out into a passage that was nearly blocked by stalactites. The hanging formations reached to the ground, making so dense a forest that he could not see the way ahead. He was forced to squeeze slowly past each obstacle, while the far-smaller imps raced back and forth to check his progress.

At last the ceiling rose higher, so that the icicles of stone hung clear of the rocky floor. Small creatures scuttled by, but Yarkol could not give names to these misshapen things. Some had long, scaly forms; others, round-bodied and armored, walked on multitudes of jointed legs.

The passageway turned sharply. He heard a growing din of shouts and jeers. And then he looked down a narrow gallery of incredible length, its walls lined with many ledges of stone. Imps sat on every perch, the creatures so numerous that some were constantly being jostled from their seats, falling several levels down and then angrily climbing up again.

"Welcome to this humble grotto, Ulaansh," said a high-pitched voice that rose above the noise. The greeting seemed to come from the gallery's far end, though Yarkol could not see details at that distance. Able to stand fully upright now, the Hakhan advanced quickly, all the while trying to ignore the boisterous audience. He used stepping stones to cross a stream of bubbling, moss-colored ooze. He bypassed a pit filled with luminous magma. At last, reaching the end wall, he gazed up at a single kobold who had a broad seat all to himself.

"I am Gilgil Yellowface," the privileged imp said in a voice distorted by a nasal twang. The creature spread his hairy arms. "And this is one of my *lesser* amusement

269

halls." Sitting, Gilgil was larger than the other imps, his head more prominent, his torso plumper as well. He had bulging cheeks and a chin so long that it rested between his legs. His curling bare toes dangled just beneath the shelf.

Yarkol felt something brush past his leg. He glanced down at a fat creature that he could only call a lizard, its body banded in orange and yellow. "That is my champion," said the chief imp. "You interrupted some wagering, but now we'll continue." Suddenly the Hakhan heard frantic peeping behind him. He turned and noticed three small toads cowering at the edge of the arena. These were Throat creatures, he surmised, unlike any toad he had seen before. Their heads and chests bristled with spines; their black tongues flicked nervously.

The lizard hissed and faced its prey. From every tier, Yarkol heard wagers shouted. The imps were betting on the order in which the toadlike things would be eaten, and the excitement sent many more spectators tumbling from their seats.

Gilgil's pet sprang forward, but the nearest toad rose on forelegs, puffed up its belly, presented its quivering spines. The lizard eyed the transformed creature nervously, backed away a step, while the uproar from the onlookers grew. Then, as the lizard hesitated, a second toad attempted to creep past it to safety. Instantly, the banded tail swished, slapping the hapless victim against the rough wall. A moment later, Gilgil's champion was gulping down its first kill.

The Hakhan turned to shout up at Yellowface. "Is this how you see me?" he asked. "A creature to be toyed with?" His words were drowned out by a new round of wagering, and he heard nothing from the imp until the last toad was gone.

After a time the hall quieted. "Now, Ulaansh," Gilgil began. "We tire of these amusements. We look to a larger arena."

"You have the whole Chirudak people to serve your whims," Yarkol replied. "You've enticed them to leave home. Now make them play for you!"

The kobold grinned while wisps of steam trickled from his ears and nostrils. "Let me explain what we are after, Ulaansh. Otherwise, the day will be lost in bickering." Gilgil raised a knobby finger and every imp turned to him with rapt attention. "The Throats, you must understand, are but the edge of our realm. We are spread throughout the eastern lands. The caverns there are not cramped like these. We have room to spare—enough, even, for our northern cousins. But without men to pay us homage, our existence there is bleak."

"If my clan were to finish—"

"Your Hakhans are niggardly with their offerings! To live above our realms we want Chirudaks—people not afraid to show their respect for us."

"Then use your trickery to bring them across."

Gilgil waggled his finger. "That is the one thing we cannot do. Not without your help. Do you recall your service to the Small One?"

Yarkol glared at the imp but gave no answer.

"I'm sure you remember. Now here is our challenge. Use your spirit hands for this task. Complete the Path. Then the nomads will go to the eastern lands, and your people will be safe again."

"And the work of my clan, the labor and suffering of generations—"

"You must choose, Ulaansh. Help us, or take your chances with Jornood's barricade. You can refuse us and keep the Path for Dolmi Clan, but you cannot be sure that a Dolmi will ever use it."

The Hakhan bowed his head. In his nightmare he had

271

watched the first Chirudaks try to use the unfinished route. Discovering the doom that awaited them, the frenzied nomad warriors then turned south to shatter Jornood's lines, swarm up the hill, break open the doors. Yarkol still saw their wild-eyed faces as they ran through the corridors in search of more Dolmi victims.

"Your answer, Ulaansh? My imps lose patience."

"Patience?" he cried. "You've waited an age for this moment!" He reflected again on the visions and found reason to doubt what he'd seen. Surely Dolmi House was empty now, like the other keeps that he had passed. His family had moved away to safer quarters.

But how long could any Hakhan remain secure? Once Jornood's shield fell, the entire south would lay open to Chirudak vengeance. The scenes of destruction would repeat many times.

Yarkol braced himself for what must come. "Yes, may the High Ones curse you," he bellowed. "Yes, I'll try your demons' labor. But in the lives that follow, may you know my pain. May you suffer as I do, a thousand times over."

"Some of us would gladly suffer," Gilgil answered, "to be freed at last from *this* life."

17

Do imps dream?
Only with their eyes open.
—Chirudak folk saying

Leaving Gilgil's arena, Yarkol followed his guides on another tedious journey beneath the Throat. He crawled through narrow steam-filled crevices, jumped bubbling pools, squeezed between rounded stalagmites. After a while each obstacle resembled one he had passed already.

At every turn hobs rushed ahead of him, scurrying across his feet or darting under his legs. The crowd that streamed by included many of the northern breed, with their woolly hair and pendulous lips. Gilgil had invited his cousins, Yarkol realized angrily, so that all might enjoy

273

the spectacle to come. They would be waiting when he reached his goal.

At last he squeezed out into a round, low-ceilinged chamber and heard shouts from a thousand impish throats. Bent over in the cramped space, he looked about at his unruly audience. One hob sat on another's shoulder, and some were stacked three and four high, the topmost heads butting stone.

Gilgil Yellowface stood apart from the others, his belly puffed out, his earholes still dribbling wisps of steam. "We stand beneath the Kumiss Bowl," he said grandly, pointing a crooked finger upward.

Yarkol saw only a pitted ceiling that glistened with moisture. "The name means nothing to me."

"That is what we call it, Ulaansh. The central obstacle of your Rya Basin. There's a crack in the ceiling—down that way. You might want to poke your head up and have a look."

Rya! Then he stood beneath the eastern limit of the Path. Though weary of squeezing and stretching his spirit bones, Yarkol's curiosity drove him to crawl to the far end of the chamber. Glancing up, he noticed a crack that seemed to run along the entire edge of the roof. "Go quickly, Newborn," shouted the chief imp. The Hakhan thrust himself into the crevice and began to climb.

When he reached the surface, he immediately recognized his surroundings. Before him lay what Gilgil called the Kumiss Bowl, a cauldron filled with milky, foaming water. A boiling spring poured into and through the depression, eventually winding its way westward to vanish beneath the crust. Where Yarkol stood, one spur of the Path ended at the Bowl's rim.

He recalled why the builders had retreated to try other routes across the Basin. At first they had planned to dump rock and rubble to create a walkway here. But attempts to quarry stone nearby had failed when every small excavation opened a new fumarole. To drag enough fill from the closest source would take years.

Yarkol shook his head at the painful memories this scene evoked. Shortly before his illness, he had treated a worker for severe burns here, but later the man had died. And so many others had fallen, scalded in mud pots that lay beneath the fragile crust or blasted by steam.

He turned his attention to the goal of all this effort—to the solid ground that lay just east of the Basin. To his spirit eyes the night scene appeared brightly lit; he saw wooded hills and meadows already rich with new grass. Here spread the territories of legend, the gift he must hand Nurtaj. The bitterness of that thought almost made him reconsider his offer.

But he turned his attention back to the task he'd been set. To the south of the Bowl lay treacherous mud flats, to the north a field of geysers. He saw no way to remake this landscape to suit the imps' purpose.

"We are waiting, Ulaansh." Gilgil's highpitched voice filtered up from the depths. Yarkol muttered an oath, squeezed back into the crevice, and returned to the kobolds underground.

"Now you see your obstacle, Hakhan." Gilgil stood near one long wall of the chamber, his arms raised, hands poised as if he were trying to push the roof higher. "The Basin could be lifted, if we had the power."

Remembering the surface features, Yarkol understood that this chamber lay directly beneath the southern edge of the Bowl. If, as Yellowface urged, the roofstone could be tilted, then the contained water would spill toward the north and west, away from the Path. The source would still flow, but the Kumiss Bowl would dry up at one end, leaving a safe way over it. What a simple—and totally impractical—solution. "I moved a small rock once," the Hakhan said. "But a thousand hands like mine, working together, could not lift this ceiling."

"Perhaps you have gained strength, Ulaansh." Gilgil strutted back and forth, inspecting the rows of his grinning subjects. "A few of my stalwarts are quoting odds that you succeed. Long odds, I admit. But the slab is cracked around the rim and may break free." The Yellowface stared at the ceiling while his hobs whispered frantically to one other.

Yarkol, feeling foolish at being set such an impossible feat, positioned himself at the center of the southern wall. "Let us try then," he said angrily. He splayed his bone fingers and pressed against the overlying rock. At once he heard a deep hum arise from the surrounding kobolds.

The Dolmi gave a tentative push and saw his wrist bones bending—proof that they were useless for such a task. Yet the humming grew louder, and suddenly he felt strength pouring into his body. The imps drew closer, surrounding him, their ugly faces everywhere he turned.

He pushed again, feeling the strain, his bones rigid now despite the pressure. But the weight was enormous. No force could possibly budge the slab. The imps' chorus became a rumble that he felt in every limb. All other sensation faded as he gave himself up to the vibrations.

His thoughts returned to the shrine and to the shaman's dance he'd performed. Something had reached him just before he woke, an influx of power that did not come from imps. His spirit had been touched and nourished—surely by the High Ones, by the mountain gods he had ignored for most of his life.

But to tap that nourishment, he must drive himself again into frenzy. He must lose his rational self as he had done in the dance. The kobolds' din grew ever fiercer, roaring through his soul to blot out all the world.

And then the madness came on, forcing him to struggle like a caged animal. He snarled and arched his back; he squirmed and strained and heaved. He wanted only to break from his cell, to straighten his legs, to walk free under the moons of heaven. A relentless burden pressed him down. Yet for a moment the weight shifted, seemed to ease . . .

Yarkol wondered if he was dreaming or awake. He had become a mere observer, with no control over his perspective. He did not know if he still possessed a body—spirit or otherwise—for he could not choose to look at himself.

For a time he hovered above the Path, not far from the infamous Pinched Worm turning. Below him a steady procession of riders streamed across the bleak landscape. Swiftly and smoothly the nomads moved in single file, their mounts never glancing aside. Between the riders and in perfect formation flowed the sheep, the goats, the strings of laden oxen. Not a creature faltered or strayed out of line.

His view began to shift, moving from one end of the crossing to the other. At Hot Pan Clearing vapors clouded the path, yet the horses did not miss a step. Up the slope of the Bridge of Summer, the pace never slackened. And at the Kumiss Bowl, whose bottom had acquired a strange cant, the animals climbed nimbly onto an expanse of dry, solid rock.

He noticed the sun cross the sky, set, then rise again. He counted the days and wondered how much longer he must watch. Below him moved one tribe after another, each with its own colors, its unique style of adorning saddle and blanket. The animals wore bells—some deep-voiced, others jingling. In one group the women plaited their hair in five braids; in another they used six. Was Greatwing passing now? he wondered. So many faces reminded him of Etoudoori.

More days went by, bringing rainstorms and bright noons, misty nights and cold mornings. For a time he drifted far east of Rya Basin, over the rich lands that lay beyond. He watched the tribes spreading across their new territory, the herds feeding hungrily. Lakes and rivers abounded here; everywhere the soil appeared dark and fertile.

But always he returned to the eastern border of the Throat and to the large white yurt that stood on the heights beyond. Often he saw Nurtaj astride his horse, watching as Yarkol did, the slow progress of the crossing. But the chief's expression did not show the sense of triumph that the Hakhan expected. Nurtaj stared grimly ahead, ignoring the greetings of those who passed him.

At last the landscape began to blur, as if reflected in a wind-whipped pond. Then the images vanished altogether, and Yarkol tried to grasp what he had finally seen. The end of the procession! The hazardous crossing was done.

"Ulaansh," a highpitched voice sang. "You have proved yourself equal to our test." Yarkol's vision was clear again, and he stood once more in Gilgil's arena. He had regained his trance-body, his spirit bones apparently unharmed by his fierce labor. But recalling what he had done made him groan aloud.

His thoughts turned to his fleshly form. Knowing how much time had passed, he felt an urgent need to hurry back. He wanted to see with human eyes that the hobs had kept their bargain—that the nomads were gone and that Dolmi House stood untouched.

All around him the ledges were crowded with scrambling imps. They were waiting for some new cruel contest, he imagined, and already starting to make wagers. Yet he detected a deep melancholy behind their boisterous play. "I am finished forever with your kind," he shouted at Yellowface. "Show me the way out of here."

"Gladly," replied Gilgil. "We have a small transaction to complete, and then we'll give you your escort."

"You've delayed me too long already. My body—" A roar echoed behind him. Startled by a noise he had never heard from imps, Yarkol turned toward the far end of the gallery. The animal sound came again, and this time he discerned its source. A huge white bear was shambling toward him from the distant entrance. *The Kag? In this place?*

"Do not be alarmed, Newborn," assured the Yellowface. "He has merely come to make payment."

The Hakhan's ire grew. "Then you had a pact with Nurtaj after all."

"He offered a trade for our services." The imps began to shriek their laughter. The oncoming bear, however, showed no amusement at these comments. Drawing nearer, it suddenly reared up, scraped with needle claws at its chest, ripped away a flap of white hide. From the opening, a birdlike figure came fluttering out.

"For *your* services?" Yarkol cried. "Now I know why I was lured into this. To fulfill your bargain. To win what you wanted above all else."

"The gods will pay well to recover what is theirs," Gilgil answered, his gaze turning upward to his new prize on its perch above the throng. "Now many of us will obtain the souls that we long for."

The Hakhan shook his head bitterly, recalling how he had tried to negotiate with hobs at the nomad camp. "To keep Chirudaks in the north, I would have made the same payment."

"But we are an honorable lot, Newborn. Our cousins made a bargain with Nurtaj first, and we were part of that agreement. We could not go back on our word."

"Then it is done." *The end of all Dolmi dreams.* Yet the Hakhan people survived, and the threat of northern

279

invaders would never come again. That achievement, he knew, must be balanced against the rest.

Yarkol turned to leave the hall. A sprite jumped down, and the Hakhan expected that this one would serve as his guide. But suddenly Nurtaj was blocking Yarkol's way, his huge back humped, nape hairs bristling, red eyes afire.

"You have won," said the Dolmi to his foe. "What more can you want of me?" For reply, the bear rushed at him, jaws gaping to show enormous canine teeth.

"Stand back!" Yarkol bellowed. But the beast knocked him to the ground with a swipe of one huge paw. Yarkol squirmed away before the bear got a grip on him. "This is your doing, imp!" the Hakhan shouted. "You can stop him."

"We have no strength against human spirits," the chief hob answered.

"Then find me a weapon of iron!" Yarkol continued backing away from the bear's advance, but he was slowly being pushed toward Gilgil's end of the hall. And from there he saw no escape.

The chief imp shouted an order. "My champion can help you, Newborn. It will take but a moment."

Yarkol had no time to wait for aid. The bear reared up and fell on him, began to savage his ribs—first with its teeth and then its paws. The Kag's spirit-body possessed weight and strength that outmatched Yarkol's, but the Hakhan had greater flexibility. He clamped his hands over the beast's red eyes, gripping tightly though the head began to thrash. He stretched his body and slipped free of the clumsy embrace, then scrambled toward the opposite corner. He saw Gilgil's lizard coming after him, dragging a curved knife that it held between its jaws. The weapon glowed blood-red from end to end.

"There is a question of payment," said the high imp as Yarkol reached for the weapon.

"I've already done more than enough for you."

"We must make a trade. Even for such a small thing as this. It is part of our nature."

The bear was almost on him again. "When I get back to my body, I'll bury offerings. Salt. Pollen. Silver."

"No, Ulaansh. You know our price. Nurtaj has already paid it."

"So he has." The Hakhan tried to dodge, but the approaching bear blocked all escape. The great jaws snapped at his hands as he fell to the ground again. The paws began groping at his rib cage, trying to squeeze through to the fluttering thing within. The Kag's purpose, he thought, was to destroy Yarkol's gift so that both men would share the same bleak future. He felt his ribs bending . . .

"Then take it!" the Dolmi shouted to Gilgil. "May it free you all to live as maggots." Yarkol felt something soft brush his sternum as the birdlike thing slipped out. He glanced down for an instant and was chilled by the sight of the empty hollow within his rib cage. "Now bring me the knife!"

Nurtaj ceased his attack and stood back warily as the lizard dragged the weapon to Yarkol. But the Hakhan realized at once how small an advantage he had bought. The hilt possessed no grip of horn to protect his fingers. He must grasp ribbed steel to hold this weapon.

He recalled the strength that the imps had given him. Now he had only the power of his spirit-form, a body that was pitifully vulnerable to iron. The bear roared and came a few steps closer. Yarkol snatched the knife from the lizard's jaws.

The Hakhan shrieked from the pain that shot upward past his wrist and into his forearm. He lunged at the beast's neck, evoked an answering howl, but the weapon slipped from his burnt fingers. At once Nurtaj brushed the blade aside with his paw, then bent down to grip it between his teeth. With a swift toss of his head, he flung the knife up toward the closest row of spectators.

Panicked imps scrambled from the path of the oncoming missile. The blade skidded along the abandoned ledge and came to a quick halt. Yarkol was scaling the wall to go after it, finding handholds and footholds on the narrow perches, when heavy paws hit him from behind.

His grip was precarious. He tried to stretch himself, but Nurtaj wrenched him away. Then the bear went at him with renewed fury, crushing him from above, pressing him down into the rocky floor.

"You have your victory, Nurtaj," the Dolmi gasped. "How will it help to destroy what is left of me?"

The bear growled, and Yarkol heard words buried within the rumblings. "Your lies turned Vuotol against me. My victory is tainted. I did not bring all my people across."

Yarkol had no more time to argue. He strained for finger holds—knobs of stone on the floor—hoping he might pull himself free. But the bear changed tactics, gripping his breastbone with its jaws and dragging him back down the gallery. Suddenly Yarkol remembered the magma pit. The lava within had glowed to his spirit eyes with the same fiery sheen as an implement of iron.

Nurtaj was planning to throw him in! The realization sent the captive Hakhan into a frenzy. Yarkol did not know how far he could stretch his arm, but his only hope lay in reaching the lava before Nurtaj got there. The molten rock must be rich in iron. If he found a cooled fragment . . .

Yarkol sent his hands scurrying like spiders along the floor, grasping every rough projection to stretch out his bones. From above he heard imps shrieking their wagers from one tier to the next.

Racing against the bear's lumbering progress, his hands scrambled on. The arm bones stretched until they were as thin as whips, and yet his fingers kept moving. He angled his vision, trying to guide his hands to the target that lay so far ahead. Then he felt a sudden warmth in his fingertips as he neared the vapors.

He scrabbled around the rim, but found no solid bits of ironstone. Nurtaj evidently realized what Yarkol was doing, for he lifted the skeletal body free of the ground and began to charge toward the pit. The Dolmi had no time to find courage; he plunged one hand down into the pool of magma.

Then there was no bear, no gallery, no thought. All that existed was the fire in Yarkol's hand. He shrieked as he dragged his arm back, the agony filling him, becoming his entire being. Time seemed to slow, and distance appeared lengthened beyond all reckoning. For an eon, Yarkol's hand came on, carrying its load of molten iron.

Then the magma slammed into Nurtaj's hairy throat. Yarkol saw the jaws gape open, felt the body sag. In a moment he was free, racing back for the shelf that held his weapon, leaping upward, grabbing with his one good hand for Gilgil's blade.

The fiery touch of the knife meant nothing now as he gripped it with all his strength. Nurtaj staggered toward him, reached up with his white paws flailing. Yarkol sidestepped the blows, dropped onto the creature's back and plunged the blade deep into its neck. He cut between the vertebrae, slashed all the way through to the throat. Even then, he would not stop, butchering until the great head fell onto the stone floor and the bear's body lay still.

Then Yarkol flung the weapon high—far higher than where Nurtaj had tossed it. He saw imp mouths gibbering, but one plump face remained frozen in disbelief. The bright weapon arced perfectly to its target. The blade plunged into Gilgil Yellowface's belly, sending the high imp tumbling from his perch.

Wailing in unison, the other hobs dropped down to

cluster about their leader. Gilgil lay writhing on the floor, the knife protruding from his plump middle. "Pull it out, Ulaansh," the kobold cried, his voice a bare whisper.

"You ask a favor?" Yarkol laughed. "We must make a trade. Even for such a small thing."

Gilgil hissed and his lizard darted forward. Yarkol watched the fat creature struggle, saw the imp wince as the blade only twisted in deeper. "Help me, Ulaansh. I'll give you . . . what you want. Even . . . what we won from you." The imp nodded toward Yarkol's empty rib cage.

A chorus of jeers greeted Gilgil's offer, and Yarkol understood the sprites' anguish. Holding Yarkol's prize as well as the Kag's, many more imps would exact from the gods a chance at another life.

"Fools!" the chief cried to his followers. "There's no other way . . . to save me."

Yarkol glanced at the sea of downcast faces. To these wretches, his one soul was worth thousands. His gift from the gods must be extraordinary even for an ulaansh. If the imps gave up this prize, then they must find other victims—perhaps many—and repeat the cycle of treachery. "I won't go back on my bargain," Yarkol said firmly.

"Then we'll give you our treasure. Silver. Gold."

"Something more important, imp. Your people have plagued mine long enough."

"A truce, then." Gilgil's face, once a sulfurous yellow, had taken on a shade approaching black.

"A hundred-year truce," demanded Yarkol. "And your cousins must be bound as well. No sprite will trouble humans . . . or their animals or belongings for all that time."

"Ten is possible," rasped Gilgil.

"I am in no hurry." The Hakhan turned and began to stroll from the chamber.

"Thirty."

"Tomorrow, you may feel more generous."

"A hundred-year truce!"

"Meaning what?" Yarkol returned to hear what the chief imp offered. With prompting, Gilgil recited a formula that seemed to cover every possibility. Satisfied at last, the Hakhan braced himself, bent over the glowing hilt and jerked the blade free. "I have let you off lightly, imp," he sighed as the weapon clattered to the floor.

When Yarkol at last reached the shrine and regained his body, he was startled first by the fierceness of his hunger. Gazing up at Dzaminid, who stood watching him, he felt a deep hollow in his stomach. Next he noticed the pain from his singed hands. He glanced down and saw bandages covering the fingers that had dipped into magma. The other hand hurt slightly, but the skin showed no damage. "You will recover quickly," the shaman said. "The suffering of a spirit body is not fully carried to the flesh."

Yarkol could not guess how much time had passed while his body sat in trance. Now, daylight streamed into the chamber from the opening halfway up the wall. He saw that Dzaminid had somehow recovered his peaked hat and robe-of-bones; he carried himself with his old air of confidence again. "You are also changed," Dzaminid continued, as if he sensed Yarkol's thoughts. "Do you understand what has happened?"

"I gave up . . . my soul."

"Perhaps." The mystic touched a finger to Yarkol's cheek. The Hakhan felt skin flaking away, and a surprising roughness on the lower part of his face. He reached up and stroked . . . *stubble.* The start of a beard.

"Your mark of rebirth is almost gone," said the shaman. "Now you know what you have lost."

"My gift—"

"Flown away. You are an ordinary man again, with the

285

usual hungers and failings. But I cannot say for certain if your soul is lost as well. The gods must decide that."

Yarkol could barely speak. "And what . . . of the Kag? Nurtaj also . . . made the sacrifice."

"I can only tell you the fate of his body. They found him dead in his yurt this morning, with his head sagging at a peculiar angle." The shaman glanced knowingly into Yarkol's eyes.

"Nurtaj . . . dead."

"He'll be thoroughly mourned. But in truth, the people will be relieved at his passing. We no longer need a Kag. We must now bind the wounds he opened and return to our former way of life."

"Then you—"

"I am what I was. The shaman of Bloodcreek tribe. If anything, my powers have been strengthened." Dzaminid glanced aside at the symbols that covered one wall. "Perhaps this place—" He cut himself off. "No more talk until we get some food into you. Have you forgotten that a man needs to eat?"

With the shaman's aid, Yarkol rose and walked a few paces across the chamber. When he reached up toward the entrance, a woman's slender hand descended to pull him out. "Etou." He emerged into open air, took her arm for support as they climbed to the copse above. In a clearing he saw a well-used campsite, a small fire burning. Etou had hot broth waiting for him.

He sat with his back against a log, lifted the bowl and began to swallow greedily. Dzaminid arrived and pulled back Yarkol's hand. "Slowly! Think of your stomach, healer."

When the broth was gone, the Hakhan smiled weakly at Etoudoori. She stared at him with a curious expression, then knelt and cupped his chin in her palm. "Soon, I think, you'll look like a proper man again."

I may feel like one also, in time. But now he felt only

286

turmoil. Glancing southward through sparse branches he saw the distant towers of Dolmi House. The keep still stood.

"Be careful of your thoughts, Hakhan," the shaman warned. "Look at yourself before making plans." Dzaminid brought a water bucket. Yarkol studied his reflection, and saw that his face retained a youthful appearance despite the emerging beard. He resembled not his earlier self, but his eldest son.

"Dolmi Clan survives," said the shaman. "Bitter, but with few losses from the struggle. If you wish to return, you might pass yourself as a distant kinsman."

Yarkol noted Etou's troubled stare. "That is no easy decision." He leaned back and closed his eyes, trying to grasp what this new change meant. Now he was free of the drives that had possessed him; his future was truly his own. "I must speak with the physician Hirchil Zarad," he said thoughtfully, glancing at Etou's brilliant eyes again. "Is my mount well? I may have a long ride ahead."

"You mentioned Zarad to me earlier," said the shaman. "I had no need to send him your message. Even so, I know where to find him." Dzaminid turned and pointed toward the distant towers. "He is there. In Dolmi House, tending the wounded."

"Wounded? Then Jornood attacked—"

"Thank the High Ones that the battle was brief. A strange fire swept the barricade, and after that the Hakhans were forced back by stampeding cattle." Dzaminid grimaced in mock surprise. "The soldiers regrouped to defend the keep, but our warriors did not follow. They stayed by the Path until all had crossed."

"I must ride," Yarkol insisted. He leaned forward, meaning to stand up, but at once fell back against the log.

"Tomorrow." Etou sat beside him, her warm hand touching his. "Go tomorrow, when you can stay in the saddle."

"Tomorrow. Yes." Yarkol closed his eyes for a moment. "And you, shaman?" he asked drowsily. "Where will you go?"

"I must serve my tribe, as always," Dzaminid said with a laugh. "And now that we have no Kag, my life will be peaceful again. I am eager to go home."

The Hakhan nodded, smiling faintly, sharing the same longings. A nomad needed no fixed place; wherever his tribe camped was home. But Yarkol had neither family nor tribe to welcome him.

18

*All of history is changed, but the gods
still watch over us.*
　　　　—Shaman Dzaminid (Bloodcreek tribe)

T he sky was overcast, the
air cool as Yarkol rode slowly up to Dolmi House. On the
day of his leavetaking he had not expected ever to approach this place again. Even now, though freed of his
wanderlust, he found the high walls overbearing. As he
passed beneath a watchtower, he shivered with a sudden
chill.

Yet Dzaminid's words echoed in his thoughts. Perhaps
Yarkol's kin might accept him as one of their own. The
possibility of returning to the Hakhan fold flitted through
his imagination, bringing a wry smile. But then he glanced
down at his mountain pony, his Chirudak saddle and

blanket, his nomad-sewn trousers. If he had come to reclaim his heritage, then he was outfitted poorly for the occasion.

At the gate, two soldiers challenged him. Never, in his lifetime, had the entrance been guarded. Did they think Nurtaj's men might yet return? "I have a message for Hirchil Zarad," the rider said quietly. "He will be eager to hear news of an old friend named Yarkol."

The soldiers grumbled, eyeing him with wary curiosity. At last one turned inside and called to a servant.

For some time, the men merely stared at each other. "I am unarmed," said Yarkol. "Harmless, as you can see." The soldiers made no reply, but kept their hands by the swords.

Yarkol sat quietly, recalling the last time he had seen Hirchil Zarad. He'd meant to return the gift of silver but the nomad guards had long ago taken his valuables. Perhaps today he had something more important than silver to offer Hirchil.

Suddenly the old physician appeared, scowling, slightly out of breath. "What do you know of Yarkol?" he demanded, as he came forward with a shuffling gait. Then he stared, seemingly confused, as if straining to recognize a face. His eyebrows shot up. "By the Great Horse!" He began to laugh.

Yarkol dismounted, and the two clapped each other on the shoulders. "I've heard of spontaneous cures," the physician said in a hushed voice. "But this is the first case I've witnessed."

"I'm healed, but I'm not the man you knew." Yarkol felt a sting of tears.

"Come inside and talk. Leave the horse." Zarad shouted an order to the guards, and one took the mare aside. "Ah, Yarkol. So much has changed."

"I know about the Chirudaks," he replied, following the

290

physician past the stables. But he had no intention of explaining his role in recent events.

For a moment, surrounded by solid Hakhan walls, Yarkol could almost believe that nothing had altered. Brown-tailed chickens trooped about in search of scattered grain. Mastiffs stood watch in the distance. And before him lay the outbuildings where he'd been left to recover from his illness. As his gaze swept the barren, puddled ground, he recalled too his last sight of Merig. The thought that she might appear now set his heart hammering.

"We must go somewhere to talk," Zarad said, turning toward the closest outbuildings. "Come in here. One patient went home today." He led Yarkol into a musty servant's room, and the two men sat on the edge of the sagging bed. "Now tell me how you'll use your good fortune." The old physician's eyes gleamed moistly.

"Do you call me fortunate?" Yarkol forced himself to meet the old man's gaze. "Look at me. I'm neither Hakhan nor Chirudak now. I belong nowhere."

"But you are young. If you were to make an effort, you could regain what you've lost."

"Not my children. Not Merig."

Hirchil sighed. "She has remarried," he replied softly. "The priest insisted, and I could find no reason to argue against him."

Yarkol's breath hissed through his teeth, and for a time he could say nothing. He summoned a vision of high mountain trails, of icy peaks, of riding until body and thoughts grew numb. In the high country he had almost forgotten her. "It is for the best," he managed.

"Don't despair, Yarkol." Zarad clapped his hand on the younger man's knee. "Here is my advice. Ride west—far from here. Many clans will welcome you and ask no questions. You have not forgotten your skills?"

The Dolmi looked down at his hands, the right one still bandaged. He tried to see himself resuming a Hakhan way of life, but all he could imagine was a priest, reeking of incense, reminding him of his duties. "These hands can serve again, yes," Yarkol answered slowly, "but my future does not lie within stone keeps."

"Then where can you go? What can you do?"

"Hirchil, put aside my personal troubles and think of the plight that all Hakhans face. We are short of land, vulnerable to famine. But I've seen what lies beyond the Path."

"Chirudaks!"

"And more territory than the nomads can ever need. Now that the Path is complete, our people must use it."

"I've heard others say the same." A troubled look came over the physician's face. "What a strange business this has been—land heaving up just in time to provide a crossing." He lowered his voice to a whisper. "Some mutter that the old gods were behind it."

Yarkol shook his head, smiling. "Whatever the cause, I cannot say the outcome was undeserved. We were arrogant to think we could take the whole east for ourselves. There is land enough for everyone; Hakhan and Chirudak need not quarrel over it. We can make peace with our cousins."

"I dare not call them cousins. Even so, I know a bit of history."

"Our people must not turn away now from the crossing. Let them send scouts to survey the terrain. Let them seek accords with tribal chiefs, offer trade—"

"What you suggest is not easy, after so many years of distrust."

"It must be done. All our hopes depend on it." Yarkol blinked, trying to rid himself of tears that blurred his vision. "You asked where I was going, and now we both know. I must prepare the way for Hakhans. I'll be the first

292

of our people in the east, but others must follow. Do all you can to encourage them, Hirchil. Tell Merig to send my sons."

"As she had hoped to do all along." He shook his head sadly.

"Keep this thought, Hirchil. The Path is a Dolmi work from one end to the other. My clan has reason to be proud of it." Yarkol could say no more. He stood up and turned to the doorway, his thoughts now focused on his waiting horse. He needed to feel the wind on his face.

"I hoped you would stay longer." The physician rose also, and the younger man turned to give him a parting embrace. Then Yarkol was running, across the yard and out through the guarded gate.

Yarkol tried to keep his thoughts away from Dolmi House as his mare cantered along the track. Ahead lay the scraggly copse at the edge of the Throat. Approaching the campsite, he felt himself begin to tremble. *Because of Etou?*

The shaman was already on his way to Bloodcreek tribe. Etou had remained, but she too was preparing to leave for the eastern lands. Yarkol's absence had been brief, he thought. Yet he could not find her roan as he entered the woods. For a long moment of agony, he convinced himself that she was gone.

"Etou!" His voice was as nervous as a youth's in his first courting.

"I am here, Newborn-no-longer." Suddenly he caught sight of her on the far side of a clump of leafless bushes. She was standing beside her mount, tying her saddlebags shut. A streak of sunlight glimmered on her dark braids. "I do not know what to call you now," she said dolefully.

He studied her face, recalling how she once had reminded him of a woodland fox. Now her features ap-

293

peared softened, comforting to a man in need. Yet the sight of her did nothing to calm him. "I am no longer an ulaansh," he said, "but I am not my old self either. At best, half of me remains Hakhan. I must find a new name." Were his cheeks still damp? He wiped his face on his sleeve.

"Call yourself Singed-fingers."

He glanced at his wrapped hand. "A name that I deserve. And one that will be less painful if I hear it from your lips."

She mounted her horse. "I followed you until your work was done. Partly out of duty, partly . . ." She did not finish her thought, but lowered her gaze. "Now that your task is over, I belong with Greatwing tribe."

"And I belong nowhere. Yet I have a purpose that takes me eastward."

She faced him again. Her eyes caught the light and he saw that they were damp as his own. "You would be welcome among us. Even the half that is Hakhan." He recalled frigid nights in the mountains when they lay innocently together, huddled for warmth. She spoke of him as a child then. He felt like a child no longer.

"It is *your* welcome that matters, Etou."

"Then come with me," she said, her face brightening at last. "Come home to Greatwing tribe. We know how to honor our heroes."